Date
Due

ct to a

D0563792

PS
3503
.I722
L3X
1937

Binns, Archie, 1899-
    The laurels are cut down.   New York,
The Literary Guild of America, 1937.
    332 p.  22 cm.


    I. Title.

                 6/12/79

# THE LAURELS
## ARE CUT DOWN

ARCHIE BINNS

# THE LAURELS
# ARE
# CUT DOWN

THE LITERARY GUILD OF AMERICA, INC.

*New York* 1937

COPYRIGHT, 1937, BY ARCHIE BINNS

*All rights reserved, including the right
to reproduce this book or portions
thereof in any form*

*1072*

PRINTED IN THE UNITED STATES OF AMERICA

*We shall go no more to the woods*
*The laurels are cut down,*
*My fair lady.*

PS
3503
-I722
L3X
1937

# The Beginning

A FTERWARD, Tyee Bay raised its first white generation, which did the things all generations do, with an unjustified feeling of discovery. And like most generations went to war. Some of them returned to argue whether it had been worth the trouble, while others remained silent in the land of the enemy.

But that was not the beginning. There was a still earlier generation, consisting of one half-breed child, marking the change from red to pale civilization. And there was an earlier war for which the entire white population of the bay, consisting of William Walter, enlisted. In the spring of 1861 that stout Pennsylvania German prepared to leave the silence of the river-like inlet and the great forest for the confusion of war. Mr. Walter was a quiet, methodical man. He had taken up his donation claim on a southern reach of Puget Sound out of a love of tranquillity and solitude. He had no taste for confusion of any sort, or for war. But he was a whole-hearted American. Accordingly, he packed his knapsack, tested his strength and endurance in various ways, and pronounced himself, at the age of forty-five, as fit as any man twenty years younger, except for his scarcity of teeth. It would be necessary, he decided, to bake his particular variety of soft bread over bivouac campfires.

He delayed his departure a day to whittle a rolling pin of cedar. The rolling pin subsequently traveled in his knapsack when his battery advanced and retreated and advanced in the wilderness; when the wheels of his caisson jolted over the shallow, undistinguishable graves of comrades and enemies; over dead arms that broke and raised their hands out of the mud; while his fellow artillerymen answered the salute of the dead with the comment: "There's another soldier reaching up for his back pay."

Having finished his rolling pin, he boarded up the windows of his shack with split cedar shakes and wrote on the door with a lump of charcoal:

Will be back when the Union is saved.
William Walter

As an afterthought he changed it to read: "Will be back, God willing. . . ." His parting act was to take affectionate leave of his young orchard. He had already arranged the defense of each tree—four cedar posts joined by a lattice of smaller strips, a protection against marauding deer, the only cattle of the neighborhood. With every contingency provided for, he began his fifty-mile journey over dim trails through the wilderness of the Olympic Peninsula. Grays Harbor, on the shore of the Pacific, was the nearest recruiting station.

When William Walter marched out of sight, the bay was again left to the Siwash Indians. Mr. Walter was a just man and a good neighbor. Also, he had learned the secret of never watching an Indian. By that token the Siwashes knew he was without fear. And in the years of his absence they refrained from molesting or burning his lonely cabin.

In September of that same year the half-way generation arrived at Collins Point, the entrance to the inlet. Captain Collins was then an old man, ten years past his final voyage around the antarctic Horn. Mrs. Collins was thirty-one, having crossed the Plains in 1850. She, too, was Pennsylvania German, but Mr. Walter had not come to say goodbye to her before leaving for the War. He was unable to forgive her devoted admiration for Captain Pickett, from Fort Pickett on San Juan Island. He could not forgive her for having entertained him when secession and war were imminent. George Pickett was a Virginian and a Democrat, which amounted to treason under the circumstances. Mr. Walter was a red hot Republican.

Captain Collins was a Republican who had carried slave cargoes in his youth and learned tolerance from the unforgiving sea. He had been around the world more than once and seen that everywhere men's enemies are poverty and themselves and the devouring years—not Southern Democrats. He claimed to know a man when he saw one, and he saw Captain Pickett as one of America's best. He was untroubled by the soldier's admiration for his spirited young companion. It wasn't given to many men to possess the full fire of life. Still fewer had that fire controlled by such exquisite chivalry. Captain and Mrs. Collins knew the unwritten part of George Pickett's life, but nothing they knew was at variance with his reputation as a perfect knight.

The Collins' only other neighbors, the Indians, could not distinguish between Republicans and Democrats. But they agreed with Captain Pickett that Mrs. Collins was the finest woman in the wilderness. Although she was childless, they called her the "White Mama" and ran to her with their troubles.

It was not by accident that Collins Point was the destination of the long black war canoe; the long high-stemmed canoe with twenty paddlers. Heading south from Bellingham Bay, it had crossed the wide Straits, into Admiralty Inlet, narrower, but still like a great river. Twenty red women paddling, with the twenty-first caring for the child. Sometimes he slept and sometimes he stood by his kneeling grandmother, looking solemn-eyed at the vast river of sea water winding between virgin forests. A small, delicate child of four, wearing a calico dress and little buckskin moccasins. The dress was of old-fashioned calico, with the dark-blue border used to outline the square-cut neck and bottom hem. It was the dress his dead mother had made for him with the last of her slight strength. Neatly cut, but sewn with crooked, childish stitches by a girl who had never used a needle before or was able to use one afterward.

Once when the child was looking over the side of the hollowed cedar canoe he reached out and touched his grandmother's hand. "*Hi as keekly chuck*," he told her. (There is deep water under us.) To the old woman it appeared a profound thought. She took it as an omen that he would become a man of great wisdom.

When evening overtook them they drew the huge frail canoe up on the beach and camped for the night. Indians of other tribes, familiar with long canoes and fierce raids of the northern tribes, took to the deep woods. Some of them, seeing the party was peaceful, came back to learn the mission of the twenty-one squaws. When it was explained they were on their way to the "White Mama," they were welcomed and feasted. Solemn pow-wows were held over the delicate-featured little boy—the grandson of the great Bellingham tyee and the son of the great white tyee. The Indians' welcome was the salute to passing royalty. In the morning the twenty women launched the long canoe and continued their journey south.

On the fourth day the women drove their canoe through the whirl-pools and tide rip off the stone point known as Cape Horn. They fought their way west between the sheer rock walls of the Narrows, against the snarling ebb of the tide, and came to Collins Point.

Mrs. Collins was reading aloud from "Adam Bede." The Captain was lying on the couch with his eyes closed, listening to her fine voice. Beyond the edge of the page appeared a bare Indian foot on the rag rug. She looked up, unalarmed, to see the house invaded. According to their rules of courtesy, the squaws had come in silently, without knocking. The white woman marked the place in her book and rose.

"Captain," she said, "they have come!"

"*Klahowya?*"

"*Klahowya, tilacum?*"

"*Nika Klahowya!*"

"Where is the boy?"

He was brought forward in his soiled calico dress and she knelt beside him. "Jimmy. Jimmy Pickett!"

His wide black eyes appraised her. "Papa went to war in a great ship," he announced in the Chinook jargon.

"Jimmy, would you like to stay with me and be my son?"

He answered with a baby version of the shrug which was part of the word, "*Klo-o-n-nas?*" (Who knows?) Then he began making approaches to the gray cat, *Tenas pusspuss mitlite* (little cougar that lives in the house).

The twenty-one women ate half a deer and many smoked salmon bellies while the grandmother and the white woman talked in Chinook jargon, mostly about Captain Pickett, who had married the old woman's daughter, Morning Mist. He had married her "Boston." The Hudson Bay traders, before the American soldiers, had married many Indian girls, but not "Boston." They married them for a night or a week or a few months. Then they had gone away and never come back to see their papooses. Captain Pickett had married the chief's daughter "Boston," and he had made his soldiers marry their girls "Boston." The white tyee was "Boston" in all he did, even with putting down the Indian uprising. "Boston" was the Siwash's term for fair play and integrity, dating from some early dealing with a New England conscience.

In the course of the potlatch the grandmother told the "White Mama" of the captain's devotion to her daughter. He was as tender as a woman, she declared with wonder. She repeated it several times, not expecting it would be believed. He had cried like a woman when his little Indian wife was buried at Sea Home. Morning Mist was beautiful, she said, but small and not very strong. She had never been well after the child was born. The white chief had brought doctors from far away, but none of them could do any good. She had died within the year.

Mrs. Collins had heard of Morning Mist from Captain Pickett. He saw her first on the morning of his attack on the Bellingham Indians. He had rushed the village with his full force and taken them by surprise. Squaws and children had screamed and run for shelter while the men debated the use of bows and flintlocks against the heavily-armed force. Morning Mist was coming from the spring with water, not knowing the village had been invaded. Voices called to her to drop the jar and hide. The expression of her child-like face didn't change to betray the moment she realized what had happened. But in that hidden moment she decided it was already too late. She walked past the line of rifles and the glittering company with the air of being utterly alone and untroubled. She didn't ignore the soldiers. They didn't exist.

When she was opposite Pickett, he asked her, in Chinook jargon, to wait. Morning Mist turned and looked at him with wide, surprised eyes, as if she suddenly realized there was someone near her. He sheathed his sword and bowed to her. Their fingers touched as he took the water jar.

"It is for my father's house," she explained, looking up at him profoundly without resisting.

"I will carry it for you, child."

7

The barrels of muskets bristled from the windows of her father's plank house. He had barricaded himself in, with some of his men, swearing he would never open to the white soldiers. But he could hardly refuse to open to his favorite daughter. The door was un-barred and the two went in. The chief was polite. He appreciated the strategy, but would not surrender.

Pickett, with his sword already sheathed, had not spoken of surrender. He now suggested both sides call it a day and stop fighting, with honors even. Their informal truce was never broken.

Captain Pickett's surrender to the small Morning Mist was more formal, but it was not a matter for history. Neither was her whole-hearted surrender, which ended in death on a stormy January morning while the captain was bringing a new doctor from far away.

In the afternoon the squaws launched their canoe and began the long journey home, each with a gift of china or silverware. They said goodbye to the "White Mama" and the grizzled sea captain on the beach and paddled toward the east without looking back.

Jimmy Pickett was left in the home his father se-lected. He had planned to bring the boy himself, but there had been a long delay before he was relieved of his post. He felt it was his duty to serve the American Army faithfully until he could go with honor and fight it to the death. His last act before taking ship for the east was to arrange for the canoe journey which placed his son in the wise hands of the "White Mama."

Mrs. Collins was the ideal foster mother for the boy, and he was the ideal child for her. The son of George Pickett, to whom she was devoted, and of the Indians whom she knew and loved. Captain Collins raised no protest to the adoption. He did not feel he had the right to interfere in the affairs of life which he was about to leave.

Jimmy Pickett's only baggage was a small metal chest, dull red in color, fastened with many rivets. It had the appearance of great age. The grandmother said it had been given to the first chief of the tribe by the Thunder Bird, when the world was new. According to tradition, it was the chest in which the souls of men were placed at the time of creation. The forbidden chest which Coyote opened, letting escape the souls which could never be recaptured and bringing death into the world. Later the chest was declared to be of ancient Japanese workmanship. In which case its arrival among the Indians is lost in the centuries and the mists of the Pacific.

Besides his Indian trinkets and toys brought for him by his father and fellow officers at the fort, Jimmy's chest contained certain items. A careful pen and ink drawing of Sea Home, where Morning Mist slept in the land of her fathers. A letter from Captain George Pickett, U. S. A., stating to whom it might concern that James T. Pickett was his lawful son. And the white dress gloves he wore at his wedding with Morning Mist, the token of a gentleman of honor.

That was seventy-five years ago. General Pickett has joined the thousands who fell about him in the shell-threshed field of wheat and on the volcanic slope of Cemetery Hill at Gettysburg. Mrs. Collins is dead since the beginning of the century. Jimmy Pickett is dead long ago. *Ahncuttie man konaway memaloose.* Chivalry is dead.

Still the waters of the Pacific swell and ebb through Admiralty Inlet and the great reaches of Puget Sound, daily retracing the journey of the long canoe. Here and there in clearings on the evergreen shore the story is handed down by word of mouth: the forest idyll of America's most glamorous soldier, and the story of Jimmy Pickett who has been lost out of history all these years. And lost out of life. But here and there the White Tyee's children of the spirit survive—a spark to unselfish patriotism, and sometimes a cross.

# BOOK ONE

# I

THE TIDE was going out, a gray river of sea water sliding toward the east between hills and evergreen forests heavy with snow. On the north shore, a mile to the west, blue wood smoke rose protesting from a terra-cotta chimney and hung in a little cloud above the fishing shack. The shack where Captain Miller waited for the spring to open the ice. He was going back to the Klondike.

On their side of the channel, the boys considered their salvage with the high seriousness of youth.

"We've only got to fix that bow," George pointed out.

The port bow of the Indian canoe, hewn from a red cedar log, had been knocked in, leaving a hole that would embarrass flotation.

"I got an idea," Alfred volunteered. "We could nail a piece of tin over the hole, on the outside. There's that oil can I was going to use for a aquarium." He knew George wouldn't reject the suggestion immediately and scornfully, after the habit of elder brothers.

"I don't know, Alf." George considered the sea-inviting hole in the little dugout, pulled up on the clean, wet gravel of the beach and moored to a post near the snowy bank. "Someways I think tin might do the job. Then again, I don't know. Maybe we could cut a piece of wood to fit, if we could fasten it good enough."

"Maybe we could put tin outside the wood."

"Georg-i-e! Alfred!"

"All right, Ma!" George's shout was shaded with annoyance. "Tin on both sides of the wood, maybe. First we got to shape the wood."

"I don't suppose we could go to the Klondike in her when she's all fixed up?" The Klondike had been much in their minds since the gold rush started.

George shook his head regretfully. "She's too small. Ma would never let us go in her."

Alfred had been afraid of something of the sort. "Captain Miller and another man went in a canoe."

"Georg-i-e! Al-fred! Come this minute. You'll be late for school!" Mrs. Tucker's voice carried a warning note.

"All right, Ma, we're coming!"

The boys shuffled their feet in the motions of obedience. "Honest," George lamented, "sometimes I wonder what women are good for!"

They raised their eyes from the dugout on the beach and looked up the sullen tide, retreating between hills and forests of snow. Far away a boat had put out from the opposite shore, the rower standing and facing forward, fisherman fashion, pushing on the oars. An ample figure filled the stern.

"Mr. Harper's taking his mother over to the Jacksons'," George interpreted. "Mr. Jackson must have hoisted the flag."

The brothers turned from the beach, up the narrow trail they had tramped in the snow.

14

"Ma'll be wanting to go and see the baby," Alfred stated.

"I know."

Their mother was waiting at the back door, with their lunches in bright, five-pound cottolene pails, and a green bottle of milk.

"Where did you boys disappear to? You know it takes longer to walk through this deep snow." The smile on her thin face was almost beautiful. It suggested one of the moments when she glimpsed the shadowy headlands of the world in which boys live.

"We were just having a look at our canoe." Casually, George shouldered his strapped books.

The understanding smile went out. "That deathtrap! If you ever try to go out in it—"

"Goodbye, Ma!"

"Goodbye!"

They hurried across the yard before their mother could make some disastrous vow to which her conscience would bind her.

Silence closed in, distantly punctuated by the sound of Pa Tucker hammering in the barn.

Mrs. Tucker watched them out of sight with pride and doubt. The boys thought nothing of walking a mile through the deep woods to school. She had her qualms every morning, and every afternoon until they were home. But now they were only dim misgivings. How would she have felt about it if the school had been organized two years before? Or earlier, soon after her first meeting with the forest? She remembered that like a picture she had once seen, or something that happened in another life.

That was the day after she and Pa Tucker were reunited in Seattle. A friend had got him free passage on a sailing ship from New Orleans. He had come ahead to spy out the land. His enthusiasm and his long absence brought her three weeks after he arrived. He had just found the very place for them; a little farm and house on Hood Canal. There were many acres of wonderful virgin timber. She pictured a snug little place on a placid reach of water one could call across. She didn't visualize the timber, having grown up on the Iowa prairies.

They took a fine steamer out of Seattle and traveled half the day to Union City, which turned out to be a tiny village. Hood Canal was not a canal but an inland sea, miles across. The place which had taken Pa's eye was ten miles up the Canal from the steamer landing. They had to hire a guide and a skiff. Mrs. Tucker was afraid of Indians and afraid the twenty-mile boat trip would be too much for George. He was a baby of two. At the jerry-built hotel they had a trustworthy woman to look after the baby. The woman was brought in: a full-blood Siwash dressed in American clothes of many colors. She came in smoothing up elbow-length white gloves which contrasted with her large bare feet. Mrs. Tucker decided to expose George to the perils of the deep, but the young Indian woman took him from her arms and entranced him with Chinook jargon. Leaving George in the hands of the Indians from whom she had tried to save him, Mrs. Tucker went with her husband and the guide.

In the middle of the afternoon they landed on the

beach in front of a cabin and a little clearing. The clearing was four or five acres surrounded by magnificent fir trees, five and six feet through and two hundred feet tall. Pa Tucker saw them as potential timber, waiting to be felled, at the very water's edge. Here was a small fortune to be had for two thousand dollars. The Ohio man who owned it had been left a widower with two small children. He couldn't find anyone suitable to care for them and was going back east.

After they had looked through the neat cabin, Pa Tucker proposed a visit to their neighbors at the little settlement half a mile inland. On his earlier trip he had been too much entranced by the timber to think about neighbors. He was wise enough, though, to understand that women need company. Mrs. Tucker proposed that her husband and the guide go without her. She would rest and look about the place. She hadn't any doubt they would buy it, and she wanted to start planning. He took her at her word and left her—changing the course of their lives.

She enjoyed it at first, planning how the place could be made comfortable and home-like. It was a fine, well-built cabin.

Then it seemed to her that something about the floor made her footsteps sound unnaturally loud. She stood still a while, puzzled. No, it wasn't the floor or anything in the house. It was outside, where something had stopped. Outside she discovered what it was. When her husband and the guide had left to go inland, the sound of human voices had stopped. Everything had stopped. Or rather, there was nothing else to hear. The silence of the forest had taken charge again. She looked up at the vast, forbidding trees which had been growing there before any white man had ever seen America. Not a branch or a needle stirred. No birds sang. Nothing moved. Except for the gigantic trees, it was a dead forest, and the trees overwhelmed her with their indifference.

It was only mid-afternoon, but the dark forest had already shut away the sun. In the little clearing there were no birds, no butterflies. She was the only thing that lived or moved. And she felt ghost-like, or in a dream. Wandering about the clearing she stumbled over a mound. The grave of a small child. A neglected rose bush was growing at the head of the little mound. That finished her.

The men came back from inland with glowing reports of good neighbors. They were going to organize a school, Pa said, and it was all arranged that Mrs. Tucker would be the teacher. It was wasted on her. All she could say or think was never, never! Let's get out of this awful place!

Pa saw she was beyond argument. They got out. The following day they took the stage to Forest City, another tiny village. Everyone there had land to sell. In the end they bought from Mr. Walter.

Now here she was in another clearing, between salt tides and the forest. Only the timber was poorer and Pa Tucker no longer talked about logging. She knew they would have been better off on Hood Canal. He realized it, too, but never reminded her of the fact. Perhaps he knew it was his fault, leaving her alone with the forest so soon after the Iowa prairies.

The boys' footsteps slowed as they passed the barn, with its entrancing sound of hammering. Their father was making a sled for Hyak, the Indian pony.

"I hope nobody beats a drum while he's hauling wood!"

"I hope not," Alfred answered earnestly.

Their father had bought the buckskin from Mr. Walter, who was a conscientious man. Going over Hyak's points, good and bad, he had ended by observing that the pony went crazy when a drum was beaten. Why? There was no saying. Hyak had been brought from the Horse Heaven country east of the mountains. Mr. Walter knew nothing of his past history, and little about the Indians of that region. Only Hyak went crazy at the roll of a drum.

Horses were scarce along the bay, and drums still scarcer. Mr. Tucker hadn't thought much about it. Nobody thought much about it, until Alfred tried it out. He had never been told, or was too young to remember. He came around the barn, beating a new birthday drum. George was swinging idly on the pony's tail. Hyak was patient and docile—except when a drum was beaten.

The unshod hoofs kicked George insensible. The buckskin cleared the fence, screaming, and ran into the woods. He didn't come back for two days. Hiding, maybe, from some phantom attack.

So the boys hoped nobody would beat a drum while Pa was hauling wood.

The comforting sound of hammering followed them as they went up hill on the skidroad, along the narrow snow path their father had broken for them the day before. It was a mile to the Burtons' house, where school was held—half of it uphill—and they needed their breath.

As the road suggested, the land had been logged off, but years before, by the first loggers who picked and chose. They had taken only the finest trees, not one in ten and nothing smaller than five feet through. Their efforts were attested by the road and an occasional twelve-foot stump, notched on opposite sides. By using springboards and beginning their operations at that height, Paul's men had saved themselves the trouble of cutting away the underbrush.

The sound of their father's hammering died away as they walked through almost virgin timber. The silence of the trees and snow was broken only by the slight squeak of their footsteps and their panting. Half way up the hill they passed the South Field— a detached, stumpy acre their father had hewn and burned into being because the land there was easier to clear, by comparison. They paused for breath near the zigzag rail fence, staring with thoughtful idleness across the white-blanketed field, with its occasional stumps rising like aloof gravestones.

Alfred puckered his brows in thought, looked up at his older brother with eyes that were dark and solemn in his pink face. "What do you suppose it was like here, long ago, when there were only the Indians?"

"Sort of wild, I guess. The Walters should know." The Walters, farther up the inlet, were the first settlers. Doubly the first. She had been the wife of Captain Collins, who first settled Collins Point. Mr.

Walter had taken up the first donation claim on the inlet, alone. When he returned from the Civil War she was a widow, bringing up her half-breed foster son. They had joined forces and built the big house where she had grown old and he had grown still older.

The boys passed the farthest boundary of the field and were again shut in by the silence of the forest. George whistled as he marched ahead. It was the loneliest part of their road. The two-hundred-foot firs, touching their branches overhead, turned the world into a snowy twilight. George stopped whistling. The sound had not been too successful—a tiny tune which seemed to diminish the small figures marching between ranks of giant trees under primeval snow. Human voices would be more reassuring.

"Alf, do you remember your geography lesson?" George asked his question without looking back.

The day before the younger boy had blundered when Miss Bun called on him. Miss Bun, their teacher, was a person who should be guarded against disappointments. Coming from the distant state of California, she was like someone from another world. So young and so sympathetic and beautiful that she seemed to have no special connection with the hard-working mothers of the neighborhood.

"I know every bit of it," Alfred declared, "as well as when you went over it with me."

"That's good, Alf."

"And I can bound the United States now: Canada, the Atlantic Ocean, the Gulf of Mexico, Mexico, the Pacific Ocean." He lagged behind, slipping his arm through the handle of his cottolene pail and pulling the geography out of his book bag to verify his boundaries. Correct. As George had pointed out to him, it helped to start at the north and go round to the right, through the east and south to the west. Closing the book, he felt himself grabbed roughly. He thought his brother was playing a trick on him. Something he seldom did. "George, don't!" He looked up with a shocked gasp, but even then he didn't believe it. He was in the grip of a lean, yellowish animal. Would his mother come in when he woke up? He tried to draw away from the phantom in the dream forest. The sharp stab of a claw in his shoulders told him that, dream or reality, he was being hurt.

"*Ma!*"

Slowly the yellow face came toward his and he was pushed over in the snow. Part of its head was out of sight, below his chin, tearing at his muffler and pinching his neck. Its hind legs were ripping his overcoat. His father was hammering in the barn again. *Thump, thump.*

"Go away, you brute!" George was bellowing to the accompaniment of thumps. "Go away!" Alfred's chest was jarred with each thump.

He woke up, lying in the snow. The yellow monster was gone like a bad dream. George was standing above him, his face white, staring after the vanished apparition, with the heavy green bottle of milk grasped threateningly in his hands. He had seen it, too!

Alfred got up, crying wildly.

"Alf, did he hurt you much?" George put down the

bottle and felt him anxiously. The child didn't know whether he was hurt or not.

"I'm scared!" he wailed.

George scowled into the dark, snowy forest. "Damn it, Pa thinks I'm not old enough to carry a gun, so I have to fight a cougar with a bottle of milk!"

He began picking up their scattered possessions. Shaking with sobs, Alfred tried to help him. The inside of his sleeves and mittens were warm and flowing. When he picked up his geography, lying open in the trampled snow, the blood from his mitten reddened Alaska and flowed over into Asia.

"George," he whimpered, "there's blood on my geography."

"It doesn't matter." George refastened the handle of his brother's lunch pail, which had been torn from his arm. "Let's get out of here!" He spoke suddenly, with determination.

"I want to go home!"

"All right, Alf, we're going home. Can you walk all right?"

"I want to run!" Alfred sobbed.

Fear didn't overtake them completely until they were in sight of the opening of the South Field. The suggestion of human habitation and safety brought out the terror of their experience in the forest. They ran down the hill in the full panic of retreat, with Alfred in the lead. Once he gasped back, "George, I'm bleeding!" George's white face nodded and they continued down the snow-covered skidroad, with their feet flying faster and faster.

23

Some of Alfred's wounds were deep and he had lost a good deal of blood. More soaked through the strips of clean sheet, torn up for bandages. The Tuckers had done their best, but it was a question if their best was good enough.

Mr. Tucker came in from the kitchen, slipping bright cartridges into his smoky Winchester rifle. He considered the spreading stains of pink, centered with red, and decided something more had to be done.

"Ma, you and George take Alfie to Mrs. Harper, while I look for that damned cougar. Don't bother to dress him; just put blankets round him while I get the boat ready."

George remembered something. "Mrs. Harper isn't home, Pa."

Pa's dark face frowned. "Where is she, then?"

"At the Jacksons'. Alf and I saw Mr. Harper taking her over this morning. Didn't we, Alf?"

Alfred nodded through carbolic fumes. "Mrs. Jackson's having her baby. Ma, how does a woman know when a baby's coming?"

"Hush!" Mrs. Tucker said reprovingly.

Mr. Tucker frowned, annoyed, at the staining bandages. Then he looked at his wife. "Take him to the Jacksons' then. I guess Mrs. Harper will have time for both of them. George can help row. A boy who licked a cougar bare handed will get you there all right."

It was George's first intimation that his father considered he had done a good job of looking after his younger brother. Personally, he thought he should

24

have acted more quickly. It seemed to him he had stood in the snow for a period of minutes, staring at the sight of a starved yellow creature in the act of eating Alfred. And when he did act, it was not with the best judgment. He hit the cougar with his lunch pail, which only produced a tinny clang. Even after he had found himself using it, he hadn't realized the possibilities of the heavy, loaded bottle. Why, he should have been able to break the animal's skull with one good blow! Except for the fact that his arms still ached with the effort of wielding the bottle, he would have been convinced that he had only fanned the creature lightly.

"Under the circumstances," Mrs. Harper said, "it is just as well I had a delivery case, with plenty of boiling water and my hands sterile. The sooner Master Alfred has some stitches in him, the better."

Mrs. Harper, a large, handsome woman of middle age, was threading a curved needle with white cotton. Her keen, clear eyes were more like a man's— like a doctor's—and her hands were uncommonly steady and precise. She threaded a second needle and took both to the kitchen where a fire crackled and water made a bubbly sound.

When she returned, bringing with her a smell of fresh carbolic acid, she smiled at Alfred. Not a sweet, soft woman smile. A strong, fine one that made him feel big and brave and a part of the grown-up world. Alfred followed her with his eyes, hoping that she would smile at him like that again. She walked around the room, with the air of having nothing to do for a minute. He saw her pause before a photographic enlargement of a bridal couple on the bare wall, look at it, and then turn away with an impatient sigh, as if she didn't like the picture, or the aftermath of weddings which was going on in the next room.

Alarming gasps and moans. Mrs. Harper consulted the gold watch pinned on her fine bosom and went out. There was the discreet sound of a closing door, but the moaning cries penetrated the thin partition.

"Ma, doesn't she like the picture?" Alfred looked at his mother wonderingly. It had never occurred to him that a picture in a frame could be anything but good.

"Hush." His mother gently smoothed back the hair from his pale forehead with one long-fingered hand. She was grateful for Mrs. Harper and also in awe of her. The widow was the daughter of a Boston surgeon. She had come to that remote arm of Puget Sound with her husband, who was going to make his fortune in timber. Only he had been killed by the first tree felled in his logging camp. Mrs. Harper stayed on in their temporary cabin with her son. Why she stayed was something of a mystery. Once she had told Mrs. Walter that whenever she had planned to go back east, she was prevented by a confinement or a desperate injury in the neighborhood. That could not have been the literal truth. But it seemed true that she stayed because the people needed her. She made long trips in every kind of weather and never turned down an appeal for help. But no one knew her very well. And no one had ever succeeded in paying her for what she did. Most people no longer tried.

26

When the stitches were being taken in Alfred's shoulders and chest, it was George who held his hand. The cries from the bedroom had become louder and more frequent and Mrs. Tucker was in there, looking after the woman who was being so unaccountably hurt in the act of having a baby.

"Just hold your brother's hand tight," Mrs. Harper said, "and don't watch me. Look at a knot in the ceiling."

"Yes, ma'am," Alfred agreed dutifully. After a moment: "Mrs. Harper, which knot shall I look at?"

"Any one will do."

The needle stab decided him on a knot that was like an eye, with a countless number of eyebrows rising above it. He clutched George's warm, calloused hand during the repeated stabs and stared at the knot with his breath quivering.

"Ow, *ow!*" he whimpered with each stab, but dared not cry. Tears would have blinded him and obscured the knot, which he must keep in sight. It was like a stone dropped in the bay, with ripples running away from it. The knot was like the pain of the needle in his shoulder, with other pains running away from it, over and through his body. The cotton thread rasped through his flesh and tore at his shoulder. . . .

"There," Mrs. Harper's voice was brisk and pleased. "*That's* sewed up."

"I—I'm glad you're done. Can I stop looking at the knot?"

"There's some more to sew up, Alf." He was glad it was George who told him. "You were awfully good."

27

There was more to come; much more. Long before it was over Alfred weakened and was lost. The knot blurred and went out in gray, blinding tears and he could not find it any more.

"Georgie, Georgie!" he wailed, "I can't find it!"

"What, Alfie?"

"The knot. *I lost it!*"

"It doesn't matter, child." The needle and thread burned through his flesh again as he choked with salt, bitter tears.

"Just hold my hand hard, Alfie. You'll be all right." He felt George's hard, hot hand clutching his in the bitter darkness. It was his last holding ground against the sea of pain and tears which beat over him. He tried to fight away at last. They finished, holding him down.

He was alone, lying under a blanket on the parlor sofa, when the Jacksons' baby was born. George had been sent outside to play; to find Mr. Jackson and visit with him. At the moment the house was an unsuitable place for males. Alfred felt the women's tabu and would have given anything up to his share in the dugout for the chance to obey it, but he couldn't be moved just then.

After a while he wondered if he had really cried at all while Mrs. Harper was sewing him up. Even if he had, his whimperings had been nothing to the cries of the woman on the other side of the shiplap partition. And it seemed that his pain had been nothing to hers, which had started long before and went on endlessly, increasing in intensity.

When he sensed the approaching end the tide was coming in again. Through the uncurtained window of the Jacksons' parlor he saw the gray current sliding westward through the inlet, like a river in a river, burdened with strange driftwood and little islands of yellow foam. The late afternoon sun shone on the flag which Mr. Jackson had hoisted as a signal that an American was about to be born. George and Mr. Jackson were standing on the beach, looking at Mr. Jackson's round-bottomed green boat. They were talking together like two men and George was pointing out how something could be done to the boat. Putting in an engine, probably. There were no launches on the bay, but George was positive they were the coming thing.

Inside the house, in the bedroom, something was happening at last. The woman's pain and cries had been like a moving tide. The tide had carried her to the Narrows, to the Rapids, where it rushed swiftly over dangerous ledges. Alfred felt himself swept into the swift tide and carried with it, beneath floating branches of trees and creamy foam. Life had been caught in the rapid tide and was moving faster and faster. The three women in the other room were all caught in that tide; they, too, were speeded up, moving faster and faster. Alfred wasn't frightened by Mrs. Jackson's cries now. He heard them, louder than ever. But they didn't seem to matter. They had been leading the way to something great and mysterious; something silent but so swift and vast that the cries dwindled in its presence. The deep, swift current in the Narrows. He was caught in it and the women in the other room were caught in it, moving like shadowy, swaying seaweed under that swift tide. . . .

Alfred snuggled under the blanket on the hump-backed sofa, feeling strangely comfortable and at peace in the tumult. He wasn't afraid to be alone, now. He didn't even have to watch George and Mr. Jackson on the beach; he wanted to be alone, even with his eyes. The gray, incoming tide was laden with strange, floating things and islands of foam. Beyond the moving tide the early sunset was like gold on the lonely, snow-laden fir forest.

In the next room they must have felt the hush of the lonely, gold-white firs at sunset. Out of the hush there arose a clear, new wail. After the noises of the woman beyond the partition, the thin new cry seemed beautiful. As beautiful and strange as the lonely, gold-white sunset firs, and part of their magic.

The magic was shattered by a new, earthy scurrying of women. Alfred's mother—was it his mother? so pale and different and fierce—ran through the room, snatching up a piece of stovewood as she went. It troubled Alfred. Why, when a baby was born, should a woman grab a piece of wood from beside the stove and run out? There were more complications and ceremonies to a baby than he had ever dreamed. Now his mother was smashing ice on the rain barrel behind the house. If they were going to give the baby a bath, surely they would warm the water first. She was back again, pulling the door shut with one foot, holding a chunk of ice in each hand. She did not even hear Alfred's question.

According to Mrs. Harper, Mrs. Jackson was having a "hemrige," whatever that was. It was strange and tiresome. All the women's talk had been about the baby, Mrs. Jackson's baby. The minute it was born and crying in the next room, they forgot all about it. They didn't seem to have noticed it was there. Or was it Mrs. Jackson who wasn't satisfied with the baby? Now she was bent on having a "hem-rige," which the other women were trying to stop.

Alfred's head was heavy and aching and he was tired. Too tired to wonder any more. He gave up at last and fell asleep.

# II

A T DUSK the entire population of the inlet deserted their homes and set out for the Walters'. Or the Tuckers', according to choice. The Tuckers' presence in the big house was something that had happened, unplanned and inevitable, like the growth of a tree. During Mrs. Walter's final illness with heart trouble, help had come and gone. Women used to town housekeeping, defeated at the start by a house where every room was twenty feet square, with ceilings almost as high. Every room but the kitchen with its fireplace to tend. Literal-minded women who never saw beneath the crusty shell of the great-hearted pioneer. Timid girls who were afraid of finding themselves alone with death in a house whose memories went back to the primeval wilderness.

Whenever the Walters were without help, Mrs. Tucker went to their rescue. A loyal and compassionate woman drawn by the same qualities in another. In the last weeks she had never gone home. She kept Alfred with her to carry messages. Mrs. Walter fancied the dark, quiet boy. When her mind drifted, she called him Jimmy.

It was Alfred who carried the final message along the shore path through a black torrent of rain, with Mr. Walter's great umbrella and lantern. While the old woman who had known and suffered so much lay dead in her big bedroom, with the Pickett relics beside her: the letters and the little calico dress, sewn with crooked, childish stitches, and the white gloves of a gentleman of honor. She lay dead beside the opened Thunder Bird chest; the chest which the mischievous Coyote God had first opened, letting escape the souls of men which could never be recaptured, bringing death into the world.

Mrs. Tucker stayed on her feet two days and nights, preparing food for the Indians who came to mourn for the departed "White Mama." She was mortally afraid of Indians, and the Siwashes came like a migration from nearby inlets and from beyond Seattle, far away. Little dugouts and long black war canoes with high prows and many paddlers, gliding into the bay; carried up the beach in awful silence by mourning remnants of tribes. They came into the house silently, without knocking, at all hours of the day and night. A hundred times, thinking she was alone, Mrs. Tucker looked up and found strange Indians in the room with her. It was then her hair started going white.

After it was all over, Mr. Walter found he couldn't do without her. Pa Tucker sold the clearing to a Mr. Hunt from South Dakota, and they all moved into the big house, which was to be theirs when Mr. Walter was through with it.

The arrangement brought Mrs. Tucker a beautiful old garden and more housework than she had ever bargained for. It brought Mr. Tucker a few less stumpy acres of cleared land. Good buildings. A variety of mature fruit trees. A mellowed place, where everything had been done for love and planned for beauty and the dignity of life; far removed from the harsh, crude clearings of the neighborhood, but little better, alas, for making a living. And the change made George and Alfred the heirs of an heroic American tradition, with its glamor and its perils.

Lanterns gleamed along the skidroad and trails, with their light casting gigantic shadows of walking legs. Voices of children drifted through the dark tunnels in the forest. From far away, to the east and the west, the inlet awoke with the creak of oars and the sound of voices. From across the bay there rose the grating rumble of a boat being hustled down the gravel slope of the shore.

The light of a lantern emerged from the woods and twinkled among a dozen walking feet. The Howards were arriving in full strength. Mr. Howard blew out his lantern and set it on the porch with a dozen others. The sound of footsteps brought Mr. Tucker. The door, which he threw open, let out a rich tumult of voices which the family stemmed like a tide as it trooped in.

Mrs. Tucker helped the younger boys with their overcoats, hanging them on the intricate rack above the high, white wainscoting in the corner of the dining room; talking to the boys all the time. "Well, Jim, I hear you were skipped another grade in school! I bet you're partly to blame for their talking about building a high school in town. When they saw boys

35

like you growing up in the woods, they decided they'd have to hurry.

"I'll take it, Arthur. It'll be another year before you can reach the top peg! When are you and Frank coming to fish with the boys? I've been expecting you every Saturday. Alfie saw Old Stubby Nose under the boathouse last week. It seems to me you boys will be big enough to catch him one of these days.

"You come with them, Fred. Off it comes! No? What a swell tug boat! You hold it in the other hand while I get this sleeve off. There!"

Mrs. Tucker wasn't like most mothers—always warning children not to do this and that, and being afraid they'd get hurt: taking the fun out of everything. She made it seem exciting to be alive. Whenever she spoke about anything the boys did, hunting or fishing or going somewhere in the boat, she made it a real adventure. Other mothers said be careful, and don't go too far, and remember what happened to the Atkinson boys. Mrs. Tucker said, "Have a grand adventure!" She knew what life is for.

Before the last Howard coat was hung up, the Jacksons came in. Mr. Jackson short and round, with shiny red cheeks. His wife taller and pale, sweet smiling. And Clarice.

The Howard boys weren't interested in girls, but they paused to look at Clarice. She was small and five and very pretty. White skin and pink cheeks; dark, Dutch-cut hair and warm brown eyes. They stood looking at her because she seemed to belong at a party where there were many voices and where life was bright and warm. At home there were no girls, and only one lamp in a room.

"*Klahowya?*" Mrs. Tucker said.

"*Nika klahowya,*" the child answered sweetly.

Mrs. Tucker knelt down and kissed her. "Who taught you that?"

"George and Alfred."

The young, white-haired woman laughed, taking off the child's coat. "Those boys will make Indians of us all! Clarice, what a pretty dress!"

It was a white dress, with a red ribbon sash.

"This dress was new once," Clarice said proudly.

Her parents smiled. Brushing out her complicated lavender dress, Mrs. Tucker said, "Mine was new, Clarice, a long time before you were born."

Clarice said respectfully, "It must be very old!"

Oliver Harper came in next. Alone from across the bay, where he lived with his mother. The children had seen him often, but did not know him very well. He was a tall, shy man, with a short brown beard. Tonight he wore great hip boots, as if he had waded the bay.

"Mother's very well, thank you," he assured Mrs. Tucker, unstrapping his boots.

She didn't ask why he hadn't brought his mother. Changing times had brought an unforeseen change in Mrs. Harper. Now there were two doctors in town, and they had horses and buggies. Better roads and gasoline launches had shortened distances. Mrs. Harper was no longer called on to save the lives of neighbors, gratis. And when they no longer needed

her skill, they hardly ever saw her. She had withdrawn, quietly, into her own life. Even the people she
had treated and nursed realized that they had never
known her very well. All the time she was giving so
much, she had kept still more of herself in reserve.

Fred Howard wandered away from the other children, clutching his boat. He went as far as the parlor
and stood there doubtfully, abashed by the sight of so
many people. Then his mother saw him and smiled
and he knew everything was all right. He started
toward her, no longer seeing all the people.

"Freddie, come and show me your boat!" The voice
was so loud and had so much authority he couldn't
disobey.

Mr. Walter was reaching out toward him from his
big chair by the fireplace. You always did what Mr.
Walter said. He was almost as old as God, with snow
white "wedding-veil" beard and long hair. Fred sat
on a footstool and surrendered his precious boat. He
was fascinated by Mr. Walter's cane, leaning against
the chair. It was a black, knotty stick with a ribbon
of white cloth tied round the middle. He was so old
he couldn't see far, and when he dropped his cane
the white cloth helped him see where it was.

"It is a tug boat," Mr. Walter pronounced. "Just
like the ones you see on the bay, towing rafts of logs.
It even has towing bitts, for the tow rope." He smiled
at Fred, who was wondering when he was going to
get his boat back. "It has machinery inside, too."

Fred looked at him with polite incredulity.

Mr. Walter touched the solid hull of the toy with

38

mysterious fingers. "It has a boiler and engines, all locked away inside."

"No," Fred answered. "It's only wood."

The old man did not hear what he said, but saw his lips move. "Yes, all locked away inside." His hearing was failing along with his eyes. The world was changing to a quiet twilight. Perhaps that was more restful, after one had lived so long.

Fred looked shyly toward the other side of the fireplace, wondering about Mrs. Walter, who used to sit there. Jim had told him she sat there smoking a pipe: shaving cut plug tobacco with a knife, filling a pipe and smoking. Fred hadn't believed him. Women don't smoke. He asked his mother, who was reluctant but always truthful. Yes, Mrs. Walter had smoked, though Jim wasn't called on to bring up the subject. Mrs. Walter had been a noble woman. If she smoked, there was an excuse for it. All the lonely years she had spent at Collins Point and on Tyee Bay. She loved people, but seemed to have been born to be alone. Most of her life she had no neighbors except the Indians. She was married twice, but had no children of her own. There had been one adopted son who meant everything to her. But when she found out he had genius, she sent him away to be educated. Sometimes he was gone for a year at a time. And while he was still young, he went away forever. It wasn't right for a woman to smoke, but in a lonely life like hers there was some excuse. . . .

When Mr. Walter gave back his boat, Fred slipped out of the parlor, with a backward look at the fire-

39

place, solemn with regret at having been cheated of his last chance to see a woman smoke.

The squeak and snore of violins being tuned up. Scraping of many chairs being moved.

"They're getting ready to dance!"

The children slipped through the dining room and crowded about the doorway to the parlor. Everything was exciting, glamorous commotion. Chairs were being moved against the wall and out of the room. Mr. Miller and old Captain Nye were sawing experimentally at their violins while Mrs. Miller, in a pink dress, sat at the piano and struck keys. Mr. Tucker walked about, sprinkling white powder on the smooth, dark floor.

John Hanson took a running step and skated gracefully along the powdered floor.

"We'll help spread the wax," he said.

The floor was instantly overrun with children, running, skating, slipping in every direction. Whooping with glee, squealing, bumping into each other, into the adults along the sides. Hedvig Hanson skated squarely against Mr. Harper, with her pigtails flying. When she saw who it was, she turned with a small shriek and skated away, pigtails flying in the opposite direction. Freddie Howard's feet slipped forward from under him and he fell with a bump on his little behind, looking unutterably amazed.

It was glorious, though it lasted only a matter of seconds. The sudden invasion of skating children took the grown-ups by surprise, until they recovered from it and took steps.

"Walter! Freddie! Grace! Mary! Arthur!" They were hailed from all sides.

Mrs. Tucker rounded them up with outstretched arms. "Who said you could make this a skating rink? Skeedaddle this minute! There are going to be games upstairs. Grace, would you like to help Alfred get them started?"

The invasion of the children was over as suddenly as it started; quick and brief as a snow flurry. The musicians clamped their fiddles under their chins and sawed away in earnest. A young man with a lock of black hair over one eye called the dances. Shouted them.

"Choose your partners!"

There was the shuffle of husbands and wives, young men and girls, finding each other; kaleidoscope of fine dresses and dark suits which had started life back east—in Iowa and Wisconsin and Nebraska.

"All join hands!"

Calloused hands and knotted ones, muscular hands and smooth young ones clasped each other around the ring.

"Circle to the right!"

The circle spun.

"Ladies to the left, gents to the right!"

Male and female they wove about the circle, gliding, skipping, prancing, according to individual taste.

"Swing your partners!" The caller's voice shattered through tortured cry of violins and the rush and crash of feet. The gents swung the ladies. One young man seized his partner about the waist and spun her so furiously that her feet left the floor and her dress flared out stiffly, exposing the tops of her patent leather shoes. The children lingering at the door watched the whirling human centrifuge with admiring awe. Afterward some of the mothers said it was a vulgar display, but the children knew an accomplished young man when they saw one.

During the intermission Lars Hanson clattered in, on his way home from Camp C, where he worked as a windfall-bucker to support his family and his little farm. Before entering the house he had muzzled the needle-sharp calks of his logging boots by stepping on two pieces of board. He sounded like a wooden giant walking. He clattered into the parlor—six-feet-seven with the boards—and greeted his neighbors. John and Hedvig hung onto his hands shyly and beamed far up at his great red beard.

He declined offers of partners with a big, easy laugh. They knew he didn't dance. Except at the camp mess shack, where the loggers sometimes danced with each other. There you didn't have to worry about floors, and splinters flew in showers under the thudding steel-fanged boots. He would come back to the party after changing from his working clothes: the calked boots and corduroy trousers and coveted blue flannel shirt. Not that the boys and young men didn't own shirts of the same kind, but Mr. Hanson had earned the right to wear his logger-style. The front was tucked into his trousers, the tail left out and twisted into a curious knot which stayed in place all day. The arrangement gave perfect freedom to the wearer's back and looked like the docked tail of a fine horse.

Mr. Hanson clattered out as the fiddlers struck up

and the caller's voice rang out above the storm of crying violins and flying feet.

"Alfred, please tell us a story."

The children were scattered about one of the big, white-painted bedrooms upstairs, after the last attempt at a game, which had ended in anarchy. Alfred and George had planned to slip down to the bay and have a look at the Nyes' launch. Maybe take the cylinder head off the engine to settle a disputed mechanical point. Instead, Alfred found himself looking after the children. Grace Miller, who was supposed to help him, had gone downstairs on some errand and forgotten to come back. Probably she was making eyes at George, whom she fancied. Everyone said Alfred was very good with children, though he was beginning to doubt it after trying to amuse so many different ages all at once. He looked at Jim, serious-faced, reading a book.

"I don't think Jim wants to hear a story."

Jim turned a page and looked up. "I don't mind."

The others crowded around.

"What is the story about?"

"It's about the first man who logged here."

"Paul?"

"It might be." It was a story Mr. Walter had told him and George, sitting in front of the fireplace.

"Tell it, Alfred."

"We want to hear it."

"You tell good stories."

"Well," Alfred began, "this is the story about the time Paul courted Alice Price."

43

"Alfred, who was Alice Price?" Clarice couldn't remember very far back.

"The Prices lived way down the bay, where the Millers are now."

"I remember Alice," Jim remarked. "She was a funny old maid who tried to act like a girl."

"This is about the time she was young and very beautiful," Alfred explained. "When Paul was doing the first logging around here. Paul was big and strong. Bigger than anyone you ever saw—"

"Not bigger than my Daddy!" John Hanson insisted.

"Paul was bigger than anyone nowadays. When he built the skidroads round here he just walked through the woods with an armful of skids and dropped one every six feet. He could carry enough for a mile in one load."

Clarice's eyes glowed as she looked up at the young storyteller. "My, he must have been strong!"

"Yes," Alfred assured her, "he was a champion!"

"Well, that was about the time the Prices moved here and built their big green house with all the gables. Alice was a young lady then, maybe nineteen. And she was very beautiful—"

"Beautifuller than the Sleeping Beauty?"

"As beautiful, anyway, I guess. Everyone stopped to look at her. And all the men who weren't married wanted to marry her. First the Prices lived back east in Omaha. They left there and moved to Denver because of all the young men falling in love with Alice. Her father and mother loved her so much they didn't want her to get married. Well, it was just as bad in

Denver. The young men behaved the same way, only there were more of them. The Prices didn't have any peace at all. So pretty soon they had to move again—"

"It must be a lot of trouble for people to have a very beautiful daughter," Mary Hunt decided.

"It's the most trouble in the world," Alfred assured her, "specially when her father and mother want to keep her for themselves. The Prices moved to Salt Lake City, and that was worse! Even the men who did have wives wanted to marry her, because they were Mormons. They left there in a week and went to San Francisco. That wasn't much better, because it was a very wicked city. So they moved up here and built their house with all the little rooms and gables.

" 'Now,' they said, 'we'll have some peace at last!' They were sure of that because there wasn't anyone to fall in love with Alice. The only people here were the Walters and the Indians.

"Well, the Prices felt pretty safe. And when there were just three of them with so many rooms it was like living in a castle. Only Alice wasn't happy. She used to sit in the garden all by herself—"

Jim Howard cleared his throat and said, "Alice Price was always sitting in the garden, under the big balm-of-Gilead tree. She was queer."

Alfred nodded. "That was afterward. This is about the time when the tree wasn't even planted. There was just a garden. One day when Alice was sitting there, very beautiful and lonesome, she looked over the fence. There was a big, handsome man, carrying a great armful of skids. They smiled at each other, and she asked who he was and what he was doing. He said

45

he was Paul, and he was building a skidroad. He was starting logging back in the woods. When he threw down the skids to talk to her, Mrs. Price thought it was thunder. And she sent Mr. Price out with an umbrella to hold over Alice.

"Paul started hauling logs to the bay with his forty yoke of oxen. All day long they could hear Paul hollering 'TIMBER-R-R!' or swearing at his oxen. And when he was passing the garden he would stop and talk to Alice. The Prices would have moved again, only they couldn't. They'd spent all their money building the big house. And they were scared of Paul. Once he waded out in the bay and caught a lot of salmon for Alice. Mr. Price threw them away on the beach. Next time Paul came to the house and said he had a fish for Alice, Mr. Price told him to throw it on the beach and not bother them any more. Paul threw it on the beach. But this time it was a whale, too big for the tide to carry away—"

"Alfred, I remember the whale!" Hedvig exclaimed. "It smelt something awful."

"That was later," Alfred explained. "It came ashore by itself, or maybe Paul is still sore at the place.

"Well, Paul and Alice fell in love. And when Paul had logged the biggest trees and was ready to move his camp, he told the Prices he wanted to marry Alice.

"They were afraid of him, but they couldn't bear to part with Alice. They said she was their daughter and nobody was going to marry her. Alice cried and Paul swore and hollered. He talked to them out in the garden, because if it had been inside he would have

46

blown the roof off the house. Mr. Walter, up the bay, heard everything Paul said.

"He told them he was going to build a house for Alice at his new logging camp, farther west. When the house was built he would come back and take Alice. When he was leaving, he drove his balm-of-Gilead ox goad into the ground. If it wasn't there when he came back, Paul said, he would do something terrible.

"After that the Prices never had any peace. The old folks were afraid all the time, expecting every day that Paul would come back for Alice. And she was waiting for him; worrying because he didn't come. In the spring, the goad had leaves on it. After a while it grew into a big balm-of-Gilead tree. And Alice changed into a funny old maid, sitting under the tree, waiting for Paul—"

Clarice slipped her hand into Alfred's calloused paw.

"That's a sad story, Alfred. Didn't Paul ever come back for her?"

Alfred hesitated, looking into the fire. "Some people say he didn't. Mr. Walter says he did."

"How did he, Alfred?"

"Well, I don't suppose any of you remember the hurricane—"

Jim did. "I counted eight trees falling at one time. The wind made a kind of road through the woods near our place."

"Yes," Alfred agreed. "Only Mr. Walter said it was Paul rushing through the woods. He was coming for Alice. The road of fallen trees went straight to the

47

Prices' place. The wind took part of the roof off the house, where Alice was dying. And it twisted the top off the balm-of-Gilead tree, just as if a giant had tried to pull it up. It was Paul, coming back for his bride and his goad."

"Is it true?" John wanted to know.

"Of course, it's true," Mary Hunt insisted. "Haven't you seen the balm-of-Gilead tree?"

Alfred suggested: "Maybe if somebody followed the road of fallen trees he would find the house Paul built for Alice. It must be a big castle, when it took so many years."

"But the hurricane came from the ocean," Jim objected. "It capsized a lot of ships."

"Maybe Paul's new logging camp was across the Pacific, then," Alfred said.

"Well, kids, how about something to eat?"

The door had been thrown open, letting in the sound of crying violins from downstairs; the rush and stamp of feet. *"The crow hopped out and the bird hopped in! All join hands! Circle to the left!"*

George was standing in the doorway; a big boy of fifteen, almost a man, in long pants, with his face flushed and a lock of thick yellow hair hanging over one of his sea-blue eyes.

"How about something to eat, kids?"

They scrambled to their feet. George swooped Clarice up in his arms, holding her triumphantly, like a prize doll.

"Hungry, Clarice?"

"Yes." She smiled back at Alfred as they all trooped

48

downstairs. George held her high in one arm, as lightly as the gigantic Paul carrying away his bride.

Oliver Harper went home early, with his great hip boots. He wished his mother hadn't made him wear them against the damp of the beach.

He pushed his boat down the rattling gravel slope. The pale moon was setting beyond the black fir tree tops on Thunder Bird Point. While the people danced the tide had gone far out, leaving the fleet of boats stranded on the beach. He rowed past the Nyes' heeling launch, standing up in his boat, fisherman style, facing forward and pushing on the oars. Up and down the inlet salmon were leaping and falling back in the dying moonlight. One struck the side of his boat with a thump but did not fall into it. Other men sometimes had salmon jump into their boats. It had never happened to him. No unusual good fortune ever happened to him. He rowed toward the steady light in the window, where his mother was waiting for him. There were no other lights. Everyone but his mother and himself was at the party. All human life on the inlet was concentrated in the two houses, the Tuckers' and his mother's. Everyone but himself, rowing through darkness from one to the other. And that was as it should be. The first settlers had brought a fine civilization with them. That had died, and the later comers were building a new, inferior one. He had been lost, somehow, between the two. Between the one that was dead, for all his mother could do or say, and the one from which she had turned. In a different way, he was

49

like his old, half-breed playmate, Jimmy Pickett. Jimmy had once said he belonged somewhere out in the dark between a dying fire and one that had just been kindled. He couldn't go back to the one or forward to the other, belonging half to each. He had shown Oliver how it was with a diagram.

It was nonsense, of course, in Jimmy's case. Jimmy had gone far in his thirty years. Farther than most people ever go. School in Olympia. Art school in San Francisco. A good job with the *Post Intelligencer* in Seattle. A better one with the *Oregonian* in Portland. Paintings signed *J. T. Pickett*. Paintings that collectors fancied and the owners wouldn't sell. There was something about them that became a part of yourself. Jimmy went far. Mrs. Walter had put everything she knew and had behind him, and he went on from there. Went out of the woods like a skyrocket. Then he was gone.

The last time he had seen Jimmy. The spring evening before he left for Portland. The two of them idling on the beach in front of the Walters' house. Skipping flat pebbles across smooth silver water. Jimmy slight and straight, with his delicate face and wonderful glowing eyes. In the dusk, he looked like one of his own pictures, where there was so much darkness, and such a cry of light.

"I worked hard in Seattle, Oliver. I expect to work still harder for the *Oregonian*, and for my art. There's only work for me. There would be a woman, if I were a white man or an Indian. These crosses don't belong. We won't have any more of them." Skipping a pebble which made ten diamond splashes before sinking in the silver water. "Love goes into my work. There's room for all I have. Pictures will be my children. . . ."

In the morning Oliver saw the open cutter, the *Plunger*, under sail. Mr. Walter's dark, big figure at the tiller. A slender one, standing up, waving. With a breath of air and the drain of the outgoing tide the cutter drew away toward the sunrise and disappeared behind the high woods of Skookum Point.

When it was gone, he looked across the tide and saw Mrs. Walter. A tall and lonely figure on the beach, standing as still as a statue, with her face turned toward the east. Behind her, the big white house against its background of unbroken forest and tremendous silence.

That fall, Jimmy was dead and buried in Portland before Mrs. Walter knew anything was wrong. Dead. Probably because of his fixed idea that he belonged out there in the dark. Burned himself out with work and died of consumption quicker than the old lady had died of heart trouble. Good old Jimmy. There was something about the spring night that made one think of him. That painting of his. The one that was almost all darkness, with a waning moon setting beyond Thunder Bird Point, taking all the light with it. Somehow it broke your heart to feel it going. As if you would die when the light went. You might say Jimmy did. Perhaps he didn't want to, after all. Good old Jimmy. . . .

There weren't any boys like him now. But there were smart boys like Jim Howard, who would go up out of the woods in their own way when the time came. And there were boys like George and Alfred, who would make something of the woods. His mother didn't have the patience to see that. The neighbors were all a mixed lot to her and the children young barbarians. She was living in the past and Boston. Boston of the past. If she went back there she would probably find it a mixed lot.

The light had all gone from behind Thunder Bird Point. Jimmy's moon had set long ago. The salmon leaped and fell about Oliver's boat as he rowed through the darkness between the many lights of the big house and the one steady lamp in his mother's window.

# III

MISS PEABODY, the new school teacher, had been invited to supper by the Jacksons. Clarice was bringing her home after school.

"We go this way," she said. They turned off the Arcadia Road onto a rough wagon track through the woods.

"Aren't you afraid to walk through the woods alone?" Miss Peabody asked.

Clarice swung her lard-pail lunch bucket deliberately.

"I'm eight," she pointed out. "Anyway, there's nothing to be afraid of."

Miss Peabody shivered, half-playfully. "Aren't there bears and things?" She clutched her umbrella tighter.

"Bears don't hurt you unless you hurt them first," the child assured her. "I wouldn't do that. A cougar is the only animal that would attack you, and then he'd have to be starving." She stopped to pick a handful of huckleberries from a convenient bush. "This is my special bush. It likes me to stop and pick some of its berries when I'm coming home from school."

They started on again, Clarice reaching up to pour some of the small purple berries into her teacher's doubtful hand.

"Clarice, how do you know when a cougar is starving? Couldn't that happen any time?"

"Oh, no, Miss Peabody. Only when there is deep snow and he can't catch any game."

"I see." The teacher smiled down at her companion. "What do you do when there *is* deep snow?"

"Daddy takes me then. He pretends he's a new pupil. We have lots of fun. He asks me what grade I think he'll be in and I ask him questions to find out. Sometimes it's the first grade, but usually he does better."

"What do you like best in school?"

"Drawing. I like to draw ladies, only I can't get their legs right."

"Clarice, a lady doesn't have legs!"

"Really?" The child's wide, dark eyes were incredulous. She considered her companion from the waist down until the teacher began to feel naked. "What happens to your legs when you grow up?"

"One doesn't speak of a lady's legs. It isn't nice."

"What would you call it if a lady broke one of her . . ." she hesitated in perplexity.

"You would call it a limb," Miss Peabody explained.

"Oh, like a tree! The lady broke her limb. The boy climbed out on the big limb. . . ."

"Exactly. Now let's think of something else."

"There's Rosie," Clarice pointed out. "She's our cow." On the other side of the rail fence a cow was grazing in the hilly pasture, picking grass among the rocks and stumps of the half-cleared land. "It's good of cows to give milk, isn't it? Still, they haven't anything else to do, except eat. They don't have to work. We have a horse, too. His name is Charlie. He's a gelding and he can't be a mother or a father."

They came in sight of the river-like inlet, green and calm between its wooded shores. In the distance the Olympic range, a long snowy barrier against the sky.

"You do have a beautiful view, Clarice."

"That tallest one is Mount Elinor. Do you know what Daddy says?"

Miss Peabody hoped in her heart it wouldn't be anything ribald.

"Daddy says if they would only take those darned mountains away he would move to where he could make a better living."

"Clarice, you mustn't say 'darned.'"

"I don't. Daddy does. Only that's not what he says. I thought you'd like 'darned' better."

Miss Peabody quit the subject. "Would you like to live in some other place?"

"I don't know what other places are like," Clarice pointed out. "I was born here, right in that house. Only it wasn't painted then. I was born in the winter of the big snow."

"The stork finds his way in any kind of weather, doesn't he?"

Clarice ignored the pleasantry. "Daddy hoisted a flag when Mother got her pains and Mrs. Harper came over. Right in the middle of it the Tuckers came in with Alfred. He'd been clawed by a cougar on the way to school. Mrs. Harper had to do a lot of sewing on him. I'm glad he didn't die. I love Alfred too much."

Miss Peabody thought she had noticed something of the sort. "Girls aren't supposed to love boys," she reproved gently.

"Really, Miss Peabody?" The little face was vivid with disbelief.

"Not unless they're brothers and sisters," the teacher qualified.

Clarice looked puzzled. "Daddy says brothers and sisters can't marry each other. That's called insect."

The teacher was startled. "Clarice, dear, you aren't supposed to think about marriage until you're grown up. It isn't nice for little girls to think about such things."

"Don't you like Alfred?"

"He's very nice."

Miss Peabody boarded with the Tuckers, who had the one comfortable house she had found in the neighborhood. It made her think of the southern mansions she liked to read about, where people are poor and proud, and very hospitable. The impression had been strengthened by George and Alfred. The boys drew her into discussions of the Civil War, which was fresher in their minds than in hers. And they showed a strong sympathy for General Pickett, who had been a rebel.

"Alfred plays end on the football team," Clarice was saying. "George is fullback."

"Yes." Miss Peabody had seen the boys kicking and throwing a football at the edge of the orchard.

"Last year the team played Elma. They thought George was too big. It isn't his fault if there wasn't a high school in town until he was seventeen."

56

"No," the teacher agreed.

"Our team would have won if Bull Martin hadn't hurt himself. The Elma substitute they borrowed didn't know the signals."

Miss Peabody said, "Football is dangerous."

"Bull wouldn't have got hurt if it had been on our own field," Clarice explained. "He didn't know there was a stump behind the goal posts." After a minute she added, "I'll be glad when I can go to high school. I like town."

The teacher shivered. Her mind was still trying to digest its first tough impression of Forest City. The business district was half a street of wooden buildings, with lean-to porches over the board sidewalk. The other side was given over to railroad tracks, sheds and a round house. The splintery wooden walk was crowded with smiling Indians, eating candy, and fierce-looking, drunken loggers with bedding rolls on their backs. The sidewalk was narrow and close to swinging saloon doors which fanned out great alcoholic breaths. A bearded giant had staggered out of one to confront her, savage-eyed, reeled away and collided with a post to which a calico pony was tied. Looking back, fearfully, she saw him raise his broad-brimmed hat to the post in a salute of profound dignity.

George and Alfred, who had rowed her to town, didn't seem to notice the terrifying giant. They walked beside her as gentlemanly and serious as if everything sordid were hidden from their clear young eyes. Like the child who was now beside her, they seemed to think of town as a fine place, with points of interest.

"Watch!" George had said in answer to her anxious question about a drygoods store. "Watch the man on the first car!"

What appeared to be a runaway train, loaded with immense logs, was looming up at the far end of the street, with men standing on the logs. A crouching figure, low on the first car, leaned out perilously and pulled a lever as it went past.

"See him?" George shouted above the banging ragtime on a saloon piano, and the jolting rumble of the train.

The first car of the train swerved toward the street, showing the ends of logs, like piled-up cannon balls. It swerved again and came on, the train swinging from the far track to the near, angling its stiff joints.

"Flying switch!" George shouted above the din of the endlessly passing train.

Alfred shouted gravely, "It's against the law!"

The heavy, crashing roar of the train was the most brutal sound the teacher had ever heard. It was more than sound. It blurred her vision of the men, standing easily on the topmost logs, against the smoky sky. It shook the board sidewalk, faded the ragtime piano with the clattering of store windows, and rattled her teeth as she tried to speak. In the street a team of white horses with a black vehicle raced the logging train in a cloud of yellowish dust. As the horses galloped by, she saw that they were drawing an empty hearse. . . .

Miss Peabody looked wonderingly at her pupil. "So you like town?"

"Of course. Don't you?" The child opened a big

gate, and they approached the neat white house. "I have a garden, I'll show it to you. Daddy!"

A round little man in overalls and campaign hat was hurrying toward them across a prosperous cabbage patch. "There is no justice!" he called as he came nearer.

The teacher was startled by the greeting.

"How do you do, Mr. Jackson?" she said apprehensively.

When the little man bent down to give Clarice a kiss, she took off his hat and put it rakishly on her own head.

"Daddy got this hat when he went to war."

Bareheaded, Mr. Jackson went on to explain. "Working outdoors, I am always thinking. My brain works as well as my arms and legs. I believe ideas are as important as cabbages. Cultivating the cabbages, it came to me that there is no justice. I'll prove it!"

"There is a Spanish bullet-hole in this hat," Clarice announced, tilting it on one side. "They couldn't shoot my daddy."

"Miss Peabody, you are a woman of education. Do you think we have any justice?"

It was quite the strangest greeting she had ever received. Justice, hats, cabbages and Spanish bullets all mixed together.

"We have courts, Mr. Jackson—"

"Courts!" he lamented. "That is what I am talking about. Last Tuesday it was testified in the Superior Court of this County, in the year of our Lord nineteen hundred and—"

"John, *will* you stop!" Mrs. Jackson had come to

the rescue. She was a thin, dimly-pretty woman, taller than her husband. "Keeping Miss Peabody out here with your ideas!" Her look suggested that she was proud of her incorrigible little husband.

He patted his wife's arm. "I was going to show her the cabbages. Miss Peabody, would you like to see how cabbages grow in this country?"

The teacher agreed readily. She felt sure that the little man's cabbages would be safer than his ideas.

At dinner Mr. Jackson appeared less alarming, with his hair neatly brushed over his forehead and a big linen napkin tucked under his chubby face. The teacher felt her courage rise among the heartening array of chicken, jelly, four kinds of vegetables, cole slaw and pickles, with two kinds of pie and coffee in the offing. . . . After her second helping of chicken, she made bold to inquire if the Jacksons attended Divine Worship. Two Sundays had already passed without the Tuckers making any move toward church. If she brought up the subject, Mrs. Tucker would undoubtedly assure her that the boys would be glad to take her. But she hesitated about interrupting their mysterious Sunday occupation of bringing in crooked timbers from the woods.

"We used to go to church," Mrs. Jackson said apologetically, "but we've rather got out of the habit."

"I didn't like the funerals," Clarice said emphatically.

"We decided it was a bad influence for a child," Mr. Jackson explained.

"Mr. Jackson! *Church* a bad influence?"

Mrs. Jackson hastened to add: "The funerals were so dismal."

"There was a funeral every Sunday," said Mr. Jackson.

"Practically every Sunday," his wife modified.

"Once there were three funerals in one," Clarice put in.

Mr. Jackson went on, "We decided it wasn't a good idea to let Clarice see how Christians treat their brothers."

A voice inside the teacher said, Be very, very careful, Louella Peabody! This man is full of dangerous ideas. He's only looking for an excuse to let them out. So she only permitted her voice to remark, "Oh!" Inside the man's own house she wasn't quite willing to believe the rumor that he was a Socialist, but she sensed that something was very wrong. And she saw why Clarice was both a joy and a despair. The brightest child in her school, and in some ways the most disturbing. Other children were slower and more groping, but once an idea was drilled into their heads they accepted it, whole. Clarice Jackson grasped the same idea easily—then pulled it to pieces and wanted to know why. Sometimes she was satisfied with the explanation. And sometimes she was polite and doubtful. Miss Peabody could see now it wasn't her fault, poor child. Her education was being muddled by her eccentric little father.

After supper they sat in the simply furnished parlor, which had the air of being used every day. Clarice had been persuaded to bed. Apparently she was never ordered to do anything. Miss Peabody longed to shake her while she protested and made delays. But in the end she said goodnight cheerfully and went upstairs to put herself to bed, with a lighted candle in one hand and an ancient, home-made Brownie held against her breast.

It was the time for confidences between parents and teacher. Mr. Jackson started it, sitting on the hump-backed sofa, smoking, unrebuked. He asked, with his chubby face anxious, "Does Clarice enjoy herself at school?"

The teacher had never heard of that as the primary object of education. When she admitted that Clarice enjoyed herself thoroughly, Mr. Jackson seemed well satisfied with his daughter's progress.

Mrs. Jackson, knitting a sock, asked: "Does she get along well with the other children?"

Clarice was inclined to be rather headstrong and lordly, but the other children seemed to regard her as someone special. Miss Peabody thought she got along with them fairly well.

Afterward the mother thought to remark, "I suppose she does well enough in her studies?"

Miss Peabody had counted on telling the Jacksons that Clarice would be at the head of her class in everything, except for her preoccupation with the recitations of the classes above her. But this off-hand attitude took the wind out of her sails. Apparently, from their point of view, "well enough" left nothing to be desired! The teacher left nearly everything she wished to say, unsaid, and led the conversation to safer ground. She asked about the chief crops of the neighborhood.

"Everything grows here," Mr. Jackson explained, "and nothing sells. All of us are still looking for a money crop."

"It's cabbages for us this year," Mrs. Jackson said. "If they don't sell, it'll be something else next year."

"Poultry might be a good idea, if we could raise our own feed."

"Strawberries do well. But there's nothing in them if you have to hire pickers."

"It's a risky business, even if you have the children to help," Mr. Jackson thought. "Strawberry picking has driven many a boy to the logging camps."

"Mr. Howard tried raising beef cattle," Mrs. Jackson recalled. "But after a few years the cattle ran wild and had to be hunted like deer."

"It may be dairying, if we ever get enough land cleared."

The teacher inquired about apples. She had been distressed by the sight of beautiful apples under all the trees at the Tuckers'. Once she had seen the boys fighting a friendly duel with apples for ammunition. Otherwise the fruit lay in the grass, undisturbed.

"Everybody has tried shipping apples to the commission houses in Seattle," Mrs. Jackson said. "Nobody ever got anything back but the freight bill."

Miss Peabody was bewildered by the vague state of agriculture in the neighborhood.

"We have no business to be farming here," Mr. Jackson declared. "We'll never get out of the woods. The next generation will find our work useful, but that doesn't help us."

"Pioneers," Miss Peabody said.

"No," he insisted, "damn fools!"

63

"John!" His wife looked up sweetly from her knitting.

"Damn fools," the little man repeated, "caught by something in the climate or the scenery. We know we can't make a living here, but we try. None of us has enough land cleared. That costs a hundred dollars an acre. Or a year of a man's time if he does it himself. None of us ever has a hundred dollars to spare—"

"None of us ever has a hundred dollars," his wife corrected.

"And a man's life isn't long enough for him to clear a decent sized place."

Later they talked about Mr. Walter, whose memory was held in such veneration at the Tuckers'.

"There was a real pioneer," Mr. Jackson said. "When he was here alone in the early days, the Indians from British Columbia sometimes came into this bay, raiding, in their war canoes. The Siwashes here have always been peaceful. When their Canadian cousins appeared, they would pack their lunches and light out for the tall timber. You can still find heaps of shells way back in the woods where our Indians ate clams while they waited for the enemy to go away. No, it was purely an Indian affair. The Canadian war parties never disturbed Mr. Walter. . . . "

Mr. Jackson was an intelligent man, and quite entertaining. But there was no way of knowing beforehand how he was going to take a subject. When his wife brought up the matter of perpetual motion, he dropped out of the conversation and looked displeased.

"The old man spent his last years trying to perfect

perpetual motion," Mrs. Jackson said. "One of his contraptions was for making water go around forever through a lot of tin funnels. There was a water-wheel, too, wasn't there, John?"

"I don't remember." He didn't seem to be trying.

"Anyway," Mrs. Jackson went on, "it stood on saw-horses behind the barn. It didn't work, of course."

"Didn't anyone tell him it couldn't work?"

"Everybody did. But he was as stubborn as he was good and gentle. He would smile and point out that the same thing had been said about steam engines and flying machines."

"And did he think flying machines would work?"

Mr. Jackson started to sputter, then checked himself.

Outside the lamplit room, in the black night, rain roared on the roof, making everything cozier inside.

Mrs. Jackson smiled reminiscently over her knitting. "Once one of his perpetual motion machines did go. The old man was having a nap when one of the cows went into the shed where he had a perpetual motion machine, and got her horns caught in the contraption. Mrs. Walter saw it. She was a wonderful woman, with a great sense of humor. She woke her husband.

" 'William, your perpetual motion machine is going!'

"He said 'Who-o-o!' the way he did whenever he was excited.

" 'Hurry,' she said, 'it's going fast!'

"He hurried out in time to see his machine going, on the horns of a cow!"

They laughed and pictured the scene, and laughed again. But the teacher thought there was something sad about it, too.

"Think of it! Wasting years of his life trying to do the impossible!"

Mrs. Jackson said, "He believed in it until the end. Strange, that anyone so wise and fine could have believed in anything so ridiculous—"

There was an ominous snort from the couch. Miss Peabody was startled by her host, with his face red and his chest swelling.

"Ridiculous?" the little man cried, "what's so ridiculous about believing in perpetual motion?"

"Now, John—" his wife murmured while she purled rapidly.

"What's so ridiculous about believing in perpetual motion?"

"But Mr. Jackson," the teacher remonstrated, "it can't work. We learned that in physics. The friction—"

He snorted like an angry bull. "If it's ridiculous for an unlettered old pioneer to have believed in perpetual motion, what about our captains of industry, who should know better? What about the men who believe they can go on forever exploiting this country? Killing men every day with rotten gear and rotten methods! Burning up two acres of timber for every acre they log! Leaving a trail of dead men and burnt desolation! Taking everything and giving nothing. Believing there will never be a day of reckoning! Never a day when there will be nothing left to exploit and destroy! God Almighty, if that isn't belief in perpetual motion—"

Miss Peabody felt as if she were falling headlong, leaning forward to resist the storm of words that had suddenly ended. Dead silence, walled in by the million little drums of rain. Mr. Jackson's head was raised, listening. His look was gentle and inquiring. Mrs. Jackson had put down her knitting and half risen. The teacher hadn't heard anything but the torrent of words, suddenly cut off, and the invading sound of rain. It was spooky, like the beginning of a ghost story.

Then she saw Clarice come into the room, like a little wraith in her white nightgown, with her dark hair disheveled from sleep. She was asleep. Her eyes were almost closed and her face set in an expression of dreaming grief. The child pattered over to her mother and put up one hand toward her reassuring face, looking at her with strange, clairvoyant intentness. Her hand hovered near her mother's cheek, but did not actually touch it. No one spoke or moved. The hand withdrew slowly, like a motion made under deep water. The expression of dream grief became puzzled. Clarice looked about until she saw her father. She went over to the couch and looked intently, the same way, with her hand hovering near his face. Like something insubstantial that would disappear if touched. Her father smiled encouragingly and her hand sank slowly to her side. The expression of grief faded. She turned and pattered out of the room. Mrs. Jackson caught up a lamp and followed, unnoticed, to light her up the stairs.

"Fast asleep!" She said when she returned, and set down the lamp. Her faded face was quite lovely. "She won't remember anything about it in the morning."

"Poor child," Miss Peabody said. "I remember the terrible nightmares I used to have when I was young."

"This one was real." Mr. Jackson observed heavily. He looked over at his wife, who nodded.

"It was real once," she corrected.

The teacher's eyes opened wide behind her thick glasses. "You know what she was dreaming about?"

"Haunted by the sins of her parents," Mr. Jackson explained.

It sounded mysterious and alarming.

"She heard Daddy's voice," Mrs. Jackson explained, "and she dreamed we were quarreling. She came to have us make it up. We used to quarrel a great deal when Clarice was small. Her birth nearly killed me, and I was warned never to have another child. We loved each other, and we didn't know what to do about it. It lead to some terrible quarrels—"

"We didn't know how to warm ourselves without burning down the house," Mr. Jackson put in.

"Whenever we quarreled, Clarice would come between us and make her father pick her up. Then she would put her arm about my neck and draw us together, and say, 'Let's all love each other!' We hardly ever quarrel now; never like that. But she still watches over us, even when she is asleep."

"She has a loving heart," Mr. Jackson said. He looked at his wife with a sad, boyish smile. "We want to be a credit to our little girl, don't we, Mother?"

When it was time to go, the teacher put on her rubbers and said goodbye to Mrs. Jackson. Her host was waiting, in a slicker and campaign hat, with a lighted lantern in his hand. She raised her umbrella on the porch and water from the eaves thundered over it. They splashed through water on the path and set off in a black pour of rain. Miss Peabody knew she would be wet through before she reached the Tuckers'. It seemed a suitable ending to the strangest evening she had ever spent, where her well-settled ideas had been turned upside down and her hosts were insubstantial faces in the dream of her stubborn and wayward little pupil.

# IV

THE forest has its beauty of damp gloom. Cultivated fields have their green or golden beauty. Even when the things that grow there cannot be sold for money. But there is no beauty or comfort in land changing from the wild to the cultivated. From the burning of slashed brush to the last, exhausting battle with the stumps, work is done in a bath of fir charcoal, powdery and choking when dry; miserably sticky, wet. Funereal, seeping black that finds its way through clothes and into work gloves. There is not one object on which an itching nose can be rubbed without being blackened and made to itch more. By that, you appreciate that the simplest comforts are not there.

This acre would be the tenth they had helped their father clear. And it was the toughest of all. It was on the hill west of the skidroad. Paul Bunyan had passed through that acre on his dash to claim Alice Price, leaving a swath of windfall trees twenty feet deep. Alfred figured that on this one acre Paul's errand of love had left them one thousand and thirty tons of fallen trees to unravel. George couldn't find anything wrong with the figures, but he hoped there was a mistake somewhere.

Now, the new acre was half cleared. The brush was gone, along with the limbs and tops of trees. The standing trees were felled, and green and dead alike bucked up into lengths that could be handled. The acre's black battle ground was massed with pyramids of logs, ready for burning. They piled them up four high with the help of the horses, blocks and tackle led to convenient stumps, skids, cant hooks and peavies, and a great deal of sweat that channeled blackened faces.

"We'll finish this pile," their father said, "and call it a day. We've time to get this log out of the way and get home before the rain."

The air was heavy with electricity. White thunder heads pushed up rapidly from the dark bank of clouds above the tree tops in the west. O, welcome summer storm, to wash off this sweat and end the day's dirty work.

They attacked the last log for the pile, too far away for the tackle to reach. Pa used the ancient cant hook, George and Alfred the spike-pointed peavies. Pa always used the cant hook and insisted it was as good a tool as any. It wasn't, but at work he treated his sons somewhat as guests.

"All right, heave!"

They surged on cant hook and peavies. The log stirred and turned on the blackened ground. Shifting their holds, they kept it rolling. Pa Tucker sang as he worked. Winterly attacks of tonsilitis had crippled his naturally good voice. But in his favorite work song it all but rose above its handicaps:

> Oh, Shenandoah, I love your daughter,
> Hoo-ray, you rolling river!

The brothers exchanged a look. Scepticism, bordered with respect, out of blackened, sweat-run faces. Straining on the peavies.

*It's full ten years since first I sought her . . .*

The log stopped and rolled back a few inches.
"All right, shall we have a blow?"
They rested on their peavies. George took the mattock and leveled a hump of earth which had stopped the log. The snowy thunder heads were towering up and up into the sky, a miracle of cool purity to men working in sweat and charcoal grime.
"All right, shall we tackle it again. Heave!"
Black, sullen cylinder just stirring under all their strength and leverage. Come on, tear your heart out! Keep it going!

*Oh, Shenandoah, I love her dearly,*
*.Hoo-ray, you rolling river!*

Pa Tucker was no sailor, but he cherished the memory of his voyage from New Orleans to Puget Sound, when he had come to spy out the west. The voyage of his life. As a supercargo, he had escaped the sorrows and hardships of the crew. Came through scotfree, if you overlooked the fact that the voyage led him to the Olympic Peninsula and a lifetime of expiation in which he cut down and cleared away enough timber to have built a thousand ships.
He made the voyage in the *Sarah Lord*, a beautiful little Maine-built barque, with bucko officers and a tough, hard-driven crew, eight of them shanghaied. An able seaman had been lost from the fore yardarm, and an apprentice died after a beating. They worked

through the Strait of Magellan, which sounded worse than Cape Horn. Forever anchoring and weighing and dragging anchors. Raked by sleet and hail. Lying on their beam ends under blasting williwaws from the mountains. . . . In zero weather, seeing a Fuegian woman standing up in a crazy canoe, taking off her one skin garment to wave to the ship. . . .

But the one thing which really impressed the young plainsman was "Shenandoah." It gives you some idea of Pa Tucker that after twenty-odd years he remembered the chantey best, and still sang it when he worked. It was in the song that the voyage found its voice. It was in talking about it that he found his, and told his sons some of the things he had learned from life. And told them about what he had not learned. The enigma which had caught his imagination—and defied his mind. Their father wasn't a wordy man. He found talking an effort because he felt deeply, and he was shy even with his own family. But when he told about the chantey he took a long time to get to the point. You must feel the things he felt. If your mind wasn't the way his had been, what he saw and heard wouldn't mean anything.

You must remember the starvation diet of bad food. The brutal officers. That seaman who fell to his death because he had been forced into unnecessary danger. The seventeen-year-old boy who was beaten and found dead in his bunk. Remember half the crew was shanghaied. White American citizens bought and sold openly, with the aid of drugs and kidnappers. You must keep those things in your mind, but not dwell on them too much. Save them for the final picture.

74

The barque was two weeks in the Strait of Magellan. Two weeks of storms and killing cold and misery and danger. Once they almost cleared the Strait. Came in sight of Cape Pillar, and were driven back by a screaming gale to an anchorage opposite Desolation Island. Hung on there for three more days of misery and danger.

On the fourth day, in the afternoon, the weather moderated suddenly. The wind went around to the east. All hands were called to weigh anchor and make sail. The barque was like something living, under the breath of spring. Furled sails burst open their buds and blossomed. Near its setting, the sun broke through the clouds, shining on the vessel and on the faces of men as they came into the light, tramping around the capstan.

The First Mate was good natured because the break in weather had come during his watch. He called for a chantey. There had been no singing on the way south, or in the bitter Strait. A greying sailor started it, sullenly at first:

*Oh, Shenandoah, I love your daughter,*

Thawing men, straining at the capstan bars, answered with a muffled chorus, like a slave song,

*Hoo-ray, you rolling river!*

One man had been knocked down a few minutes earlier and he tramped about the capstan in silence.

*It's full ten years since first I sought her,*

The song caught him in its tide. Coming into the light, he raised his head, with blood still on his face, and added the finest voice of all.

Pa Tucker had been seasick on that ship. He had

seen cruelties and injustice and cold-blooded murder. He hated the ship. And he was troubled to find that he also loved her. There was part of the mystery. Greed had found its expression in the swift sailing ship, almost as beautiful as anything God could make, and in human slavery. And the shanghaied, brutalized sailors matched the ship's beauty with a song like "Shenandoah." How can you account for such things? He would end with a helpless gesture before the baseness and grandeur that is in men.

That was the mystery. But the boys' father thought he did see some meanings in the experience. One of them was that sailors, men who work out of doors for other people, are betrayed by moments of beauty. Like that afternoon, in sight of Desolation Island and the Evangelistas. That is all they get out of life: the feeling of their own strength; the warmth of the sun on their faces, tramping around a capstan; the beauty of a moment when sunset and ship and song are intertwined.

You boys have seen the loggers, with their bedding on their backs. With nothing to show for their dangerous work in the woods. Nothing but a bottle and a stagger. Or pockets rolled during a drugged sleep in the back room of some dive. You have seen them, drifting between Forest City and Olympia, without enough money to pay their steamer fare. Drifting without past or future. . . .

They always knew what was coming. The solution was a farm, hacked and burned out of the forest, with the sweat of gigantic labor, through the slow agony of escaping years. That is the solution, boys.

Their father overlooked the fact that they weren't

boys any more. Under his grime, George was a blond giant of twenty-five. Alfred was nearing twenty-three. Since leaving high school they had been helping their father clear land and work the farm, on shares. And most years their share was not a hundred dollars in cash. Not a dollar a week each for this backbreak and sweat and grime. Over she goes! Come on, keep her rolling. Tear your heart out.

> *Hoo-ray, you rolling river!*
> *I'll work for her and pay you yearly. . . .*

"All right, there she is!"

The sullen, black log rolled over the waiting chain, toward the skids. George was up on the pile, hooking the chain into the steel block, with its frayed wire cable. A great, blackened figure on the blackened pile of logs. With snow-white clouds boiling up in the smoky sky above him.

Now it was the horses' turn to have a taste of how men work.

"*Get up! Hi, there, Ned!*" Out of sight, behind the pile of logs, Pa shouted and lashed them with the ends of the reins.

The brothers guided the log. First with peavies, then with their hands as it rolled up the skids. Getting behind it, adding their strength to the horses' and the purchase of tackle. Checking it with fire-blackened stones when the invisible horses wavered.

"*Get up! Hi, Ned! Get up, Jan!*"

The log was almost chest high on the skids. One more good roll. Come on, tear your heart out! Alfred saw his brother's face. White streaked black, with the grim grin of a strong man using all his strength.

Ha!

"Hi, there, Ned!" Surging on the cable.

*Snap!*

The free ton of blackened fury leaped back on them. You don't think. Your quicker body does what it can.

The brothers looked at each other quietly. Lying on the blackened ground between the skids.

"Hell!"

Was that thunder, or the log still going?

They got up and saw it roll to a stop, sullenly, at the place from which they had started it by hand.

"It ticked my nose," George said.

"Boys, are you all right?" Pa came running around the pile of logs. Face white where it wasn't black. "Was it the chain?"

"I guess so." George picked up the end, where a riveted link had carried away, flicking it with a gloved thumb.

"I thought it was a good, strong chain," their father said sorrowfully.

It was a good, strong chain, except that some of the repaired links were a little haywire.

"I'll put in some new ones before we use it again. If I had ever thought—" Pa looked ashamed. He often talked about the way rotten gear was used in logging camps until it broke and killed someone. And he was upset that his own sons had nearly met a home-made death by the same practice.

They rode down the hill on the two sweaty, blackened gray horses. Pa riding Ned, with the disgraced logging chain like a heavy black serpent coiled about the hames. George and Alfred riding Jan, like a couple of squaws with one pony. Or two poor knights on one

horse. Feeling young and ridiculous when they could
feel anything but sweat and weariness. But it was the
only way to get their father to ride home. He had
wanted them to ride a horse each, while he walked.

Not talking. Thinking thoughts they hadn't energy
to put in words. Past the acres they had cleared. Almost too tired and weighed down by the coming
storm to feel satisfaction. Pa, riding ahead, stopped,
looking at the field of vetch and rye. Grasshoppers
going *crik-k, crik-k*, among the grain. The tangled mass
of purple and green, heavy as the sky, threatening to
bear the pale gold rye stalks down to the dry earth.

With a stir of passion in his voice, their father said,
"Boys, that's the finest stand of vetch we've ever
had!"

"It looks good."

"It certainly is."

Reassured, he rode on, with his head held a little
higher, under his blackened, ten-year-old felt hat.

The rye and vetch did look good. And it was about
their only money crop—the part that was fed to the
cows. Cream could be sold for cash. With forty more
acres cleared, they could keep a dairy herd and make a
comfortable living. Two acres was a good year's
clearing. In twenty years, O, my big brother, we'll
have a fine farm. With a fine herd of cows to milk.
Only twenty more years of fire and charcoal dust, and
sweat and backbreak. If something haywire doesn't
let go at the wrong moment. It wasn't anything. They
skinned out of it, without time to think. But afterward it focused attention. You can stand anything
you're going to live through. Save yourself trouble

79

by not noticing all the ugliness. But it jumps out at you when you have a peek at lying smashed in sweat and black filth.

Usually it was George who was impatient with this kind of farming, where you would need two lifetimes. One to clear a farm and one to work it. If Alfred had been willing, they would probably be working in a logging camp, or homesteading in Oregon; or, more likely, trying their luck in Alaska. Alfred knew how his brother felt. And he knew how his father felt. He loved Tyee Bay, down there beyond the orchard. Green, tinged copper by the gathering thunderstorm. The big white house, built by a man who had no meanness in him. The orchard so rich and varied that when its fruit couldn't be sold you knew there was something wrong with the world, not with the orchard. He loved the trusting, generous flavor of the place. But how make it secure? It was everywhere, but out of reach. Like trying to take sunshine in your arms.

The other boys of the neighborhood, from ugly clearings and jerry-built houses, had felt the charm of the place. Its promise that life will be a rich adventure. They had looked up to George and Alfred, expecting them, in some magic way, to produce the keys to that promised richness. George and Alfred, as poor as any of them, and as troubled in their hearts.

George, in his bursts of impatience, had wanted to strike out for one place or another. Alfred had encouraged him into staying to see if they couldn't make something out of the farm. Now, he did not know. He had been held by dreams, his own and other people's.

They did not seem to be made more real by adding laborious acres. Even if he and George some day became successful dairy farmers, something might be missing. The flavor of life. They might become quite prosperous—and have nothing worth sharing with those who have faith that life will be a rich adventure.

In front of him, George's big back sighed.

"You don't see it, Alfie, but it's a hell of a life!"

Thunder crashed through the darkening sky.

"I see it all right, George."

"Enough to have a shot at Alaska with me?"

"I don't know about that." Alfred had always wanted to go up north, ever since the Klondike Rush in their boyhood. Only, later, there had been other things he wanted to do still more.

Close ahead of them Pa had dismounted, stiffly, from the big work horse, to open the barnyard gate. Alfred slid from Jan's back to close the gate.

His father insisted on unharnessing Ned. George was looking after Jan. Big drops of rain smacked scatteringly on the roof.

"Better get into the water before you get wet," George said. "I'll be right after you."

The misery of sweat mixed with charcoal dust decided him.

"All right, I'll see you in the bay." The long grass in the yard ran in waves under the opening wind. He snatched two pairs of cut-down overalls from the line in the back yard and ran for the boat shed as the skies let go. A curse on clearing land! He couldn't even put the home-made bathing trunks under his arm without getting them too black to put on when they came out of the water. So ran with them in his hand, getting wet. Arrived in a burst of speed, thunder and lightning and redoubled rain. Welcome boat shed!

"*Excuse me!*"

He almost collided with a naked woman. Her startled face looked like Clarice Jackson's. But Clarice was only a kid. He started back into the downblast of rain.

"Alfred!"

When he turned at the door, she said, "I didn't tell you to look at me!"

He looked away.

"I was going to say, you mustn't go out in all that rain because of me. You can look at it and talk to me while I dress."

"Thank you, Clarice." Dutifully he watched the downward fury of the rain.

"Your mother said you were all back on the hill clearing land."

"We were, but we came home to get out of the rain."

"I might have thought of that."

"How are you going to get back to the house without getting wet?"

"I won't, unless I wait until it's over." Then she said, "I suppose you were going to have a swim."

"I need it, all right. I'm black enough! But there's no hurry. George will be here in a minute."

"I'm making a lot of trouble, aren't I? Just by being a woman."

He heard her pause in dressing.

"George isn't coming yet, is he?"

"No." Peering through the gray dusk of rain.

"I'll slip into my bathing dress again. Then I can go through the rain. I wasn't going to get your mother's house wet, but I'll have to now."

"You know you're welcome. But how will you keep your clothes dry?"

"I'll come back for them with an umbrella. No, there's a bucket. I'll carry my clothes under that." After a minute she said, "You can turn around now, Alfred."

He turned, reluctant to show his grime.

"I didn't mean to be so much trouble!" Such a nice kid, in her wet bathing dress. She smiled at him, folding her dry clothes to carry under the bucket. Not embarrassed. Not noticing the black on his face, which must look like a minstrel show.

When she was gone, he undressed slowly. Thinking, nice little kid. Probably never will be much bigger. Seventeen, and going to the University this fall. . . . He hung his blackened clothes on a ribband of the unfinished sloop that stood in frames. Just as old as these scars. It doesn't seem like seventeen years. It was nice, talking to her and looking out at the rain. What did we talk about? Not much. But it was nice. I think she liked it, too. Fine little kid. "I'm making a lot of trouble, aren't I? Just being a woman." He tried to forget her proud young breasts, and remembered them more. A sweet little youngster I've known all her life. . . .

He walked about the skeleton boat, frowning thoughtfully at the stout frames. A good job, as far as they had gone. What a difference! The black hell of

83

clearing land was hideous all the way through. A boat was beautiful at every stage of building. A good stout job, as far as they had gone. She was part of their life, too. He and George had started collecting knees and curved timbers when they were still kids. For the big schooner they were going to build for all the boys of Tyee Bay. If the dream had shrunk to thirty-two feet, she was still the ship of their lives. Fit to go anywhere. . . .

When George came, talking about having a shot at prospecting in Alaska, he would say, "I'm with you. We'll finish the sloop and shove off."

# V

Near midnight they decided to camp.

George swung off his pack and settled it on a convenient ledge of lichen-covered rock. "Looks like as good a place as any to hit the hay."

Alfred put down his pack more deliberately. He ran one hand over the dark growth of beard on his lean, shy face and looked about. "You don't think we ought to keep going until it gets dark?"

That was their favorite Alaskan joke. Not to be taken seriously when darkness was several weeks away.

"All right if you say so." George broke out the hand axe, certain his brother would not say it. "Anyway, it looks like rain."

Clouds were driving swiftly across the ceiling of the little valley in which they had stopped. A narrow, secret valley east of the glaciers; so wild and silent you felt sure no human being had ever been there before. Coarse grass and boulders along a little stream from the flower-edged snow field. Stunted shrubs and rock walls sloping up to the gray, driving sky. George's axe rang with clear precision as he lopped off boughs of stunted hemlock and dropped them in a dark heap. Alfred chose a level spot of high ground and pitched their tent. The site was in the lee of the cliff, and the back of the tent to windward. Not that there was any wind down there, though there was plenty on the ridges above. When the tent was anchored, he studied the thickening strip of sky and took up his prospector's pick. George finished with the boughs and came with his pick to help. Together they dug a horseshoe trench on three sides of the tent. They were used to being wet. They were used to such rain as they had never known at home. But there were limits. They weren't used to having their belongings washed away. And the rain that was making up promised to be something special, even for the Archipelago.

George's pick clanged against rock. There was more rock than soil. He picked up a fresh chipped bit and squinted at it with mock hopefulness. "It would be just like us to find nothing prospecting and then shovel gold to hell out of our way pitching camp."

"No," Alf thought, "it would be our luck to find nothing prospecting and make our stake picking blueberries with the old men—after we ran away from berry-picking at home!"

For a week they had been sampling the interior of the island, in perfect accord. They couldn't have said which one suggested the expedition, but it had been in both their minds before it was put into words. Improbable, of course, that they should make a strike there. But everything about gold-hunting was improbable. It was true, but just as improbable, that other men had passed up rich and unsuspected fields near home and gone, with infinite difficulty, to die by freezing on Wild Creek or the flats of the Chandelar. And if the brothers did make a strike so near Sitka, how convenient that would be. It was one of those famous off-chances in which neither of them had too much faith. But they did have faith that sooner or later, here or somewhere else, they would strike pay dirt. Alaska was the land of hope. In that northern country American optimism reached its fullest growth. Even the aged sourdoughs of Alfred's joke gathered blueberries with infinite optimism. With their stakes from berry-picking they would pack their war bags and hit the trail again to make strikes of infinite richness. They had it all planned, except what they would do with their millions.

They finished the horseshoe trench and spread hemlock boughs in a deep mattress for their blankets. They cut firewood of stunted spruce and hemlock, and still there was no rain. Instead of turning in at once, they poked leisurely about their little valley. It was a personal place. So shut away from the world by its walls of rock; shut away from the universe by racing gray clouds. Something like an island of one's own. The kind of place where you decide to stop when you see it, and leave with regret. Afterward, probably, you wonder why you left when you did. The way you wonder, caught out in a gale, why you left a snug little harbor. Maybe what you went searching for was in the little harbor. Anyway, that was what you found to remember. They hadn't said anything about it to each other, but they knew it was their little valley.

"No gold," George said. He washed a pan of gravel from the little stream and looked satisfied at proving his statement.

No gold, of course. It didn't matter. With a swing

of his big arm George sent the sheet iron pan sailing through the air. Clang on the rocky ground before the tent. The echoes clanged back from each rock wall, unnaturally loud. As if the silent little valley had been frightened, not used to the sound of metal. The brothers grinned shyly at each other. A holiday had been declared.

Rain began to fall. Not heavily yet: soft easy drops, wondering when they were going to have a chance to land, falling past the rock walls so long. There was a kind of perverse pleasure in wandering about in the rain at midnight. There was something in their joke about waiting until it got dark. The feeling, sometimes, that they could go on forever without sleep.

At the foot of the eastern cliff there was a break in the rock, like a niche for a saint. Or a place where a sinner could stand out of the wet. They stepped in, on dry ground, out of the increasing rain.

"Just as if we didn't have our tent," Alfred commented. "Still, we shouldn't pass up anything free."

The back of the niche was a separate rock. George stepped around it and disappeared. "Alf," he called, "there's a cave here."

They struck matches and found they were in a cave, perhaps twelve feet high and twice that wide, with a roughly level floor. They couldn't see how far back it went.

"Better look and see whether the grizzly's in or out," Alfred suggested.

Two more lighted matches showed their footprints in light dust at the entrance weren't mixed with any others. The matches curled and died, leaving them in deep twilight.

"We'll have a look at this place in the morning," George declared. The cave made him forget and think darkness had come at last.

They stood in the niche, watching the loosed rain batter down into their valley. It hammered their little brown tent, out there in the grayness, and filled the horseshoe trench. Rivulets spurted from everywhere and dashed toward the little stream which was growing bigger.

Too bad we pitched camp out there, Alfred thought. It would be nicer in the cave, where the biggest storm could never touch us.

George looked at him and knew what his brother was thinking. "*Klosh spose mesika chaco copo oleman house?*" (Wouldn't it be a good idea to move into the old house?)

Moving north, they had come into the region where the Chinook jargon of their youth still lingered. It was like capturing the first zest of life.

"*Klosh*," Alf agreed. "*Hiyu snass! Hiyu chuck! Sail house klonas kock-shut snass.*" (Good. Much water. Much rain. Maybe the tent will be wrecked.) The barbaric sound was like a stimulant.

They stripped, piling their clothes in the niche, and put on their boots again.

"We'll get our war bags first, then bring the boughs in with the tent."

"Good. Shall we go?"

They ran out, gasping cheerfully as the cold downpour struck their naked bodies. George looked like a great, muscular doll in high boots: gleaming white, with golden brown neck and forearms. Yellow hair streaming with water. Ridiculous and beautiful.

Alfred's lither, dark scarred body tingled under the breath-taking, wild pelting as they leaped about in the rain, bringing in their gear.

The wood was brought in; last of all the hemlock boughs, reasonably dry in the bundle of the struck tent. It had been thrilling out there in the hammering rain, but they had enough. They rubbed their bodies to a glow and started to make camp again. George nursed the half-wet wood into flame while his brother made a mattress of the boughs and spread their blankets.

Rain roared into the valley outside while they sprawled luxuriantly and stared at the brightening flames. This was their secure harbor. The shelter of the mountain, bright warm fire, and soft bed of boughs. This must have been why they didn't turn in at once when their tent was pitched. They must have felt what they hadn't guessed—the final security their little valley had to offer.

"We'll have a good look at the cave in the morning," George said again.

Alfred didn't feel curious about it, either. It was so right there should be a cave in their little valley. They had half known it was there and weren't much surprised at finding it. Like a dream which changes from probable to improbable so easily it all seems natural. Maybe they were in something like a dream, after going all day and half the night without sleep. Keeping on because they were young and strong and undefeated.

"Wouldn't it be nice to strike pay dirt in our valley, Alfie?"

Nice? Of course. Only things don't happen that way.

And the valley had done pretty well by them as it was. The rain roared outside the doorway of the cave, roared like one continuous sea, and inside they were warm and dry and luxuriously sleepy.

George was lying full length, with his face resting on one heavy, bronzed forearm. His blue eyes were very dark in the firelight, and they had that look. A kind of twinkle that was such a part of him. He was big and powerful and conscious of his strength. Sometimes, when he was angered, he would have a wave of violence and seem about to break anything, anyone, except his brother, to pieces. Then there would come that twinkle in his eyes and a half-grin and he would be good-natured again. . . .

The fire burned up more brightly, its light touching the ragged roof of the cave. Volcanic flaw, probably, like a bubble. Or a pocket of softer stuff eroded. In a little while George's blue eyes would close—if his own didn't first. Probably they wouldn't know which fell asleep first in the brightening fire which their eyes were too sleepy to see.

Then Alfred found they weren't alone in the cave. Queer, but not as startling as you would expect. Like sitting in a restaurant, talking to a friend until you forgot there were other people. Only when you stopped talking you became aware of them. Over there in the shadows, beyond George, a figure sitting asleep against the side of the cave. Nothing to be startled about. A man sleeping so quietly you hadn't known he was there. Someone else who had come in for shelter from the storm. An Indian, Alfred thought. They would be more likely to sleep that way.

91

He didn't know how to tell George without making it seem startling when it wasn't. It was as natural as everything else. First the little valley, then the cave, then someone sleeping in the cave. A natural sequence, each thing leading to the next.

George was looking at him now, questioningly, without moving a muscle. Wondering why his brother was looking past him steadily into the presumably empty dusk. George wasn't the inexperienced kind who would jump up or blurt out "What is it?" He was asking with his eyes if it was anything dangerous. Alfred signalled that it wasn't, but he didn't want to speak until both of them had seen it. George didn't make it out at first, and Alfred wondered if he had been seeing things. Then his pupils adjusted to the dim light and he saw it, nodding just perceptibly. He looked back at his brother and grinned. *"Tilacum."*

Really, it was amusing. Their slight surprise would be nothing to the other fellow's when he found that while he slept they had moved in and camped. Alfred poked the fire to a brighter blaze and they walked over quietly to have a look.

The man was shrunken almost to a skeleton and his head was bowed on his breast more deeply than seemed possible. He appeared naked, like themselves, but it was hard to say in that dim light. There was nothing to be afraid of. The shrunken figure appeared interested in nothing but sleep.

George touched its shoulder cautiously. *"Memaloose!"* The old word echoed somewhere back in the cave.

They brought a flaming stick of spruce to make a

closer examination. It gave them a feeling of importance and gravity. They were the law and the coroner and the human voices to make the last pronouncement on what was once another human being. Also they might learn something of importance to themselves. If there had been foul play, or if it was the kind of cave where one took shelter and never left alive, they would be on guard.

When they made their examination they didn't feel so important. Plainly the figure had no interest in their pronouncements. If it had come here for shelter, it was from some other storm, ages before. It had dried up to a mere mummy, brittle to the touch.

George stooped and picked up something from the dust.

"His prospector's hammer."

It was a chunk of roughly-chipped black stone, grooved about the middle, where a handle had once been lashed.

The brothers had heard of such things in Alaska. Mummies and tools of the Stone Age, found on the islands of the Archipelago and the Aleutians. Men from Asia who had discovered Alaska before the coming of the Americans or the Russians, or the Indians before them. Or perhaps they were the first Indians.

Farther back in the cave they came across another mummy. A woman, this one, with her head sunk toward breasts that were mere flaps of dried skin. There might have been others, still farther back, but there was no rush about exploring. Evidently they were in a tomb.

Alfred threw the dying brand back on the fire and

lay down again. The rain thundered outside. George said nothing for a while, frowning into the fire. Then his eyes twinkled and his frown softened to a shy grin.

"Well, Alfie, they're not bothering us, are they?"

"No. They're quiet neighbors."

"I didn't think I'd like them, at first."

"I didn't, either."

"But it still feels like a good place to sleep."

"They found it a good place."

It might have been the effect of having gone so long without sleep. Alfred didn't exactly feel old, but he knew at last that some day he and George would grow old and die. He had been told that since he was three, but he had never quite believed it. It had seemed too improbable, when he could remember back to the beginnings of America. His part of America. He had known the first white people who ever lived there. Attended the first school—learned his lessons in the Burtons' parlor before the first school was built. At home, he and George shared the room built for the first half-white child of the neighborhood. When you have been there since the beginning, you build up the feeling that you will go on forever and be there at the end.

Take a great, modern city like Seattle. It looked as if it had been there forever. But it hadn't. No white man ever lived there until six couples and their children were put ashore from the schooner *Exact* on a November day near Thanksgiving, when the breaking waves dashed as high as they ever do on Elliott Bay. That handful of pilgrims found itself in a wilderness as unexplored, among Indians as hostile, as earlier

94

pilgrims found at Plymouth. Now, the settlement of twenty-four had grown to half a million. And some of the men walking in its crowded streets and riding in automobiles on its boulevards, could remember back to the beginning. They had been among the first pilgrims from the schooner *Exact*.

When you have been there since the beginning, part of you builds up the feeling that you will go on forever. Everything will go on forever, bigger and better. You move forward, always doing new things. When life gets tame, you build your own boat and shove off for Alaska, a still newer country. You anchor in an island harbor. Camp in a wild valley in the interior, in a cave where you think no one has ever been before. And there, at the end of the earth, you are caught at last. In your mind which was fooled by a new setting for the story of man, who is born, tries to escape death and is overtaken. You and these mummies of ancient men who died going through the motions of what you thought was a fine, new adventure. Generation after generation, turned loose like rabbits. Running with hope in their hearts. And after them the overtaking hounds.

It made a difference, he thought. Getting the facts straight. Charting the limitations. Then you could do something about it, within limitations. It was all right, coming to Alaska. They had to try making money somewhere. But Alaska had its limitations. He wouldn't ever fool himself that it was a fresh adventure. A new world where he could go on escaping. He had started with one country, as near the beginning as possible, and he wanted to see that one through. As far as he went. He loved Puget Sound and Tyee Bay. That was home, and always would be. He would like to say to George, "Let's go home to our own country." That is what he would do if there was any way of making a living at home. The kind of living which would be an adventure in which all the boys of Tyee Bay could share; and all the people.

That was their dream—George's and his. Sailing to Alaska in their own boat was part of that dream. When they struck pay dirt. . . .

George was asleep now, his shaggy yellow head resting on one big arm. Gleaming in the light of the dying fire. Roar of the rain like a long drawn out sea. Steady undertow of sound. It had gone on while the fire blazed up in the cave, showing the men of ancient times sitting just outside the circle of light. It roared on as the fire sank and the ancient men faded back into the shadows.

The fire sank lower and the rain roared on. Alfred lay beside his brother in the tomb and slept like the dead.

BOOK TWO

# VI

Aweek out of the mouth of the Yukon, the *Tyee* reached through Unimak Pass. Alfred came on deck, climbing over the sliding panels, pulling the hatch slide behind him to preserve what heat there was in the cabin. Cold, rolling gray sea. The mountains of Unimak luminous white. A banner of steam flying from the cone of Shishaldin, high above George who was standing up, steering with the tiller between his knees, flourishing his arms.

"Well," he said cheerfully, "what's the word?"

Alfred had been sliding the parallel rulers over the chart.

"Looks as if our best bet is to keep sou'east till we can reach under the lee of Sannak, toward Shelikof Strait."

George squinted at the compass and then nodded agreement with the decision, which his brother immediately qualified. "That is, if the wind holds east."

"It'll hold," George maintained. "Sometimes I wish it wouldn't. It's such a damn cold wind!" He squinted up at the luminous peaks in the gray sky. "I'll be glad when we get away from those mountains. Gray and white are the coldest colors in the world."

Alfred agreed. The smell of fallen snow was like a threat of more to come. "Want me to take her a while?" he suggested. "There's fresh coffee below."

"Not yet," George insisted. "Wait until I finish my trick, then try to keep me from it!" After a minute he resumed his good-natured complaining. "Sometimes I wish we were keeping her straight for Cape Flattery, with no danger of running into anything but weather. Every time I see kelp waving at me from a sunken rock, I feel it's something personal."

They had been over that more than once. The first time, before they followed the white procession of ice out of the Yukon River. They had been over it several times since. And each time they were overawed by the prospect of two thousand miles of open ocean and violent spring gales. They had no business to be there so early in the year. It became their business to make use of all the shelter there was and work their way into the inside passage.

Their week in the Bering Sea had been tame. Tamer than they had thought of hoping for. No more wind than *Tyee* could use with one reef down. No obstacles but the fog and floating ice. George, who liked to make decisions on impulse, was almost ready to believe it proved something—and to decide that spring gales were overrated in the Pilot Book. Alfred's more thoughtful mind decided if you don't get what is coming to you on schedule, you are sure to get it later with interest. And because he had often been right, George accepted the decisions of his younger brother.

By three in the afternoon the *Tyee* had lost the mountains of Unimak in mist. They had enough offing, they decided, to lay their course south of Cape Pankof. Alfred, who was at the tiller, kept the sloop heading sou'east a quarter of an hour longer, for luck. Experience had shown them that with a sea running it was no good trying to make distance on anything finer than a reach. Alfred's tendency was to broaden the reach. When good measure had been satisfied, they went about, George handling the head-sails, belaying the sheets with his big, mittened hands. The *Tyee* forged ahead powerfully on the new tack, taking the seas at half breast with an easy motion. Steering was largely a matter of keeping a hand on the tiller. There wasn't enough occupation for one man.

George clapped his mittened hands, stamped his feet and decided to go below. "It's chilly enough when you get cold," he said. "Stamp on the deck if you need me to put on more sail." He slid open the hatch, stepped over the sliding panels and descended the ladder. For a moment his blond face, ruddy with the cold, grinned back at his brother. Then it disappeared like a jack-in-the-box. The companion slide closed and Alfred was alone with the sloop and the gray arctic sea.

Before the end of the first hour of his watch, he could no longer keep the *Tyee* footing on her course. She was headed a point, then two points to the south. The wind was backing toward the nor'east. By the end of the hour he gave up hope of weathering Pankof and laid a course south of the Sannak Islands. Eased, the sloop sailed faster, rushing diagonally up and down the short gray seas. An occasional crest leaped at the weather chain-plates and sent an icy shower over the deck, stinging the face of the muffled helmsman. The wind was hardening as it backed into the nor'east. Hardening, with a sting of cold.

Alfred stamped on deck, glad of the excuse to start the circulation in his feet. The hatch slide opened almost at once and George's head popped up.

"Want me to set the balloon jib, Alf?"

"No. Take in the jib and reef the main!"

George's head turned to survey the weather, ducked a shower of spray from the chain-plates and popped up again. "Wait till I get my oilers!" By the time he got back, there was no doubt about the weather. A dark squall was coming down from the nor'east.

"You take the tiller while I stow the jib," Alfred suggested. "I need to warm up!"

George grinned and shook his head, fastening the final clasp of his slicker. "You might get wet." On the way forward he called over his shoulder. "Then I'd have to stand your watch!"

Alfred brought the sloop as close to the wind as he dared. George cast off the halliard at the foot of the mast, swung forward, with a grip on the forestay. Swept the jib, rattling, down its stay as the bow rose with the crest of a wave. For an instant Alfred saw his gigantic outline against the blackness of the coming squall. Then he dropped on the bowsprit, muzzling the sail. The bow dipped sharply with the passing of the crest, ducking him and the sail under green water. Alfred sensed that he was gone and luffed by instinct, but the bowsprit rose with George's big dripping figure clinging on with arms and legs, gasketing the sail as if it were a monster he had fought and conquered under water.

The helm was up and the shaking sails filled and drawing again. The jib was gasketed and George coming in from the bowsprit. He came aft, dripping.

"I said you'd get wet!" Shaking water out of his sleeves. "I'm only wet in spots."

Alfred didn't stop to argue the point. "We'll take a reef in the main," he said. "Then you go below and dry off." Steadying the tiller with his legs, he passed the second reef cringle while George stood at the halliards.

"Here's your squall," George said, tying reef points. "Smells like snow."

It hadn't been only the snow on Unimak they felt that morning.

The *Tyee* rose on two more seas and plunged into grayness. No squall violence. Only a thickening veil of snow and dying visibility. Sounds were muffled, too. The rushing seas seemed farther away.

"You're not going to see your islands if this keeps up!"

"Not in time, anyway." Alfred brushed the gathering snow from his eyebrows with one mittened hand. "We'll have to keep on east until it clears, or until we're clear of everything."

George looked relieved. "I'll get below. My mitts are freezing." He disappeared down the hatch in a swirl of snow, like Santa Claus descending a chimney.

His brother settled down to the business of putting miles between the peninsula and the *Tyee*. If there was going to be a gale with snow, the nest of islands and rocks would be a deathtrap. He brushed the clinging snow from the binnacle glass and found the wind had backed directly into the nor'east. The wind for snow, according to the Pilot Book. This time it hadn't lied. They were in for something. And a good offing had become the most desirable thing in the Pacific. The little *Tyee* was forging east, up and down dim seas. Seas that were unreal except for the more frequent gushes of spray from forward. Of all the courses they had attempted that day, the easterly was the only one on which they had not been headed almost at once. If they could hold that, clear of all lee shores, Alfred would be satisfied.

Another hour, and the sloop was still on her easterly course, forging through the moving pall of snow. Snow that clung to her weather rigging and thickened, heedless of the flying spray. With all but his eyes and nose muffled in his hood, Alfred kept brushing the snow from his eyebrows and eyelashes. To keep from being petrified in one position, he often shifted hands on the tiller. Shuffled his feet in the snowy cockpit and alternately stood and sat. The cockpit floor was becoming dangerously slippery with snow. But when he tried to push it aside with his foot, he found ice. That explained the white, thickening rigging and deck. The spray was freezing as it fell and the *Tyee* was icing up. Becoming a phantom of snow and ice, staggering over dim seas, through a ghostly world.

Everything was unreal except the cold. After a while that became unreal, too. Alfred was changing to match everything else, the thickening snow on his oilskins changing him into a snow man, driving a ship of snow over a phantom arctic sea. He didn't know whether the snow was keeping him warm or petrifying him so he could no longer feel the cold. He was almost comfortable. Without feeling. Without any responsibility except to keep the *Tyee* heading east. Keep her east and keep a lookout between snow-tangled lashes, under snow-gathering eyebrows. In the sea valleys, the world ended just beyond the bowsprit. A dim gray moving slope. On the snow-swept crests, it ended a few seas away, fading from faint uncertainty to non-existence.

At four, George came on deck without waiting to be called. He looked warm and hearty and tremendously alive, like someone from comfortable civilization. Alfred felt far away, unreal. He gave George the tiller, but still felt as if he were holding it. Unable to shake the feeling of numbness.

"There's stew on the stove, and a fresh pot of coffee," George said. He peered ahead to where the world ended, twenty yards away. A dim gray slope, bearing down on them through incessant snow. "How am I going to know if we're running into ice?"

"You probably won't," Alfred told him. "Not in time, anyway."

The *Tyee*'s bowsprit rose to meet the crest, like a big, white sugar stick. The gasketed jib grown big with snow and ice. Ahead, the next sea moved toward them like a shadow, and the next like the shadow of a shadow. Beyond that there was nothing. One glimpse, and everything was shut out by a gush of stinging spray.

"Have you thought about heaving to?" George was clearing his eyes, looking at the limited scene with distaste.

Alfred had thought about it. "I don't see how we can, so close to the islands. Wind's likely to do anything. We'd better have good offing."

"All right. I'll keep her east till I sail her under, or climb an iceberg."

Below, the cabin was oven-hot from the coal fire in the little range. Alfred had thought he could never be warm again. A minute off the icy, snow-swept deck, he was fumbling out of his layers of heavy clothes. He ate and drank. Stoked the range and dropped onto his bunk. Like falling on a trap-door to oblivion.

He was awakened by distant thunder. Throbbing of an Indian drum overhead. Stamping on deck. George must have got into trouble five minutes after he took the helm. Alfred opened his eyes to darkness. Maybe he had sailed the sloop under. She was lurching and staggering heavily. Striking a match to light the gimballed lamp, he found it was ten minutes after eight. Four hours gone while he closed and opened his eyes.

On deck it was hard to recognize familiar things. The sloop deep under snow and ice in the darkness and driving snow. George like a monumental snow man at the tiller. The sea an invisible force, a muffled sound.

George's first thought was for a smoke. "How about a drag at that cigarette?" he asked. "For the last hour I've been worried that we'd sink without my getting a smoke!"

The cigarette glowed fiercely when Alfred put it between his brother's cold lips. "Think we ought to heave to, now? She seems to be getting heavy with ice."

It was even more apparent to Alfred, after his watch below. The *Tyee*'s sluggishness was frightening. "I don't see what else we can do. A few more hours of this, and we won't be afloat!" Every sea, every blast of spray, freezing as it fell, added to the weight of the staggering sloop.

The staysail sheet refused to budge when they hauled on it. The sloop had been kept at it so long that she was frozen on her suicidal course. Alfred worked his way forward with the lantern, past the snow-topped cabin, under the snow-thickened mainsail and the boom, with icicles hanging like reef points. He cleared the sheet blocks of ice and hammered the frozen sheet into partial flexibility. Worked his way aft again. He was appalled by the thickness of the ice forward, wondering how the sloop had kept afloat so long.

With the staysail backed slightly, the sloop hove to. Sailed a little, came up into the wind, shaking snow from her mainsail, fell off and sailed again.

George was numbly impatient to go below, demoralized by his bitter four-hour watch. "She's all right," he maintained. "It's all we can do."

His brother wasn't so sure, waiting and feeling how the sloop behaved. Heavy and sluggish, she was still taking spray on board. In the snow-filled darkness, it was impossible to make out the approaching seas and help the sloop take them easily. She stumbled and took one sea wrong, too far aft on the weather side. Fell over to leeward, sickeningly, with the feeling of absolute top-heaviness. The thump and crash of things they would probably never need, going adrift below and falling away to leeward. The sloop could never right herself, it seemed, lacking ballast to equal her deck load of ice. The distant, muffled sea was close upon them at last, licking the cockpit coaming.

The *Tyee* lurched and righted herself slowly, painfully. George gave a gasp of relief. "I thought we were gone that time, Alfie!"

Alfred had thought so, too. They would be gone the next time, or the time after. One more thing they could try, and they would have to try that quickly. "We'll have to run before it," he said. "It's all we can do. We won't ice up, that way. See if the mainsheet will run out." While George tested the sheet, he got the staysail drawing again and the sloop forging ahead.

"Sheet's pretty stiff," George said. "I think it'll run. I'll watch it when you give me the word."

"All right." The *Tyee* rose on an invisible sea. "Let her run!" Alfred put up the helm and held it with his knees, surging on the staysail sheet to flatten the sail and help the sloop about. She reeled heavily and began falling off, with the mainsheet running out, George helping it through the blocks with savage jerks. Alfred eased the tiller amidships. With the boom well out, George belayed the sheet, crouched beside his brother, waiting to see how the *Tyee* would make out.

Running with it, the wind seemed suddenly taken off. No more flying spray or driven snow. Everything dead still except for the rush of seas coming up astern and passing underneath. The sloop was running sou'-west, with snow and wind and sea, moving with the invisible universe. A part of the storm. If she could keep on, she must run out of it eventually, out of snow and freezing weather, to where the ice would melt from her rigging and deck. That was a matter of chance, and skill. A heavy following sea, or one sea steeper than the others, would overwhelm the ice-laden sloop. If she yawed in her course, or the main-sail jibed over, that might be the end.

George must have had the same thoughts. "How in hell can you know where the wind is?" he asked.

Alfred had been judging it by the chill on one side of his muffled face. Judging the wind was from that quarter. He wondered how he would gauge it when his face became numb. To the people at home, he and George were doubtless the most skilled and daring sea-men of their time. Actually, they were rank amateurs who had learned what they could out of books, and who had been spared to learn a little more by painful experience. According to books, you judge the direc-tion of the wind at night by feeling it on your neck. But that was no help under conditions where your neck would grow numb and possibly freeze off if it were exposed. Still, he was managing, somehow. And it was his worry, not George's. "I'll make out," he insisted. "Better get below for some sleep. You'll need it."

George staggered to his feet, still worrying. "I'm damned if I could tell if I was sailing by the lee," he complained.

Experimentally, Alfred reached over and lifted the lantern from the rough box beside the compass. In its light there was no question that he was sailing as he should, with the wind a little on the port quarter.

Illuminated, the falling snow was like a shower of arrows, showing the direction of the wind. The wind made visible. He put the lantern between his feet, where it was sheltered and still illuminated the arrows of snow. Simple, once you thought of it. Too simple to put in a book. "There you are, George. I'll tell where the wind is by looking at it."

"Good, Alfie!" George swayed uncertainly. "I'm falling asleep on my feet." He staggered to the hatch, opened the slide and stepped over. Turned on his way down the ladder and called back. "Don't call me for my watch unless we're still afloat!"

"I won't."

The slide closed and Alfred was alone with the ghostly sloop, staggering on with the moving universe of snow and wind and sea. Caught in a vast procession moving sou'west into the Pacific. In the morning, he thought, the procession would still be on the move. The nor'east wind and driving snow, and the gray sea surging underneath. Driving on with endless energy. Wave after wave. About the *Tyee*, he didn't know. The little home-made sloop had no business in that august procession. By morning she might have tired and dropped out, unnoticed. Borne down by the weight of snow and ice, or overwhelmed by the following sea.

The *Tyee* had done all that could have been expected of her, and more. She would still be a match for the sea except for the unfair load of ice that weighed her down. Too heavy to stand up to it or fight back. She could only turn her tail and drift before it. Like that picture he had seen in childhood. An Indian pony, with its head down and its tail between its legs, drifting before a blizzard, across the endless prairie. The pony always made him think of Hyak. Hyak, the buckskin pony that went crazy when a drum was beaten. Went crazy and kicked George unconscious. Jumped, screaming, over the fence. There was blood on George's head. Alfred had dropped his birthday drum and yelled with fright. Just as if he had touched a button that set off an unsuspected mine and blew the sensible world to screaming hell. . . . Hyak, with his head down and tail between his legs, drifting before a blizzard across the endless prairie. He used to wonder if the pony reached shelter. Reached shelter or dropped unnoticed from the procession.

The muffled rush of a heavier sea, rolling up astern, brought him back. He put up the helm a little, steering dead before it. Braced himself for the final shock. It was impossible that the overburdened sloop could meet it. The sea rumbled close behind and above him. Heavily the stern answered and rose up and up. But not enough, not fast enough. The sea broke with a crash and water fell on him. It roared by, into the darkness ahead, leaving the *Tyee* still afloat. Water was washing about his feet. The sea sharing the cockpit with him. Scupper pipes clogged with ice. He reached into the locker beside him for a bailer, and touched heavy rope. The stern line they had used for mooring to the river bank. That might help. Steering craftily, he worked the heavy coil onto the deck behind him. Made one end fast to the ringbolt and capsized the coil. Let the free end overboard, helping it run out, sluggishly at first, then faster with the accumulated drag. Still faster, until it brought up with a thud that made the ringbolt jump. Someone else had done that, long ago. Probably Captain Slocum. Trailed a hawser astern to steady his boat and break the following sea. It might work, maybe not. The same thing works for some people, not for others. If it didn't work, one more sea like the last. . . . The sloop was steadier, he thought, or the seas more regular. Rushing up astern and passing underneath in endless procession, hurrying after the wind and snow. A bigger one roared out of the darkness, gathering power as it came. The grandfather of them all, showing the others how easily it was done. It broke somewhere astern with a noise of thunder, the ruins of its efforts tumbling by harmlessly on each side, foaming and faintly luminous. The grandfather of them all tripped by a few words from a book.

The *Tyee* staggered on with the universal procession. Wind and sea and moving pall of snow. A cayuse, with its head down, drifting before a blizzard across endless prairies. Hyak journeying across snow-swept wastes where no drum ever sounded. Only the biting cold and snow. Pa hammering in the barn, building a sled for Hyak to haul wood home through the big snow. Alfred following George up the trail through the woods. Gigantic trees under snow. The boys like little dolls beneath them. Talking geography. Biting cold. Digging claws. Blood on the snow. Suddenly they realized the world was too big for them and ran home crying. It was a woman who was crying. Great trees under snow. Gold-white firs at sunset. A flag flying in the sunset, showing that an American was about to be born. Gold light on the fluttering stars and stripes, and the snow-laden firs. A clear, new cry. Afterward he used to wonder if Clarice Jackson remembered. No one remembered that far back. Still, she had always counted on him. Just as if there was an understanding between them. Up to the time he went away. The understanding of the gold-white firs at sunset. Indian thinking. He and George didn't get to school that day. The day Clarice Jackson was born. If he went back to school he would find Clarice there ahead of him, teaching the children. It didn't make sense. Would she tell the children about the war? Other wars? How the men from the big woods always answered when their country called them. How Mr. Walter wrote on his door, "Will be back when the Union is saved," and marched alone through the wilderness to enlist. How Captain Pickett left the happy islands to break his heart at Gettysburg. Gave himself, because of honor, to a hopeless cause, which he came within a breath of winning. Unfurling the Southern flag on the heights of Cemetery Hill, where it fluttered in the blast of cannon. Fluttered for a moment of victory and fell among the regiments crumbling into the dust.

Clarice could tell them about her own father. With a young wife and a baby, enlisting in the war against Spain because he thought it was the least a man could do for his country. And now the war with Germany. The children wouldn't have to be told about the first boys who had attended the school. They would see them all enlisting. All of them, unless the ice-laden *Tyee* dropped out of the procession, unnoticed. If that happened, people at home would wonder, but they wouldn't ever be sure. He and George hadn't written that they were coming home to enlist. They had slipped away from Fort Gibbon, where they were wintering, without telling their plans. That was a mistake. By morning, or long before, the procession of the wind and surging gray seas and the moving pall of snow might be going on without them. Then no one would ever know for certain that they had heard their country's call, or that they had been lost while making their answer.

# VII

FLOWERS, the gauge of popularity, crowded the teacher's desk and the corner table between the blackboard and windows. Wild white trillium, spring beauties, and pale scentless violets. School had been dismissed, but three of the children lingered. As a reward, they had been allowed to stay after school. "Steamboat" Harry Robinson was cleaning the long blackboard with absurd slowness and infinite perfection.

Steamboat was a newcomer in the neighborhood. His nickname resulted from the patent lunch pail with which he had appeared at school the first day; a square, tinned affair with a tank for liquids and a stack-like cup inverted on the top. In a district where shortening pails had been the style since the beginning, the contraption had been looked upon unfavorably and dubbed "the steamboat." Later the nickname was transferred to Harry. He was a sensible boy and he still carried both the steamboat and the title.

Anna Larson and her younger brother, Karl, from the new Finnish settlement down the bay, were prolonging the geography lesson. They were at the work table, poring over the relief map of North America: a three-foot-square map which the children had made with the help of their teacher. It was made of putty, colored with oil paints, and sprinkled with several dozen miniature trees: evergreens and oak in the north and east; palm trees in the south.

"Once more!" Anna coaxed. "Where shall I start?"

"Panama," the teacher decided. "Take your ship through the Canal and north to New York. Stop at four different countries on the way and pick up four different kinds of cargo."

The relief map was built in a metal tray, with its oceans and main waterways flooded with real water. Anna's brown fingers guided a match-stick freighter northwest through the half-inch-deep Caribbean. The match stick hesitated off the Nicaraguan coast, passed it and turned west to stop at the republic to the north.

"I stop at Honduras for mahogany," Anna explained.

The teacher smiled approval.

Heading northeast, the match-stick steamer voyaged to a dot south of Cuba.

"I stop at Grand Cayman for bananas."

"Good. What country is it?"

"It is an island. The English own it."

"Good, Anna."

The match stick hesitated.

"Go to Jamaica for rum," Karl whispered.

"I am running this ship," the girl said reprovingly.

It made a two-second run through the Channel of Yucatan and swung east to Cuba.

"I go to Havana for sugar."

Steamboat stopped on his way to dust the erasers. The match stick was being propelled through the Straits of Florida.

"Stop at Nassau for tomatoes," he suggested.

Anna bit her lip with annoyance. "I am running this ship!" she reminded him.

The rebuked Steamboat went on. Anna's ship passed the Bahamas scornfully and headed north. Then it bobbed to a questioning stop.

"You boys!" Anna lamented. "You mixed me up with your rum and tomatoes!" She slapped her brother tentatively and looked about for more boys to punish. Steamboat was out on the porch, clacking the erasers together in a cloud of white dust. She gave Karl another slap for him, but it failed to ease her grief. "I know better than that, Miss Jackson," she said, "but they mixed me up, those boys! That makes only three—"

Karl whispered, "You can stop at Bermuda for—" Then he saw the fierce look in his sister's face and dodged around the work table.

"I don't want to go out of my way to Bermuda for onions!" she lamented. "Not lilies, either." Then she had an idea. "Would it count if I stop in the United States before New York?"

Miss Jackson's eyes said "Yes." Anna sighed with relief and her ship put in on the Carolina coast. "I stop at Charleston for cotton." And in a few more seconds the match stick was berthed between the end of Long Island and New Jersey.

"That was a fine voyage," Miss Jackson said.

Anna smoothed back the thick brown hair from her serious face. She looked at her teacher, doubtfully, but with gratitude. "Thank you, Miss Jackson. They nearly made a shipwreck of me, those boys, mixing me up with rum and tomatoes!"

The teacher laughed. "Never mind, Anna. You didn't really let them mix you up. Now you and Karl must run along, or your mother will want to know what's the matter."

Anna was busy getting into her coat and knitted cap, but Karl still lingered at the table.

"Miss Jackson."

"Yes, Karl?"

"Is Steamboat going, too?"

The teacher was suddenly aware of Steamboat, busily clacking erasers on the porch. "Right away! It shouldn't take any boy so long to clean a blackboard and six erasers."

Karl hesitated. Then his eyes moved slyly toward the door. "Steamboat has a case on you," he confided.

The teacher was annoyed. "Karl! What makes you think anything so silly?"

Karl answered truthfully, "We all have," and marched out of the schoolroom after his sister. As soon as he was gone, Steamboat came in with the immaculate erasers.

Miss Jackson was ready for him. "Harry, I can't let you help me if you're going to be so slow. I expect to get a note from your mother, asking why I keep you after school!"

He distributed the erasers in their trough with geometric precision and came over to where she was standing by the work table. "I'll tell her I stayed because I wanted to. She doesn't care." He looked up at her hopefully, with dignity and a touch of defiance.

"I care," she reminded him. "And there has to be a limit."

Craftily, Steamboat generalized the discussion. "Funny," he remarked, "if anybody'd told me a year ago I was going to want to stay after school, I'd have said he was crazy. Just crazy." He had the air of unburdening his deepest secrets.

No one beyond the age of sixteen, she thought, could be so serious. After that there is always some touch of irony or humor. She smiled at his earnest, straightforward face, and knew that instead she should have packed him off sternly. Her smile was often misunderstood. It gave the kind of encouragement she had not intended. Brought confidences which meant too much to their tellers.

"You know, Miss Jackson, I didn't know school could be like this. I didn't know a teacher could be like you. I always thought a boy just went to school because he had to. I thought school teachers were all mean or didn't care. . . ."

She laughed and quoted from the old rhyme:
"High-heeled boots, stand-up collar. . . ."
She saw Steamboat's face aflame. Thinking of the verse she hadn't quoted:
"Wouldn't kiss a schoolmarm for half a dollar."
He broke away from his red embarrassment. "Miss Jackson, I like you better than anyone! I'd do anything for you. Miss Jackson, I—"
"Harry," she said firmly, "you are a very nice little boy. Now go home as fast as you can. Now!"
He faced her for a moment, red and defiant, then gave up. "Oh, well, I thought I might tell you." He sighed, going for his "steamboat" lunch kit.
"Good night, Harry."

There was a moment of resistant silence. "Good night, Miss Jackson." He bumped his historic lunch pail against the door frame. Jumped off the porch, through habit, and tramped across the yard toward the stile, whistling painfully.

The teacher was still wondering about him when she heard a quick, heavy step on the porch. A figure almost filled the doorway. "Clarice?" The big voice was half-questioning, half-familiar.

"George Tucker!" She hurried toward him, holding out both hands. "I thought you and Alfred were in Alaska."

He took her in his powerful arms and kissed her heartily. "Lord, how things change! Here you are, a school teacher. When I left, you were a little girl in pigtails, going to school."

"I was not," she corrected him. "You only think that because you were never very observant. If you hadn't been away, you would still think I was a little girl."

He was holding her, wondering at her vivid face. "You're not, thank God!"

"Please remember it, then, and let me go. Sit down and tell me everything, or nearly everything." She was hypnotized by his boldness and confidence. He had gone away, half-shy and half-indifferent to the girls who fancied him. He was so good-looking in his big, barbaric way, probably the best way. His eyes were bluer and his hair thicker and more golden than ever. Or perhaps it was because she had never been so close to him before.

Steamboat looked through the open doorway from beyond the stile, and grieved. He had turned back on seeing the big, purposeful stranger striding through the huckleberry patch toward the schoolhouse. He knew Miss Jackson was alone. She might need help; he hoped she would. It would give him a chance to come to her rescue and show he was a man. But she didn't need help. She seemed to like it. Steamboat didn't know the stranger, but he must be her sweetheart. He should have known she had one. She knew he was coming. That was why she had hustled him out when he was on the verge of his great adventure into the unknown. He was going to tell Miss Jackson he loved her—and see what would happen. He had almost done that the week before, then decided to wait until he was twelve. A fat chance he had of telling her now. "Wait, sure, *wait!*" he mocked himself bitterly as he turned away from the stile.

Kicking along a rut of the wagon track to the Arcadia Road, he threw pearls of disillusioned wisdom to the salal bushes: "If you love a woman, that's the time to tell her. Don't wait for *nothing!*"

"Now you must explain yourself to some extent," George and Clarice were in the schoolroom, sitting by the work table. He was guiding a match-stick boat about the waterways of North America.

"I came to invite you to a party."

"Not all the way from Alaska!"

"I was getting around to that. Anyway, you're invited to dinner at our house. Pa's killing the fatted calf. We'll have kind of a party, if we still know how."

"Nothing could suit me better. How is Alfred?"

"Good," George assured her. "He's fine." He was making a match-stick cruise up the Gulf of California. "We didn't have things like this when I went to school." His big, sunny face looked up regretfully.

"It's along the line of modern education," Clarice said. "Making studies interesting."

"The children eat it up, I suppose. *Full speed astern!*" He had rammed Guarda Island.

"They like it. Sometimes I have trouble driving them home when school is out."

"Tell me where you can buy a map like this. I want one to play with."

"I don't know if you can buy them. The children and I made this one."

"Good girl!" His blue eyes studied her face appreciatively. Now, when he was admiring her, they had their old shy, sunny look.

Clarice confided, "If I had a school of my own I would build a relief map of the world out doors. Maybe an acre big. Then the children could paddle around the continents in a canoe and have an idea of how it all looks."

She was rewarded with a crushing blow on her shoulder. "What an idea! I'll help you any time you like. Alf will, too. We've dug up half of Alaska, from Beaufort Sea to the Gulf."

"It can't be now," she pointed out. "Anyway, I'm sure you have other things to do."

George felt rebuffed. "I don't see how anything

could be more important than getting the youngsters interested in their studies." He scowled at her thoughtfully. "Maybe you don't remember, but when the schoolhouse was built, we boys cleared the yard, out front there, and we cleared the playfield. We worked every noon hour, and sometimes after school. I remember we worked for more than a week digging out a two-foot stump in front of the porch. That was the time Jim Howard caught fire."

Clarice looked puzzled. "I don't remember that."

"You wouldn't," George told her loftily. "You were too young. Well, we were digging out that stump and Jim was swinging a pick. He had some matches in his back pocket, and every time he bent over it made friction. After a while the matches went off and set his pants afire."

She laughed with him, looking out at the school yard. The window gave her a view of half the barren acre of ground, broken by unconquered stumps, the girls' outhouse, one end of the playfield, with the old ship's capstan which served as a merry-go-round. "I do wish you had left some trees," she said with regret. "If there were any shade I would have lessons outdoors in weather like this."

George shook his head ruefully. "It was too late, even when we got here. The first thing the men did was to cut down all the big trees and slash and burn the rest. That was before they started building the schoolhouse. I guess there aren't any trees left because there were too many in the first place. The early pioneers must have felt about trees the way they did about Indians. The only good one was a dead one."

123

He stared apologetically out of the window, at the barren yard, the rich evergreens beyond the fence, and the snow and blue Olympics in the sky beyond. Then he sighed and looked at Clarice, humorously and with tenderness. "God, how things move on! You were a little girl, too young to go to school, and now you're teaching the children. I never even knew you were going to be a teacher."

"I wasn't," she explained. "That's mostly accident. I had two years at the University. Then I found that Daddy had had to borrow money to help me through. I didn't like that, George. I want to be able to go where I please and do what I please, without being indebted, even to Daddy. So I dropped out to earn some money. They offered me the school. It wasn't what I planned, but I wouldn't have missed it for anything."

"I bet the children wouldn't, either."

She smoothed back her hair, with the gesture of brushing the subject away. "I've talked enough about myself, George. You haven't told me anything. How do you happen to be here, when your own father and mother thought you were in Alaska? Didn't you have a rough trip, so early in the year?"

"We were lucky!" he grinned. "We got iced up and driven away to-hell-and-gone into the Pacific. But we were lucky, we got back." He became self-conscious and uneasy. "We came home to enlist."

"Yes?" She made no other comment for a while.

He was disappointed. Now that he was home, on the verge of enlistment, he felt misgivings. The war wouldn't be like other things he had been up against. It was full of sneaky things, poison and hidden death.

Strength and courage wouldn't necessarily do you any good. An ugly business. At such a time, a beautiful young woman like Clarice should encourage a man and make him forget. Instead of that, she only said, "Yes?" She seemed to feel the cold shadow, as uneasy as himself. He stirred again and shook back his thick yellow hair. "I don't expect it will be fun, but the Kaiser has to be licked, doesn't he?"

She looked tired and troubled. "I suppose so. Only I'm not sure that will do any good. Daddy doesn't think so; at least, he didn't. He talked as long as he could against our entering the war—and was abused as a pro-German. Feeling is very strong here. All the time we were supposed to be neutral, it was almost a crime to be neutral. Now, there's no good in protesting."

George shook himself and got to his feet, towering above her. "Oh, hell! Let's forget it now, Clarice. We'll settle it another time." His half-rueful grin was comforting.

"Yes," she agreed, smiling a little, "let's forget it. If I'm going to your party, I must go home and dress." She stood up, straight and supple, with her dark head just reaching the level of his huge shoulders.

He couldn't forget it. Not so easily, anyway. He put his arms round her and drew her against him, burying his face in her hair. He felt the warmth of her body through her light summer dress. He could only forget if she helped him.

"Please, George." Her protest was muffled against his breast. "I don't know why you should be so affectionate!"

He continued to hold her, gently and stubbornly;

in silence, warming her hair with his breath, because he couldn't explain to her. He knew why, dimly, but couldn't explain. Something he read in the *P. I.* he got in Seattle. The story about German soldiers on leave. They were turned loose and told to go the limit. "Breed before you die!" At the time he hadn't thought much about it, except that it was what you would expect from a brutal, efficient people like the Germans. He hadn't thought much about it, but it had stuck in his mind. Now it seemed to have been said to him, too. He was caught in the same trap. He was slipping into the war, which was bigger and more dangerous than anything he had ever been up against. Courage and strength mightn't do him any good. If it happened that way, he would be killed and that would be the end of him. In the war he would be a plaything of greater forces. He couldn't gamble on his own judgment and savage strength. He would lose something of himself at the very beginning. He was partly lost already. He must have something to hold. He had always been independent and a little scornful of women. Now the only thing that would help was holding onto a woman. He had felt there must be something. He hadn't known what it was until he saw Clarice, grown into a beautiful young woman, just when he needed her. In a few months he might be killed. The German order had been for him, too. "Breed before you die." But he couldn't explain. So he held her dumbly in the shadowy schoolroom, crushing her warm young body against his.

"Please, George," she said again, "what did I ever

do to make you think I would fall into your arms when you came home?" It sounded very reasonable and matter-of-fact. "You didn't even give me a chance to say goodbye."

He took her shoulders in his hands and held her away from him, a little way, looking into her face longingly, with savagery. As if he might take her at once. His big hands held her shoulders firmly, without hurting, but she could feel the brutal strength in them while he was stirred by the impulse to take her then and there. If he did, she knew she would be powerless even to resent it. She was too full of admiration for his barbaric strength and directness. There was so little of that in most men. Their advances were either sly or weak and apologetic. She unnerved him a little by laughing. He didn't know the mockery was mostly for herself.

He looked baffled and inquiring.

"George, you've made a mistake," she explained.

"Mistake?"

"You must be thinking of some other girl. Remember, when you went away I was a little girl in pigtails, too young to know about love."

He scowled, wondering if she was making fun of him. His hands tightened their grip on her shoulders until she felt like a straw in his grasp. Then his eyes changed and twinkled and his big hands relaxed about her shoulders. He grinned shyly. "Don't mind me, Clarice." He drew her to him again for a moment, without using any more physical strength, and kissed her lightly. "I've been away a long time, and it's good to be home." He stood there, looking about, while she collected the door key from her desk and her coat from the rack. He seemed to miss something. When she was ready to go, he still held back. "Where's Jimmy Pickett's table?" he demanded.

She said, "I never heard of it."

George looked exasperated and half amused along with his regret. "God, you are too young for anything. That's a fact! It was a table Jimmy made when he was a boy. A little pine table with a drawer. Mama brought it here for the first teacher's desk. When the school board bought that varnished one, it was put in the corner for the water pail. It sort of helped me with my history. Made me realize history was real. Sometimes in singing, when the teacher had us bawling 'The Battle Hymn of the Republic,' or 'Marching Through Georgia,' I would see Jimmy's little table standing there. It would give me a queer, lonesome feeling. Then I couldn't sing as loud as the others, because it made me remember there were two sides to the war, with some of the finest men that ever lived fighting on the other side. We seemed like young hoodlums, walking on something, well, sacred to other people." He blushed. "I don't know if you understand how I felt."

Clarice answered earnestly, "I hope I do, George." She was moved by his revealed compassion, "I'm going to find out what happened to the table and have it brought back if it's in existence. I've always loved Jimmy, even though I never saw him."

"I guess everyone did," George decided.

As they went out into the afternoon sunshine he stopped, unconsciously, and looked back into the shadowy schoolroom, with its old, familiar smell of books and paste and maps. It seemed to have called him with a soundless voice. Like Jimmy Pickett's table, silent among the noisy conquerors, and still making itself heard. When he turned, Clarice was looking up at him with her compassionate, sweet face. Then she closed the door, gently, and turned the key.

"Memories?"

"Plenty!" He had the odd feeling of being a boy, with his schooling just ended. Leaving the schoolroom for the last time. Going away, alone, to where no one could help him, with his strength weakened. He hadn't expected this terrible feeling of weakness, which he mustn't confess even to his own brother. This hungry need for someone who could make him forget for a while. He was realizing, rather late, that even after a beautiful and heroic death a man is dead forever. He did not want to die.

# VIII

Late in June the brothers were still at home. After their wild rush south from Alaska, they were experiencing a pause before plunging into military training. Mrs. Tucker pleaded with them daily to stay at home and wait for the Draft. They would be called as soon as they were wanted, she argued. And they owed something to her, after being away so long. By enlisting earlier they would only inconvenience the Government. She gave the impression of her great hulking sons overcrowding two or more recruiting offices and distracting a Government intent on the Draft.

It was unthinkable to George and Alfred that they should wait until their country called them by name. They weren't that shy kind of patriot. Still, there were things to do after an absence of three years, and pleasant excuses for remaining a little longer. George had become sentimental about the district school, going at least as often as he was allowed to see Clarice home afterward. He thought it would be suitable to stay until school was out.

Alfred saw nothing against it, and they became involved in the closing exercises. It was George's idea that they take the children on the *Tyee* to Steamboat Island for a picnic. That was to be on Saturday, the day after school closed.

Clarice invited them both for a Thursday afternoon expedition to gather wild flowers for decorations. Some of the children might go with them, she thought.

The breadth of the invitation started everything off wrong. George had counted on going with her alone. Wednesday evening he told his brother he wasn't going. Two people who had their minds on what they were doing could pick all the flowers in Christendom. He could spend the day to better advantage cleaning up the *Tyee* for the picnic.

Alfred insisted he would rather work on the sloop than pick flowers. The whole business began to sound silly. To pick flowers or not to pick flowers. In the end they laughed about it, but George had a way of being stubborn even after his first resentment had passed. They would work together on the *Tyee* in the morning. Then Alf could go and trim hats if he felt like it, but he could count George out. There was no use arguing with him. George might be sorry he had said he wouldn't go, but he had said it, and he wouldn't.

Thursday morning Alfred woke early with the feeling that it was to be a very special day. Something immense and thrilling was to happen. Something— what? He was going to pick flowers! It didn't sound funny. It was very pleasant. Clarice and himself wandering through the woods, talking, in search of wild flowers. It appealed to him immensely. He hadn't seen nearly as much of her as he would have liked. But their few times together had made coming home worth while. Their minds seemed to go hand in hand, even though his education was a patchwork of books and life, with great gaps between, and she had attended the State University. Alfred didn't have his brother's confidence. George felt himself the equal of anyone. To him, a millionaire was just a man—if he proved it. If he couldn't, he was something less. Like that sportsman who chartered the *Tyee* for a hunting trip to Lake Minchuminia. To George, Clarice Jackson was a pretty girl with whom he would fall in love if he felt like it. He didn't see that she was different from any of the others, except that she was uncommonly lovely—and therefore more desirable. Probably that came from being the eldest, in a new country. Like Jim Howard, another first-born. He had assumed that he and his chances were as good as any —and proved that they were a lot better than most.

That's the way an American should feel—free and equal. Only Alfred couldn't always feel that way. Not about Clarice. She knew so many things he had only felt vaguely, or wondered about. That seemed part of the reason for their getting along so well and having so much to talk about—when they had the chance. There was so much he wanted to learn and she took such pleasure in telling him, as far as she was able. And that seemed to him far indeed.

Really, there was nothing silly about picking flowers. Walking through the woods with Clarice and going on with his neglected education. There would be the children, of course. They didn't seem very real. Maybe they wouldn't come. He had a powerful feeling they wouldn't. That was part of the feeling with which he woke. Part of the conviction that something splendid was about to happen.

He felt it more at noon, and waited until George went back to the sloop before changing from his soiled dungarees, and shaving. It was the least one could do out of respect to a college girl, but he knew it would be impossible to make his preparations seem casual. Impossible, with something splendid hovering over the day.

There was no reason to feel that way, he told himself. It was only the shadow of a dream. He had had a dream with Clarice in it. He couldn't even remember what it was, but the feeling had carried over after he was awake and colored everything with a fateful glory.

His mother was doing the dishes while he shaved, sitting at the table with the mirror propped up against a stone pickle crock. There was no running hot water in the bathroom yet, and shaving things were kept in the big kitchen. His mother stopped beside him, with a dish towel and plate in her hands, looking out of the window at the sunny inlet. He looked, too, with his face lathered. On the *Tyee*, anchored in the cove, George was turning the cushions, airing on deck. Turning them with exaggerated ease. Even at that distance he showed up big and powerful.

"This is the nicest day we've had this year," his mother said.

Alfred shaved steadily, with his strong, dark features emerging from the lather. "It was fine on the water," he said, "whenever I came up from the bilges to enjoy it."

His mother went to the sink, then came back with another plate. "George always had these stubborn streaks."

Shaving the under side of his jaw, he glimpsed her troubled face in the mirror. "All of us have streaks of one thing and another. I wouldn't want George any different." Shaving under his chin, "It's never done him any harm."

She said, "You always helped him out. Ever since you caught up with him. If it came to where you couldn't help him—"

When she came back with another plate, he said, "I don't know anyone I'd trust better than George to look out for himself."

But his mother was still troubled. She began talking about Clarice. "We never had a better teacher. We've had good ones and poor ones, but we've never had another one who knew as much or was so modest about it. When Clarice went away to the University, I was afraid she might find she was too good for us. But when she came back to teach, she seemed to belong here more than ever. She has a way of making us feel that what she's learned belongs to all of us."

Shaving his other jaw, he said, "I guess she's pretty good." Really, George hadn't given him much chance to find out. But it was pleasantly disturbing to hear his mother talk about her that way.

She said, "Clarice is very young, and she may change. But sometimes she reminds me of Mrs. Walter—it would break your heart, some of the Indians who came to her with their troubles. They called her 'White Mama,' but it seemed to me they considered her one of themselves, who knew more. She was so lovely to them, only sad because she was old and dying, and their troubles were more than she could help."

His mother's face always became beautiful when she spoke of Mrs. Walter. "There aren't many like that," she continued. "In all my life I've known just a few people I wanted to keep for always. Clarice Jackson is one of them. Since she came back, I've sometimes lain awake at night, thinking about her in this big house. She belongs here."

Alfred said, "I don't know how George is making out with her," closing his razor.

"I wish George hadn't got this silly streak. Or else—" Her look was strangely complicated.

He said abruptly, "You think I shouldn't go? I tried to get out of it."

"You must, Alfie! It would be dreadful if neither of you showed up."

But she was still troubled, disturbed and tender. As if the colors of his dream shone like war paint on his well-shaved face.

He was still trying to fathom it as he walked up the hill, along the rotting skidroad. Looked at sensibly, it was only a dream which had clung about him and gone on after he woke. If it had been anything more real, he wouldn't be on his way to meet Clarice—Clarice and the children.

He turned, at the edge of the old Southeast Field, where the hay would soon be ready for cutting, along the foot-wide path he and George had worn to the schoolhouse. The winding path was still hard and barren, after all those years, but the salal and young firs were crowding in from each side. Then he noticed some of the branches had been cut away. George had opened the path again, and he was profiting by his brother's work.

He was late, yet he had no impulse to hurry. He wanted to keep the shadow of the dream which clung about him. Something he couldn't even remember. He wanted to keep it a little longer. The moment he reached the schoolhouse and met Clarice and the children it would be gone. It would evaporate, and he would be fully awake and himself again.

He passed through the huckleberry patch, where the mothers used to come after school and help the children fill their lunch pails with berries. The berries plumping in, creeping up to hide the last bright inside of the lard pails while the afterglow faded from the far-off Olympics and shadows crept up over the snow. He turned and saw them there, unchanged. What had he expected? Does a man outlast the mountains? The long huckleberry branches were loaded with little hard berries. In August they would be purple clubs wedged with tender green. *Shot olalie* they were called in Chinook jargon.

Topping the stile, he saw Clarice come out on the porch. His heart gave a lurch when he saw she was alone. Straight womanly little figure in a soft orange blouse and gray skirt. She came out onto the porch with a waiting look, and saw him. He saluted, descending the steps of the stile. Her waiting look relaxed and she stood still while he came up to her; waiting, but differently. So much alive, even when she was perfectly still, like life waiting.

He felt slightly intoxicated, or not quite awake. The dream didn't evaporate as they met. It became more real. The schoolroom behind them was perfectly quiet.

"What about the children?" he asked, hoping to hell they were miles away.

"They got impatient waiting," she told him. "I let them go on alone."

He looked at her, uncertain of his voice. "Do we have to—are we to catch up with them?"

"It isn't necessary. The big boys know the woods as well as we do. They will look after the others." She didn't ask about George. He must have told her he wouldn't come—or she had known without being told. She locked the door and put the key under the mat, where the children could find it if they came back first.

"What kind of flowers are we going for?" Not that it mattered, only beyond the stile they would have to choose some direction.

She considered, walking slowly beside him. "The children are going toward the creek, for maiden hair fern and bleeding hearts. I think it would be nice if we could bring in some Indian pipes. They're rather ghostly, but I like them with brighter flowers."

"Do you know any special place to find them?"

"Anywhere in the deep woods, I should think." Clarice seemed to have lost interest in the subject.

Beyond the stile the way to the Arcadia Road was two wagon tracks, with salal and Oregon grape between fine wild grass in the ruts. The road had always been like that. People only drove to the school for the programs two or three times a year. Most of the traffic was the feet of the children who lived inland. Sometimes, at noon or recess, the whole school used to race along the wagon tracks at the swift rumble of wheels. They were rewarded by the sight of a horse and buggy dashing by. . . .

Clarice said abruptly, "It seems strange that you and George are going away to war."

He reminded her, "We came home to enlist."

"I know. Yet it doesn't seem right that the best go first."

"They wouldn't be the best if they didn't go first," he told her soberly.

"Just the same," she said, "I wish it hadn't happened this way."

He was beginning to wish that, too, but it was rather late, even for wishing. There was something sweet and religious about her being sorry. But there was something sad about it, too, like religion.

"It's hard to explain what I mean," she said. "Maybe you'll have a good time in the war. I don't suppose it can be more dangerous than working in a logging camp. Mostly, I'm sorry because of the country. Have you heard Mr. Howard's story about the Seattle man? He's very proud of it. The man looked around the Howards' clearing, full of stumps, with the woods all around."

" 'What in the world can you raise here?' he asked.

"Mr. Howard said, 'Boys.'

"He was proud of that answer. But I think there is something sad about it, too. Jim is on his way home from Oxford to enlist in the American Army. Frank and Freddie are away at sea. Arthur left the State College to enlist in the Marines. The Howards haven't seen any of them for more than a year. It's like that all over the county. This spring I've met a dozen young men, practically neighbors, for the first time. They've been away, some of them for years, in Alaska or at sea or homesteading in Montana. I might never have seen them if they hadn't come home to enlist."

Alfred said, "I guess they found things about the same as we did. There isn't much here except the logging camps."

Walking very slowly, she said, "I know. Most of the farmers on the inlet are working their places alone, and doing road work or carpentry to make ends meet. The farms can't even support the farmers, let alone the boys they raised. The country is so new people haven't learned how to make a living. When there is so much to be done here, it doesn't seem fair that the boys should have to go away to a war in Europe."

He said, "I wish now it hadn't happened. But America has been good to me. I'm ready to do my share for democracy."

"I hope it turns out well, Alfred," she said quietly. "I hope you come back safe."

"Thank you, Clarice."

It was like a sober dream. Their feet had stopped just short of the Arcadia Road's narrow ribbon of dust. They were looking at each other the way children sometimes do, wanting to know about each other, openly and with innocence. She was like this beautiful, somber country, to which he belonged. He loved it deeply, and had known it from the beginning.

But he had been away a long time. There was the feeling of belonging, passionately, with a touch of strangeness. Clarice was part of his own country. She knew it better than he did, and had thought about it more deeply. When she talked about it, it was like this strange, familiar land coming to life and speaking to him. He had always felt its beauty, even in the poverty-stricken years of boyhood. But then it was everywhere, and out of reach. Now, for a flash of time, the beauty and sweetness were gathered together in one woman. He wanted, profoundly, to hold her in his arms before he went away. He wanted to have her young arms hold his head against her breast. That longing didn't have anything to do with love-making. It seemed to him if he had that to remember, something of him would always be in this land he loved. Even if he stayed forever in a foreign country.

They stood looking at each other, solemn with the realization of the meaning of war. Then her dark eyebrows went up, inquiringly, and she turned her head a little.

It was only the wind in the trees. A dry, far-away whisper. It swelled through the tree tops a hundred feet above their heads, and went away into the distance like the echo of earth sighing.

She asked, "Which way are we going, Alfred?"

When they left the road his longing went away. Both of them changed. They were very young and impersonal, walking through the almost open country. Dry, gravelly soil nourishing sparse huckleberry and salal. An occasional madronia tree, half tropical, with smooth red bark and glossy leaves like the rubber plant. Those and fir trees, which grow in any kind of soil. Scattering firs, a hundred feet high and more, as dry and hostile as the gravel land. The ridged bark of their lower trunks blackened by old forest fires. Their dry, green, inaccessible branches sighing in some breeze of the upper air. Alfred remembered how he used to regard them when he was a child. It seemed to him the fir trees lived in a high green country of their own, where people could never climb. Only their barren trunks came down to the world of men. He still thought that way about them. He felt very young and impersonal, with no grown-up urge to turn this or that to his advantage. One of the trees ahead bore mistletoe. He pointed it out to Clarice: a thick mass of different, softer green foliage. Their way led them close to the tree. They passed under it, through the dark cross-road of its shadow, without his having any urge to touch her. There was something mocking in the thought of kissing a girl under mistletoe held up a hundred feet in the air. The tree was centuries old when he was born, and it might be green centuries after he was gone. . . .

Once he and George were cutting wood from a tree they had felled west of the clearing. Resting, they sat on the block which they had just toppled over, a round table of creamy new wood, five feet across. They started counting the yearly rings. Three inches inside the bark, the Battle of Gettysburg was being fought. Less than six inches from there, the Revolution. Nine inches farther, the Pilgrims were landing on Plymouth Rock. They never reached the heart of the tree. Six inches away, the earth was as flat as the block over which they were poring. America was an unguessed country beyond its edge. They stopped in the failing light. Groped their way back through the centuries. Gathered up their tools and found their way home through the dusk of prehistoric woods. . . .

There was no use pretending the mistletoe had anything to do with him. It belonged to the unexplored, green country from which only the barren trunks came down. They tramped on through the still, dry land. Not saying much, but talking easily and quietly when they did. Nothing personal or important. Only the sound of their voices answering each other in peaceful accord.

They had decided to head south, toward the low country east of the Howard place. The rain, early in the week, should have brought up Indian pipes in the damp woods where alder and ash covered the ground with leaf mold.

Almost unexpectedly they passed out of the dry, open country into the true forest. Cool, green twilight closed over them. Trunks of great firs stood about, huge gray columns, brokenly fluted. Their bases blurred by the starved foliage of undergrowth. The high, green country which the columns held up¯was warm in the June sun, but none of it came through.

Their mood changed again in those dim, sunless woods. Something had gone away when they left the open country. Or something had come back. They were deliberate and relaxed. No need to hurry when they were already there. They rested, sitting on the ground that was deep under fir needles and pale and black leaves which had starved and fallen.

The man and woman weren't impersonal any more. It was the two of them against the forest, with its weight of centuries. They had only each other for warmth and company. They were not touching each other, but they had joined forces.

Clarice said, looking up, "Do you think those trees are hostile to people, or just indifferent?"

He said, "They probably don't know what's going on around their toes."

"I always think of them as Gothic woods," Clarice went on. "Like being in a Gothic cathedral. No comfort where you are, and everything leading up to where you can't go."

No, there wasn't much comfort here. They smiled at each other for companionship. When their smile went away, their eyes stayed together. Saying, we have only each other in this gloom-haunted cathedral, with columns a thousand years old. Outside, in the sun, the rumble of war. No comfort there. None here, except what we make for ourselves. No warmth except each other in this overwhelming indifference.

He thought of George, and sighed. "I suppose we should go on."

Clarice didn't seem to hear him. Then she came back from somewhere and said, "Yes."

He got up and helped her to her feet. Their hands stayed together, as if they had life and desire of their own. Then he bent down, awkwardly, and put his face against her bright blouse. He heard the soft hammering of her heart.

She asked, strangely, "Why did you do that, Alfred?"

When he looked at her she was disturbed, and he thought she was angry. She had taken her hands from him.

"Because I wanted to," he said, "before I went away."

"I don't want you to go away!" She still looked as if she were angry. But she could not have been angry with him.

They were clinging to each other, desperately. As if, when they let each other go, they would be lost separately in the overwhelming indifference, and never find each other again. While he kissed her he tried to think of George, and all the trouble that would come of this. But consequences were like sea birds, beating against a gale. Their warning cries swept away by the storm.

Once she asked, "Is that better? O, my dear Alfred! I couldn't have you away at war, trying to remember the touch of a two-dollar blouse!"

# IX

ALFRED reached home long after dark. He had
seen Clarice home first, but it was dark
even then. Dusk before they left the woods.
Night in the schoolroom, where they left
the ghostly Indian pipes among the children's maiden
hair fern and bleeding hearts. He had struck matches
while she put them in a jug of water on a little table,
dimly familiar.

In the flare of the last match he recognized it.
"Jimmy Pickett's table," he said.

"Yes. I found it in the attic." Clarice didn't say
how she came to look for it or when it had been
found. But it seemed to have been fairly recently.
"Finished," she said a moment later.

The match flame died and they felt for each other
in the dark. Clung together in the still schoolroom,
as dark as the grave and solemn as an unlit church.
Solemn as childhood and innocent with the smell of
books and paste and maps. They clung together for a
minute, then groped their way out.

"We'll have to do some explaining," Clarice reminded him gently. "And I never felt less like explaining anything."

When he reached home, Alfred remembered that he
might have to do some explaining. He never felt less
inclined, or less prepared. He wanted passionately to

be alone, since he couldn't be with Clarice. Wanted to come home to a silent house. Go to bed without having to say anything to anyone. Lie in the dark and think, and remember. He didn't want to have anything to do with words. Every word he had to speak or hear would take something from him. Check his mind from reaching the meaning of his adventure. That was something he had never heard, or been told. That a woman could give a man as much adventure as the sea. The same adventure. The kind not every man might care to meet. Some men wanted their women cold and their sea calm. Afraid of aroused passion. Afraid of the grandeur of the aroused elements. It didn't matter which one. They were the same. The *Tyee* in a gale. Your job to keep your head and match your strength and skill against the headlong passion of the sea. When you knew that experience, you had lived. That must be the meaning of adventure. Something that makes you remember you have lived. The opposite of death, where you are overpowered or out-manouvered. Adventure was the same, whether with an aroused woman or the aroused sea. Your reward was the same, the satisfaction of meeting headlong passion with the best you have. Skill and endurance. Not scared by fear or dulled by overconfidence. Reaching safety through danger, peace through storm.

He was utterly peaceful now, with the tumult of the sea somewhere far away, half remembered, half heard. He didn't want it spoiled by strangers. And just now everyone was a stranger.

They were in the living room. Pa reading the inside

section of the *P.I.*, with his left foot tucked under him. The outside half of the paper laid on the table under the lamp. Brutal black headlines. German advance. Battle along the whole front. Two hundred thousand killed. The War was Pa's religion. It had converted him to subscribing for a daily paper. He often wished he was young enough to enlist and take a shot at the Kaiser. Easy enough to say and so simple, as if the Kaiser were a chicken hawk that might land on the fence and wait while Pa took down his old Winchester from the kitchen wall. Too easy and simple, to believe that would end all wrong and injustice.

Ma was knitting a sock of khaki-colored wool. Her needles flashed and clicked like sword-play in the lamp-light. George wasn't in the room. Alfred wondered where he was, but couldn't ask.

Ma looked up. "Well," she said pleasantly, "home at last!" With the finality of asking and answering all the questions that there were going to be. Making herself his ally. "Have you eaten?"

"Yes." Meaning he hadn't, and wasn't hungry.

Pa lifted his bald head from the newspaper. "These Germans! By God, I wish I was young enough to take a shot at them. Look at that. They're grinding up their dead for fertilizer! I used to think it was only the Kaiser, but they're all alike. The Allies ought to kill every man, woman and child in Germany! They strip the dead on the battlefield and tie them up in bundles for the fertilizer factory. The women grind them up."

Alfred was dubious, and impatient. "Who says so?"

Pa pointed with a sun-browned finger. "It's a dispatch from London," he said. "If it were from the French, you might think it was propaganda."

"I think I'll go to bed," Alfred observed.

Ma looked up from her knitting again. "George has gone already," she remarked. Just in case he wanted to know without asking.

He nodded, absently. "Good night, Pa; good night, Ma."

She gave him a conspirator's kiss that might have been words. "You're only young once, and not for very long." He went upstairs, wondering. Love did strange things to women. Even to the ones who were only onlookers. Probably a woman couldn't be a mere onlooker. If you need an ally in love, get a woman. Women know everything without having to be told anything and they have no moral sense. No loyalties except for you, if it happens that way. He didn't want to think about it. Didn't want to think of anything or anyone but Clarice, and another woman was getting into the picture. Maybe you can't know one woman well without knowing all of them better. That might be the joker. You can't love one without the others feeling it gives them some obscure claim on you.

George was in bed, propped up on one elbow, looking out of the window at the dark bay. He was smoking a cigar, a bad sign. Usually he didn't think about bed until he was ready to sleep, and he smoked cigars only when he was feeling rough and obstreperous. Probably because it gave him something to bite on. When Alfred came in he turned on the other elbow and jibed over his ash tray—the half shell of a ten pound geoduck.

"Well, Alf, you must have picked a lot of flowers," he said.

"Enough, anyway." Alfred sat on the edge of his bed and began unlacing his boots. He never felt more defenseless against questioning. Couldn't even protest against it.

"It's none of my business, of course," George pointed out. "Only it sounds like keeping the kids out late."

Alfred didn't like lies. Didn't find them necessary except in a case like this, where a girl was concerned. Even then, he wasn't going to tell anything that could be disproved. "The children weren't with us," he said. "They went off on their own hook. They got back before us."

George looked as if he had received a sudden jab and was trying not to show it. "It's none of my business, of course." He went on smoking and stirring his thick yellow hair. Watching Alfred's face while he undressed. He didn't look suspicious, only hurt and puzzled. If he were suspicious, he wouldn't be watching so openly. He seemed bewildered by a situation where it would be possible to suspect his brother. After a while he blurted out, "I suppose you had dinner at the Jacksons'?"

Really, it was none of his business. "No," Alfred said, taking off his shirt. "We were too late. We went farther than we realized."

"You didn't go too far, did you?" Shrewdly.

Alfred laughed, annoyed. "What kind of a girl do

151

you think Clarice is, anyway?" Then hated himself
for the hypocrisy.

"I hope she is human," George answered like a re-
proof. "I hope to God she is!"

"So do I."

"So you went too far—"

"We went farther than we realized and had trouble
finding our way back."

"Lost, eh?" George suggested.

"Something like that."

"You're a hell of a woodsman, Alf."

Alfred had finished undressing. He arranged his
clothes on the chair, with his shoes underneath. "I've
known better," he admitted.

"There are worse, too," George pointed out, per-
versely. "Where the devil were you, anyway?"

"Looking for Indian pipes. We finally found them
in the woods east of the Howards'."

George was becoming interested professionally.
The half-smoked cigar between his strong white
teeth, his lips drawn back a little, and his blue eyes
far and set. Picturing the lowland, which he hadn't
seen for years. "That's the place for Indian pipes, all
right," he decided. "You should have looked there
in the first place. Where did you look?"

It was getting exasperating. "First in the woods
below the spring," Alfred lied. He stretched himself
on his bed. "If you've a map of the township, I'll
trace our course."

George's mind was still working, annoyingly. "So
you got lost in the woods. You couldn't have had
your mind on where you were going."

"No. My mind was on what we were looking for."
God, what an ending to the day of glory. "Damn it,
George, I told you a dozen times you should come
along—or go alone. If you had, it wouldn't have
happened."

"What wouldn't have happened?"

"Our getting lost."

"I thought you were trying to be damned polite.
I didn't think you wanted me along because you were
afraid of getting lost in our own back yard."

"That sometimes happens to good woodsmen."

"But it happens to your kind oftener."

"It might have been you. I wish it had. Then it
wouldn't have mattered."

"Thanks, Alfie!"

"I mean you wouldn't have been able to say anything about it."

"Not till I found someone to say it to, anyway."

They laughed, and George subsided into good na-
ture, smoking his cigar and brushing the ash into the
huge clam shell. If he would only blow out the light.
Then Alfred would be alone. For the first time it
occurred to him that they might have been too much
together. About the only time they had ever been
away from each other was that week, long ago, when
Mrs. Walter was dying, and his mother had kept him
with her to carry messages. Those nights he had slept
here, in Jimmy Pickett's room. It was hard to remember that he had ever been there without his brother.
Wasn't he about ready to put out the lamp?

George stirred and shifted his weight to the other
elbow, great muscles stirring under his white, satiny

skin. He looked over his shoulder at Alfred. His face was troubled and doubtful. He was off again! "What did Clarice think about your bum woodsmanship, getting her lost?"

"I was wondering how long it would take you to think up the next question! She didn't say. She's a good sport."

"I know that." After a minute he asked. "What did she think about my not coming along?"

What a baby George could be when he got this kind of streak! "She didn't say. Too polite, maybe."

George grinned, with that blue twinkle in his eyes. Making him laugh helped, only he always came back to that hurt, puzzled look. He would be all right for a few minutes, then he was off again, stung by doubt. "So you don't think Clarice missed me?"

"O hell, I'm no mind reader! You'll have to ask her." Alfred hoped he would see her first. They hadn't planned what they would tell George, or anyone else, because they hadn't planned what happened. They had left themselves defenseless.

George was still upset. All their talk had got them nowhere. George hadn't asked what he wanted to know. Alfred hadn't told him. But George was getting round to the point. He blurted, "How do you feel about Clarice, anyway?" It looked as if he was as much afraid of knowing the truth as his brother was of telling.

"I think a lot of her, of course."

George gave a snort. "Hell, Alfie, I didn't ask if you respected her!"

154

Alfred said, "We could go on like this all night, beating around the bush."

"Only we won't!" George's teeth met through his cigar. "I'm asking you straight, do you love Clarice?"

"Will you believe what I tell you?"

George eyed him belligerently. "Sure, if you stop lying to me!"

"I haven't been lying."

"No, but you haven't been telling the truth."

"I'll tell you the truth, only I want to ask a few questions first."

"Shoot!"

"Since we came home, have you seen me running after Clarice?"

George said, "No." Then, with his natural honesty, added, "I've been doing that."

"Was it my fault that I saw her alone today?"

His brother took a long time to say, "I suppose not."

"Well, when you admit I've stood back and not tried to cut you out, why do you act this way?"

George's big chest swelled as he reared up in bed. His blue eyes had a million volt look. "Because, by God, I think you have, anyway!"

"Without meaning to!" Alfred reminded him quickly. "Without wanting—"

George ground out his cigar in the big clam shell. "You admit it, do you?" He was taking it almost quietly, after all. As if he could stand anything better than suspicion and doubt.

"I promised to tell you the truth. You promised to

believe me. You must believe it wasn't anything we planned or could help. If we found we loved each other, it was something we couldn't help any more than any other accident."

George scowled past his brother. "The laugh's on me!"

"More likely, it's on me!"

"How do you make that out?"

"This damned war," Alfred said. The nearer he was to it, the more of a nightmare it became. "I think the laugh is on me. Just as if you wanted a pair of snow-shoes, and for some reason or other I got them. The laugh would be on whoever got them, because we both had our tickets bought for hell."

George growled, "Showshoes, eh? Is she as cold as all that?"

Alfred didn't answer the question. Cold, no. But he felt chilled. Since he was a boy he had hoped to be in a war. He used to wish for a war, even though it inconvenienced other people. He'd got what he asked for. And he had been inconvenienced, perhaps fatally, before he was ever in it. An hour ago he had thought that by being alone he could bring back the glory of the day. Now he doubted if that could be done at all while life was undermined by war. It might be years. And then only if he lived through. And if love lived through. Though he hadn't any real doubts about love.

"You're a hell of a brother!" George burst out. "You take Clarice away from me and make a fool of me, and then, by God, you bellyache!"

"Call it bellyaching if you like. I wish to Christ it

156

never happened! What good do you think it can do me when I'm going to war?"

"Plenty good," George said. "You'll marry her. You'll have months together while you're at Camp Lewis. Maybe that's as far as you'll ever get."

A hell of a chance, with things at a standstill on the Western Front and Russia out of the war!

"You could wait for the Draft. They mightn't even take you, with me in the Army."

"I wait for the Draft! What do you think I am?"

George was scowling at the crayon portrait Jimmy Pickett had made of his father, from a photograph. There was no telling whether it meant anything to him at the moment, or was just a place to rest his stormy eyes. "Make the most of your chance," he said. "Don't bellyache to me. Even if you get blown to hell, you'll have something to remember."

"Suppose they don't make a good job of it?" Alfred was thinking of that pale Canadian boy at Ruby. The lieutenant he told them about, sent home in a basket; a blind, wriggling worm, without arms or legs. In this Christian world lives are sacred. You can destroy millions out of hate, but not one out of mercy. His wife embarrassed the return of the hero by going insane on the station platform and outscreaming the welcoming band. Whatever else happened, Clarice wasn't going to run the risk of being tied to anything like that! "What if they don't make a good job of it?" he asked again.

George stirred impatiently. "You take your chances in a war. Don't ask me for sympathy. I'd be more likely to break your neck!" He turned down the lamp

157

with a quick twist. "How about some sleep?" The springs creaked as he settled himself in bed.

Alfred was alone in darkness, at last, to think, and remember. He didn't even try to piece together the smashed bits of the day. They hung before his mind like fragments from an explosion, about to fall. His brother's stormy look, going on after the lamp had been blown out. Beauty come back to earth, gleaming white in the shadow of the old woods. Brutal black headlines. Pale Indian pipes among the children's maidenhair fern and bleeding hearts. A hundred thousand lives blown out like candles. That first kiss. Conscience and loyalty like seabirds beating against a gale. Powerless, with their cries swept away by the storm. A gentle man like his father clamoring for the extermination of the whole German race. Love. The sweep of a long sea, greater than the others, coming in to shore. Rising and falling as it swept on. Always rising higher. Until it towered up at last and shut out the sky, ending with a great burst on the shore. George was still. After a while his breathing changed, and Alfred knew that he was asleep. He couldn't sleep. The moonlight touched and left the top of the sweet apple tree outside the window—one of the trees Mr. Walter had left when he wrote on his door: "Will be back, God willing, when the Union is saved." He had come back, and gone away again.— Tugs with tiers of towing lights labored toward the east with great rafts of logs to feed the war. Dark acres of forest, glacier slow, on the dark water. The Olympic forests marching against the German Empire.

Alfred knew he had slept because he was aroused

158

by the steamer's whistle. George was up already. His empty bed and the goeduck shell with last night's mushroomed cigar. How would they face each other this morning? As enemies or brothers? He went to the window.

The *Forest Queen* was coming down fast, looming out of the light morning mist. There was a skiff waiting in the path of the white steamer; misty, with a dim rower resting on his oars. No passenger. That was George, with the *Tyee*'s tender! But why? The steamer still had weigh on her, sliding down. Gray wood smoke trailing from her tall black funnel. Red paddlewheel poised motionless. The skiff dropped alongside. The deckhands, out on the guard, hooked it with their feet, bow and stern. George looked up and spoke to them, shipping his outside oar. What message did he have for the steamer? In his best blue suit, passing up a suitcase. George! He was up on the guard, with the deckhands kicking the skiff away.

The sternwheel revolved, throwing up its cloud of white spray. Its soft thunder reached Alfred as the steamer gathered weigh. It had never really stopped. George stepped through the open freight door, and did not reappear on deck.

Why? Alfred left the window, feeling dazed and a little ill. George going away like that, without even telling his own brother! Making a bad business worse.

He found a folded note beside the geoduck shell.

Don't mind me, Alfie. I came home to enlist. It was about time I got round to it. Be good to Clarice. Take my advice and wait for the Draft.

That will be soon enough. I'm not leaving this way because I'm sore. Only because I'm afraid I might get sore and break your damn neck. God bless you.

George.

P.S. Tell Dad and Mother the best story you can think of. Will write soon.

G. T.

They got into the Army, as they had planned. But not quite the way they had planned.

George and Alfred met in a company orderly room at Camp Fremont. They had let George out of the guard house in honor of his brother's arrival.

"Jesus Christ," he said, "this is a funny Army! A man enlists to save his country, and they want to tell him when to go to bed. Stuck me in the hoosgow because I took a night off. There wasn't any work to do, either. What are you doing here?"

"I've enlisted in your Company," Alfred said. "I came as soon as I knew where you were."

George looked exasperated. Then he grinned, looking at his brother's suit. "You know best. Those civies do have ears on them." Then his blue eyes looked troubled. "Where's Clarice?"

"At home."

"You're not bringing her here?"

Alfred shook his head.

George had a lost, hurt look. "You're married, aren't you?"

"No, George. I told you I wasn't going to let her run the risk of being tied to a cripple."

"What the hell! Wasn't she willing to take the chance?"

"She wanted to, but I wouldn't let her."

George was disgusted. "A man has to take his chances. I don't see why a woman shouldn't, too." He still couldn't quite believe it. "And you just went away and left her?"

"I came here to enlist."

"You could have gone to Camp Lewis. Then you'd have seen her, anyway."

Alfred knew that very well.

"Why didn't you?"

"We're brothers, aren't we? We've been through a lot of things together. When we're both going to be in the Army, I thought it should be together."

"You make me sick!" George said. "I step out so I won't be a skeleton at the party, and you up and leave the party!" Just the same, he was glad to have his brother with him.

# BOOK THREE

# X

WAR was never like this. Maybe it was always like this, only you weren't told. There must always be uninteresting parts, like eddies away from the main stream. If you get into one of those you have no luck, and you stay. . . . That must be a Jap passenger steamer, up from Tsuruga. . . . Maybe there's a danger in learning too fast and being too good. You and George helping train other recruits. . . . Do they ever run the sampans down? . . . You put in a year at that. . . . What would it be like, sailing a boat in Golden Horn Bay? Not very good, probably. It seemed a windless sort of place. . . . The men you trained went overseas before you. Their account of war would be that they were drafted, trained, sent East on a troop train, overseas in a transport, touched up a little, and sent to the front. . . . Why did the Japs, coming to Russia's aid, send a battleship they captured at Port Arthur? . . . Your story of the war would be that you enlisted and were trained, trained other men to kill and get killed. Without finding out what it was like yourself. . . . An accident, or a dig? You couldn't tell. Some of the Russians resented it. The Japanese are a polite people. . . . When the thing seemed almost finished you were sent overseas at last. Over the wrong sea, to sit on a hill of rusting ammunition and wonder what the hell.

Blue Golden Horn Bay. A Jap steamer up from Tsuruga, sampans getting under her feet. Allied cruisers anchored in the bay. *The Brooklyn* lying at a dock. Dark Russian gunboats, without a country, the houseboats of their crews. He had seen a woman pushing a baby carriage around the deck of a rusting monitor. Vladivostok, looking something like San Francisco, with Allied flags. Surrounded by red rusting hills of hardware. Field guns and car wheels and briary mountains of barbed wire; steel rails and shrapnel and explosive shells, piled up like cordwood at a steamer stop on the bank of the Yukon, multiplied ten thousand times. Motor cars, never assembled, aging in the wood of their rotting crates. Rotting bales of cotton. A billion dollars worth of war materials, going to rust and rot on the hills from Vladivostok to Nikolosk and north toward Habarovsk. The Russians began dumping goods on the hills when they tired of building warehouses. He and George had found a submarine, partly assembled, going to rust far back among the hills, taken there by God knows what titanic, nitwit effort. It looked like the Ark on Ararat.

You didn't know what to expect in a place where submarines roosted in the hills and a billion dollars worth of ammunition had been stacked up for scenery, six thousand miles away from where an army had broken its heart and quit, tired of fighting without enough ammunition, or with none at all. In a place where things were so thoroughly sidetracked, men might be sidetracked, too.

When they had disembarked from the *Thomas*, the

27th Infantry from Manila was already going into action up the Ussuri River. A combined Allied action under the Japanese going to meet an overwhelming force of freed German prisoners and Bolsheviki, commanded by Prussian officers, sweeping south to capture Vladivostok for Germany. A buck private would have seen that the thing to do was send reinforcements. But they were commanded by a general who should have known what he was about. And he had pastured them in the railroad yards and on the hills to guard the expensive and misplaced scenery.

George still had hopes of getting in on the campaign. Alfred didn't see any sign of that. Two weeks before, the Allies had contacted the superior Bolsheviki-Prussian force. There had been fierce battles, every one a victory for the Allies, and heavy casualties for the enemy. No mention of Allied casualities, and no appeal for reinforcements. Habarovsk and towns with even more difficult names had been captured with apparent ease. Alfred wondered if the men from Camp Fremont weren't more superfluous war materials, dumped to rust on the unsatisfactory Maritime hills.

George wouldn't admit the possibility. What good is a war if you don't have someone to fight? But he looked more discouraged today, sitting on a red cylinder, the edge of a talus slope from a mountain of six-inch shells rusting against the sky. "We should have waited for the Draft, Alfie. We jumped into this war so damned hard that we came out on the other side!"

They were sitting there, wondering what the hell. A Russian officer stopped and jotted something in a little notebook. They were on their feet, saluting. The officer returned their salute, a silver pencil between his white, long fingers.

"Americans?" He was young and pale and slender, with fine dark eyes.

"Yes, sir."

"I am Lieutenant Serge Ivanitch." He put his notebook away. "I belong to artillery brigade which is just formed. I make survey of ammunitions. We have six batteries of four point seven English guns. These shells are six inch."

George said hopefully, "If you could wait while they rust a little more, they might fit."

Lieutenant Ivanitch looked blank. Then smiled. "You Americans have humor. You make good jokes." He took a case from his breast pocket and offered them cigarettes. "We are comrades. Do not stand." He sat on the rusty grass, smoking with them. "White Russians will be democratic, like Americans."

He was very flattering. The slender Russian cigarettes were excellent. Golden Horn Bay was blue and sparkling in the sunken distance, brightly indifferent to those dull warships.

"America is our best friend," Lieutenant Ivanitch was saying. "Japanese we do not trust. We think they have understanding with Germany. Japanese would take Siberia, Germany would take much of Russia. English are here for Empire. They think only of that. But America—America is noble and helps peoples."

He was almost too flattering.

Shells had been put down on a wild cherry sapling.

Must have been flat on its face. But the top had turned toward the sun and was a tree again.

"One time I was in England," the lieutenant said.

"You speak very good English," Alfred told him.

"I know English before I go to England. I speak French, too."

"We speak only English," George said.

"In England I live in London. I want to be like Englishman. Englishmen are always the same. You cannot tell if they are pleased or angry. Now I do not like that. I will be like American." The Russian had beautiful soft leather boots which he slapped lightly with his gloves. "How you like this country?"

"It's nice and warm."

"Ah, if you could see Russia before there was war and revolution!" The lieutenant sighed. "O Mother Russia!" He offered them more cigarettes.

George held a match for Lieutenant Ivanitch. Scowling sympathetically. "We want to get into the Ussuri Campaign," he said. "We don't want to stay here on guard duty."

"Ussuri Campaign is nothing," the Russian said. "That is the start. Look, my brigade it has only nineteen officers and few *unosnis*. The soldiers have not been called yet. It is only the start. You will help us free the Motherland of Communists and Jews and atheists."

George was interested, but puzzled. "We have to do all that?"

"I am follower of Father Voinoff," the lieutenant explained. "I think also Russia must be made pure."

169

"Who is Father Voinoff?"

"A priest. One time I laugh at priests. Pouf!" He snapped his white fingers. "I light my cigarette from the ikon lamp. Peoples say: 'Have some fear of God, Serge Ivanitch.' But Voinoff—" he sighed, admitting his surrender.

"What is he like?" George asked.

"Fighting priest, great orator. He was in France. Rich Russians in your Washington send him to wake up Russians here. He is like fire. Make Russia pure of Communists and Jews and infidels, he say. Like holy war. Then we have aristocrat like priests. God's officer on earth. I believe like Father Voinoff."

"Does Father Voinoff want another Czar?"

"He is Royalist," Lieutenant Ivanitch said. "But 'Romanoffs, pouf!' " He snapped his fingers. "Not fit. Admiral Kolchak, who is War Minister, is only man fit to rule Russia. Strong, like iron. Before he is overthrow, like a Romanoff, everybody will be killed!"

Golden Horn Bay, blue as ever. September sun warm on the rusting hillside. Vladivostok like a smaller San Francisco. The likeable young Russian officer, trying to make them feel at home. Just the same, a chill, a doubt. "What do the people want?"

Serge Ivanitch asked, "Who?"

"The Russian people."

The lieutenant looked puzzled, then displeased. "You do not understand. There are only White Russians. The peasants are nothing. They are good peasants, make fine soldiers. You should see them in Galicia, take German trench without cartridge. Nothing. Only stones. Germans think they throw hand

170

grenades. They stoop. Our Russians are on top of them."

George said, "I suppose they got tired of fighting with rocks."

"No." Ivanitch told him. "Not our peasants. They are good, patient. Thirty million killed and wounded. They never complain—"

"*Thirty million!*"

The Russian didn't like Alfred's tone. "Only eight million and a half killed," he said crossly. "That is nothing! We have so much peasants they could beat Germany with their hands. They would win the war, the swine, if they have not rebelled."

"No wonder," George muttered.

"No, no!" Lieutenant Ivanitch said harshly. "Not the way you think. They would not rebel; only some Jews make them dissatisfied."

Alfred asked. "What happened, that they had to fight with rocks, when all this ammunition was piling up here?"

"That is sad." The lieutenant agreed. "The Germans have agents here. They influence the ammunition to stay."

Influenced a submarine up a hill. "But how? Weren't there ordnance officers? Weren't there—"

Lieutenant Serge Ivanitch sighed. "Ah, yes. But we have always bribes. Army officers have so poor pay. Officials have so poor pay. They do the best as they can." He slapped his soft boots with his gloves, "Friendly, what you would do if you get little pay and someone offer much money just to hold back shipment of supply?"

Just to let men go up against machine guns with empty rifles? What do you think I am? A Russian?

George said, "I'd pull the pin out of a hand grenade and stuff it down his throat!"

"You American!" Ivanitch said. "You have so much heart, so much energy. You can do everything."

"Can we learn Russian?" George asked. "All I know is *nitchevo*."

Lieutenant Ivanitch hesitated. "It is difficult. The language is so rich. To learn it is like getting very rich. It is difficult."

"It's impossible." George thought.

"Russian language is like all the languages. I show what I mean. Listen. I will sing Russian that sound like French." Lieutenant Ivanitch squared his shoulders, filled his chest and sang. Something light, bright and catchy. He had a fine, supple voice.

"Very much like French," Alfred agreed. "You have a fine voice."

"I thought it was French," George said.

"Now I sing like Italian." He stood up and sang, walking between them and Vladivostok harbor in his fine soft boots and bright spurs. What he sang was showy and full of tricks. His voice was rich and deep, though he was a slender young man. And the song sounded Italian, as much as Alfred knew about it.

"That did sound like Italian."

"I thought it was Italian."

Alfred guessed that George didn't like the Russian and was making fun of him.

"Now I will sing Russian that sound like German."

"They won't think we're German spies?"

"Pouf!" Serge Ivanitch snapped his fingers. "The song is Russian. If it sound German, it is because that the language is so rich." What he sang was strong, simple and a little throaty.

"That was very much like German."

"I don't know any German lately." George had heard that one at the Orpheum in Seattle. Then he asked: "Do you know any Russian songs that sound like Russian?"

Lieutenant Ivanitch looked faintly displeased. "All Russian songs sound like Russian! It is that the language is so rich—" He was interrupted by the roar of a big gun from the harbor. Not so much by the gun, as by the Americans scrambling to their feet.

"Who's shooting?"

"They're bombarding the city!" George was eager for something to happen.

"No one bombards the city." The Russian didn't seem to think much of it. "Maybe a ship, having practice."

While they were watching, there was a flash of fire from a gray cruiser in the harbor. Then the heavy report thudded against the hill.

"The *Essex*," George said.

Alfred thought he heard the dying scream of a shell. Then the sound of its burst. It didn't seem much like a bombardment. The steamer from Tsuruga had docked. There wasn't any activity in the blue harbor except the sampans, shuttling between ships, and a tug nosing out to somewhere with a barge.

"It is the English ship having practice. Now you like to hear boatman song on Volga River? That is most Russian."

"I've heard about it. I would like to hear it."

There was another flash of fire from the forward turret of the *Essex*. Another. The Russian looked annoyed. He waited until the BOOM, BOOM of the explosions struck their rusting iron hill and rolled away to silence. Then he filled his chest and sang, starting in a firm, faraway voice that grew deeper and nearer.

Alfred thought George was annoyed by the Russian lieutenant, walking slowly back and forth between them and the harbor as he sang. Really, the song was worth more than anything going on in the bay. It swelled, deep and loud, with a wild and defiant ring. Like something he had known in imagination, through his father's eyes. The *Sarah Lord* weighing anchor in the Strait of Magellan. "Hooray, you rolling river!" The muffled roll of voices in that glorious, mournful song. The man who had been knocked down a few minutes earlier, lifting his head to sing, blood still on his face. There was something like that in the boat song. The lieutenant's voice was at its grandest in a Russian song that sounded like Russian. It was going away in the distance when it was lost in another gun roar from the harbor.

"The devil fly away with their noise!"

"I saw where that one burst!"

"That was great!" Alfred said. "I suppose it's a kind of chantey."

174

"I don't know that."

"A song sailors sing at work."

"Like that, yes. The men have harness. They are the horses to pull boats up the river. They sing and they pull. The harness cuts here." He spread his white hand across his collar-bone. "Soon men have consumption." Another gun roar, echoing against the hardware hill. "They were nice Russian picture."

George looked impatient. "If you watch," he said, "you can see where they burst! Over there, among those buildings!" He pointed toward a distant hillside, beyond the harbor, flecked with tiny roofs that caught the sun.

BOOM!

"Watch! Over that way."

"There!"

"Did you see it?"

Alfred had seen the black and white burst of a high-explosive shell on the brown, roof-flecked hillside. It was too far away to make out if anything had been hit. "They're shelling that town!"

"It is only mines," the lieutenant explained.

"Nobody lives in those houses?"

"Only miners and their families."

The brothers looked at each other. Then at the slender young lieutenant.

"Have the miners attacked the British?"

"No, no." Lietenant Ivanitch looked as if they were making a lot of fuss over nothing. "The English have practice with the guns."

What the hell?

175

"The miners. Isn't it dangerous?"

The Russian mistook their alarm. "No, no, do not be afraid. The miners have not guns."

Their turbulent silence seemed to grate on the lieutenant. "Those miners," he said harshly, "they are bad peasants. They are Bolsheviki. The way to treat such is like that." The guns boomed again.

Alfred looked at his wrist watch. "We have just time to report back to barracks," he told George. "Thank you, Lieutenant, I enjoyed your singing very much."

"That was nothing," Serge Ivanitch said. "We are comrades." But he looked troubled. When they started down the hill, he called after them. "You do not understand Russia!"

Alfred found himself hurrying. He wanted to be out of hearing, where he could think.

George growled. "Is he crazy, or what?"

Crazy? No. Alfred thought the White Russian was sincere and reasonably intelligent. He liked Lieutenant Ivanitch, but he felt chilled with doubt and a long way from home. The things Americans believed in didn't seem to mean anything in this foreign country.

George felt it, too. As they were going down the hill he said, "I hope to Christ we get sent up the Ussuri soon!" The British cruiser was continuing its comfortable shelling of the mine village. "I don't like this town. I don't like your friend, either. He can talk English, but he doesn't understand it."

George should have said "American," Alfred thought. At that moment the English were talking with eight-inch guns, and there seemed to be a difference. Or maybe the English were bilingual and understood the language of the country.

They had no luck about being sent into action up the Ussuri River. It couldn't have been much of a campaign, after all. They heard less and less about it. Then nothing. In October the brothers talked with a gray sergeant-major from the 27th Infantry. He sat at their table in a little tea shop on one of the unpaved side streets off Svetlanskaya. They talked quite a while before Alfred realized that the old regular had been in the Ussuri Campaign.

Campaign? Horse manure! Sergeant-Major Tompkins was still indignant over the insult to his profession and his gray hairs.

You can imagine the kind of campaign it was, with the American 27th kept in the rear! Sure, the Japs would fire off ammunition and send back word about Prussian regiments and Bolsheviki commanded by men in German uniform. But not even American officers were allowed up front. As if the sight of a German would be too much for them! Where were the Japs at Chateau Thierry?

Two or three times they might have had skirmishes with guerrillas. Battles, the Japs called them. *Battles!* The sergeant-major's gray moustache was wet with tea and trembling with indignation. They were never so outnumbered but what they could spare most of their troops to keep their allies from seeing what was going on! Once they fired off a few thousand rounds of ammunition and sent back word about German staff officers. When the 27th was allowed to advance again, they couldn't find any sign of battle. Only two new graves in a little open space where somebody had been cutting wood. By God, it looked as if the Japs had killed two wood-cutters and called it a battle! It was all very polite and secret. And it was all horse manure!

When they were tired of horsing around, the sergeant-major said, the Japs left some of the 27th at Habarovsk. They stationed the rest in the woods to look for Bolsheviki. His company was at Habarovsk. The Russian commander there was a Cossack, General Kalmykoff. Looks like a mangy little dog just going mad. This Kalmykoff has robbed three Habarovsk banks. He calls wealthy citizens Bolsheviki and tortures them into giving up their ready cash. Since the 27th had been in town, he'd arrested and executed six hundred people. The execution of men was private. They say Kalmykoff kills them with his saber, one at a time, in a peculiar way. Even the White Russians were afraid of him. By God, it was no joke, with someone like that at the head of affairs!

The boys had been dismayed. Weren't there enough Americans and Allies and Japanese to take care of Kalmykoff?

Any one of them could do it alone, the sergeant-major said. But it didn't look as if they would. For one thing, Kalmykoff had been armed by the Japs. And they were supposed to be paying him to help Russia in her hour of need. Anyway, they protected him with their troops. They had more troops than all the others put together, and they didn't intend to let anyone interfere with the Cossack's brand of help.

The 27th was all at Habarovsk, now. When General

Graves was up north, he inspected the companies the Japs had stationed in the woods—and sent them all back to town. The boys were sorry, because the hunting and fishing had been good. It was the sergeant-major's opinion, with a wet moustache, that the 27th would never have suffered the indignity of the fake Ussuri Campaign if their General had been in Siberia at the time. And it was his opinion, with his moustache neatly dried, that the Japs would not command any more American troops.

There was another thing, like a benediction, if the boys didn't know it already. Some of the companies in the woods got hell for arresting peasants who looked like Bolsheviki. The General told them they weren't in politics, or fighting any Russians who didn't attack them first. It may save you some trouble.

They talked it over afterward and couldn't make anything of it. Alfred dug up the newspaper clippings he had started saving when it was rumored that they might go to Siberia. According to the first stories, America and her allies pledged themselves not to interfere in Russian affairs. But the newspapers had forgotten that by the end of a week. In Vladivostok everyone assumed the troops were there to fight the Bolsheviki. And the Germans, when they were reminded of them. It looked as if General Graves had a better memory than his Allies or the newspapers.

Afterward Alfred and George were sent part way up the Ussuri Valley. They went with their platoon to guard a railway bridge over which American supply trains passed on their way to Habarovsk.

# XI

T HERE's been some row in the village back of us," Lieutenant Ross told Alfred. "I want you to take Nikolas," he was their interpreter, "and see what it's all about."
A big peasant woman with a red face was blubbering near the door of their box car headquarters. "Take two squads, with rifles. Probably isn't anything, but to hear that woman talk everyone in the village has been hung, drawn and quartered." The young lieutenant inclined his head toward the woman. "She'll show you the way, if she can see for crying. If she can't, you can find it yourself. There's only one road."

"Yes, sir." Alfred knew the way to the village very well.

"Find out what's wrong, if it's anything, and get back as soon as you can." The lieutenant couldn't spare two squads for very long. His command consisted of one platoon, housed in two box cars which had been taken off their trucks and banked with dirt near one end of the railroad bridge. Not much of a command, but he was responsible for it.

Alfred took George's squad and Willoughby's. They set off toward the east, through the scattering pine woods, over light, dry snow on iron hard ground. Eighteen men in sheepskin-lined Alaska army coats and fur caps, following the vast figure of the sobbing woman. If she was a woman, and not a great rag doll, moving on invisible wheels. Her human shape was almost lost under descending layers of a tent sized shawl and old skirts. The outer one brushed the snow, giving an impression of her gliding heavily before them without legs or feet.

"What's up?" George asked when they were out of hearing of their anxious lieutenant.

"A complaint from the peasants," Alfred told him.

"Bad?"

"It doesn't sound good." It would have to be serious when half their platoon was sent to investigate. Lieutenant Ross wasn't a man to run errands for peasants. Alfred heard him say that two days before to a British officer who dropped in to tell him how to guard the bridge. His advice had been to draw deadlines and not let the peasants near the bridge. They were a bad lot and it was best not to have anything to do with them. Well, the lieutenant was using his own judgment.

After a while George asked uneasily, "Our village?" He must have known it all along.

"Yes."

They had spoken of it as their village since they discovered it the week before, Alfred and George and Pink Byers, doing a little unofficial reconnoitering. Really, it was much like any other village—thirty or more unpainted frame and log buildings in a snow covered clearing, under a few scattering pine trees; like buildings of a logging camp at home, or an Alaskan gold-mining town, rough and pioneering.

Probably they wouldn't have entered the village if it hadn't been for Paul Bunyan. That wasn't his real name, which they never bothered to learn. But it was a good one, and it suited him.

While they were looking at the village, arguing in low voices about whether it would be safe to go any closer, someone started chopping in the woods near them. That didn't sound dangerous—a man cutting wood. Pink still thought they should go back. Any Bolsheviki they didn't run into wouldn't hurt them. George and Alfred weren't worried. Everything was so much like Washington in the early days that they felt safe and at home.

George settled it by going boldly into the woods, along a path that looked as if it had been used for hauling logs. Alfred and Pink followed.

George stopped short. The axe blows stopped.

"By God, if it isn't Paul Bunyan!" George was staring admiringly. The woodsman was staring back at him, perplexed and startled at the sight of foreign soldiers with rifles; a big, powerful figure of a man with curling yellow hair and a great yellow beard, standing beside the tall, straight pine tree which he had begun to undercut. He was looking at them with large startled eyes—blue eyes and yellow hair and fresh pink and white skin like a baby's. It made him startlingly innocent and clean, although he was dressed in doubtful rags and probably no cleaner than he should be.

"Looks like Odysseus building the raft." Pink said to Alfred.

George was in good spirits. Looking first at the

tree, then at the big, staring Russian. "You ought to be ashamed of yourself," he said severely. "Why don't you pick on a tree your own size?" He pointed a heavily-gloved finger. "Do you call that a tree?"

The big woodsman answered in Russian. None of the three understood a word. But the way he spoke gave them an idea of what he was saying. There was a pleading dignity to his speech, which became emphatic and then stopped with quiet abruptness. Just as if he said he was cutting down a tree, which was allowed. That he wasn't doing any harm to anyone and couldn't see why foreign soldiers should arrest him.

George grinned at the others. "Paul says we have him all wrong. He says this isn't a tree, it's only brush that's in his way."

The Russian nodded hopefully to the others, seeing that George was pleading his case. He stopped nodding when George threw off his coat.

"Come on, Paul, let me show you how to cut brush."

"Better take it easy," Alfred suggested. The peasant looked as if he feared the axe would be used against him.

"Come on. Attaboy!" George took the axe from him, quite gently, after all. He attacked the tree while the wondering Russian looked on.

The axe was dull, but George swung it with accurate fury. Cutting out great rough chips. Once he stopped short and pointed to the blade. Asking with sorrow, "Do you call this an axe?" The peasant spoke apologetically, and George translated it to the others.

"He says every nick in it has a name. The biggest one is 'Waterloo.' " Then he attacked the tree again.

When it was about ready to fall, Alfred drew Pink back, out of the way. George delivered a few furious blows. The tree swayed and the remaining splinters cracked.

"TIMBER-R-R!"

The tree came down with a rush and a crash that echoed from a hill beyond the village. The two woodsmen were congratulating each other, shaking hands.

George was winded from his exhibition tree-felling, but he put on a bold front. Indicated the forest with a sweeping gesture. "How about it, Paul? Shall we cut those down and call it a day?"

"Amerikansky?" the peasant asked eagerly. His fear was gone.

They all nodded and George said, "You know it, you old devil!"

Paul was inviting them toward the village, making hospitable sounds.

"He says the samovar is ready to boil," George interpreted, "and how about some tea?"

Pink was doubtful, but Alfred thought it was a good chance to get the lay of the village.

Near the edge of the village their guide led them proudly to four tiers of notched logs laid in a square, with an opening for a doorway. There were more logs, peeled and some already notched, waiting to be laid. Paul was building a house. He was telling about it eagerly and showing them why he was cutting down trees.

George appeared to find the building one of the

wonders of the world. "I'll be damned if this isn't the house Paul's building for Alice Price!" To Pink, who didn't know the legend: "Paul's going to get married." Nudging the big peasant knowingly, "The old rascal!"

The Russian smiled back at him, showing even beautiful white teeth. They seemed to understand each other almost as well as George pretended.

Then they were surrounded by peasants, men, most of them middle-aged or past; women and small children with good healthy faces. Paul was telling them something about the Amerikanskys. Perhaps about how George cut down the tree.

They were urged to enter all the houses in the village at once. Alfred wasn't sure they should visit any of them. With typhus always about, entering a peasant house wasn't a thing to be done casually. He was trying to signal a mixture of gratitude and urgent business when a flock of the older children swooped down the dirt street, into the crowd, clutching ragged books and shouting, making even sign language difficult.

"Please, where are you Americans?"

They started at the sound of a woman's voice, speaking English.

She made her way to them, holding out her hand. A tall woman, almost young, with her pale face framed by a black kerchief. "They sent for me at once," she explained, "but first I had to set the children's lessons for tomorrow. You know how it is with children."

The school teacher persuaded them to have tea in

the Elder's house. It was clean, as she had promised, and they weren't mobbed. No more people were allowed in than could be seated. The big room was more comfortable than a box car. Hot tea tasted good. It felt good, anyway, even if there wasn't any sweetening. Sugar was a hundred roubles a pound, and not to be had.

Byers seemed to have got over his fear of being trapped by the Bolsheviki, though his short, orange-pink pompadour had a frightened look. He was asking the school teacher about herself, how she happened to be there and where she had learned English.

There was nothing mysterious about it, according to Maria Rizoff. She had been governess in Habarovsk with a wealthy family that spoke English as well as Russian. After the Kerensky revolution she felt she should do something for Russia, and became a village school teacher.

Pink said, "So you cast your lot with the common people."

Maria looked troubled. "No," she said. "I cast my lot with the children. Before the Revolution it was forbidden for peasant children to learn to read and write. When it became lawful, I wanted them to have their opportunity."

They were interrupted by the arrival of a little girl in a coat years too big for her. From one of the sleeves, hanging six inches below her hands, she produced a pot of strawberry jam. The village had probably been combed for it. No one but the three soldiers would take any, until Alfred insisted on giving some to the child who brought it. She had taken off the mile-long coat and was sitting on the oven like a tow-haired doll, stealing looks at the jam with fabulous eyes. When Alfred gave her some in a cracked dish, she caught his hand and kissed it.

Maria Rizoff wouldn't talk any more about herself. Consulting with the elders, she asked what was happening in Siberia. Whether the Allies had come as friends or enemies. About the truth of terrible reports they heard. When the Allies came to Siberia, she said, the people were told they would be safe. They believed it, and most of them gave up their arms when they were asked. Now, when they were helpless, the people were being beaten and shot like criminals. Why?

Alfred had to evade most of the questions. Many of the answers he didn't know. The ones he did know, even if he could have told them, would have been cold comfort. All he felt safe in saying was that the Americans were not fighting the people of Siberia. He didn't want to add that they weren't helping them, either. Partly for Pink's benefit he asked if these people were Bolsheviki.

The school teacher didn't think there were any Bolsheviki in the village. Siberia was a backward country, she explained, and the people had suffered a great deal. Five years of war and civil war. They were sick to death of all the fighting and they had never been interested in politics. All they asked was to be allowed to live. "We have been branded as Bolsheviki," she said, "because we do not fight for the new directorate at Omsk. Admiral Kolchak was a Czarist officer. The officers in his war department are all

Czarists. He uses the Czar's Cossacks against the people. It is cruel to brand people as Bolsheviki because they do not cheer a Czar under another name and fight with him against their own people. And a brother-killing war is worst of all. The people will never fight again except to defend themselves and their families. They cannot even do that, now."

Paul Bunyan didn't seem interested in politics. He had been bursting with eagerness to ask the Amerikanskys a question, which Maria Rizoff finally translated for him.

"Alexievitch wishes to know if it is true that in the middle of America there is a great waterfall that goes up instead of down. I have told him there is not, but he will not believe me because I have never been in America."

Alfred confessed he had never heard of an upside-down waterfall. But George loyally insisted that she tell the big fellow there might be such a thing for all they knew. They had never been in the middle of America and couldn't disprove it.

Maria Rizoff didn't find the answer worthy of Americans, who should help enlighten the world—she was a teacher every minute of her time—but she passed it on to Paul, speaking very slowly and distinctly. When Paul was in the army in Galicia, she explained, he had got too near an exploding mine. He hadn't been scratched, but his hearing was almost gone.

Doubtless the village was like a great many others, except for Paul Bunyan, the earnest school teacher, and the tow-haired little girl who perched on the

oven and kissed Alfred's hand so warmly. Those
things made a difference. The boys didn't feel quite
like exiles after that. And they spoke of it as "our
village."

They had been planning to go back. Alfred got one
of the engineers to bring him chocolate bars from the
"Y" canteen at Iman. But so far the three of them
hadn't managed to get away again.

Now the lieutenant was sending them there. And
they felt uneasy and afraid of what they might find.
Alfred even forgot to bring the chocolate. It was a
dismal outlook, not brightened any by their guide,
moving ahead of them like a substantial rag phantom,
crying off and on.

"What kind of trouble?" George asked as they
neared the village.

"White Russian recruiting officers, with Cossack
troops."

"Jesus Christ!" George didn't ask any more.

They passed the wood road and came in sight of the
village. It hadn't been burned down. It looked the
same as it did the other time, except that more tiers
of logs had been added to Paul's house. The walls
were half up and there was a gap for part of a window.

People were coming toward them: men with clubs
and a few old army rifles, all talking at once; some of
the women crying.

Alfred asked through the interpreter to see the
Elder. That wasn't possible, they told him. So he took
the stories of some of the peasants, one at a time,
making notes on the main facts. They agreed fairly

well with each other and with the story the woman
had told at headquarters: somewhere between twenty
and forty Russian officers, with a company of Cossacks, had come to the village that morning, recruiting for Kolchak's army. The peasants had seen them
coming and men of military age escaped to the woods.
As a warning, the officers had punished the ten like-
liest men.

"Where can I find the school teacher?"

They would try to bring her. Or perhaps the
Sergeant would go with one of the women. Maria
Rizoff was with the Elder's wife at another house,
trying to quiet one of the children.

Alfred decided to leave the two squads in the street,
with George in charge, and go alone. The men had
heard the first peasant's testimony, before Alfred
moved him and the interpreter away, and some of
them were white about the gills.

Before they reached the house, Alfred could hear
the child; long, steady screams, with a few seconds
of silence between. When they came closer, it wasn't
really silence, but sobbing intakes of breath before the
next scream. Like an engine with something gone
wrong, making so many slow revolutions, then running wild, tearing itself to pieces.

The teacher opened the door, came out, and closed
it. It would be better not to have any unnecessary
noise in the house on account of Tanya. She had been
screaming like that for four hours and might go mad
if they couldn't stop her.

Maria Rizoff seemed to be the only woman in the

191

village who hadn't been crying. But she looked old and seared. And she winced at every scream from the house.

Alfred asked if the child had been hurt.

"She was not struck, if that is what you mean." What happened was worse, Maria thought. "Tanya is a sensitive child and she worshipped her father."

The men selected for punishment had been taken to one of the houses. The officers kept them for perhaps half an hour, with soldiers on guard outside. Then they were taken, two and three at a time, to the Elder's house. Tanya's father had been among the last to be led across the street. A few minutes later the child suddenly broke away from her mother and dashed to the house. Maria went after her, but it was a losing race. She caught her outside and brought her back, but the child had already seen through the window. . . .

"Russian people know how to suffer," she said. "They are used to suffering. But the children. . . ." She couldn't go on.

Afterward he went to the Elder's house with George's squad for witnesses. They weren't very good ones. Taking notes, Alfred was conscious of their white faces and fixed gaze, like an escaping shaft of light, going straight out of the small-paned window; level and shrunken down from the ceiling beam and up from the floor, away from the splashed walls. Nostrils, like their gaze, shrunken to keep out the sweet smell and the scorched. Bum witnesses. And yet they must have smelled and seen everything. He turned over a knife on the table, and there was a fingernail stuck to the blade. Like an answer, Pink Byers made a bubbling noise in his throat, then bolted outside. Two others followed him. Alfred told his brother to take the rest out, and finished as quickly as he could.

Along the wall of a shed in the barnyard Alfred finished the investigation. The peasants hadn't exaggerated. There were even a few details which they had overlooked.

On the way back, passing the unfinished house, George remembered his friend. "You didn't see any sign of Paul, did you?"

"No. He probably took to the woods with the young men."

"He was deaf. He wouldn't have been any good in the army."

"Those others wouldn't, either."

George didn't seem convinced. Neither was Alfred.

He halted his men at the edge of the woods. They stopped reluctantly, looking at him with angry white faces.

"There may be another man in here," he told them.

There were muffled protests that suddenly blazed into revolt. Willoughby stepped out from his squad.

"Sergeant, if you can show us any Cossacks to kill, we're with you. But if you want to see any more of what we've seen today, by God, you'll go alone!"

Alfred ordered the men to wait, and he and George went on. They passed the stump of the tree George had helped cut. The tree was gone, except for the branches and top. And other trees had been felled. They didn't see anything of Paul.

"He seems to have got away all right," Alfred said. He hoped George wouldn't notice, and put his foot on a spot of blood in the trampled snow. He didn't want to see any more, either.

But they went on, just the same, until there didn't seem to be any use. They were giving up when they heard a sound like the bleating of a hurt lamb. They crashed through the woods till they found Paul.

He was alive, and he might have been conscious. But they didn't speak to him. They couldn't. It wasn't a matter of languages, either.

Alfred and George looked at each other. They couldn't take him back. Even if their men were willing to carry him. No good adding one more horror to those at the village. They looked at each other with stricken faces, while the little bleating sound went on beside them in the snow.

George's eyes flashed, and he moved.

"Wait!" his brother said. "This will make less noise."

They went without looking back.

"Better give me that."

George returned the pistol. When they were near the edge of the woods, he stopped suddenly.

"Do you—you don't think he could have got well?" His blue eyes had a nightmare look.

"No," Alfred insisted. "No! And if he had . . . "

George gulped. "Yes," he agreed. "That way . . . "

"It was the best thing anyone could have done for him," Alfred said.

194

George drew a great, sobbing breath. "It wasn't much to do," he said, "for a friend."

It was beside their box car headquarters that an American train stopped with news of the armistice. They cheered like fools. George and Montana went A. W. O. L. looking for something for all of them to get drunk on. Their lieutenant pretended not to notice that they had been away. Maybe he didn't notice. He had gone hunting. The boys didn't find anything to drink. But the lieutenant killed four black cocks, and they had a kind of Thanksgiving in the box car. They even made speeches. George said he was writing for permission to keep his rifle after he was discharged. In case he met any second lieutenants. Lieutenant Ross announced he was getting a promotion. They were all fond of him. He was a young lawyer, with a wife and baby in Boise, Idaho. And he was as eager to get out of Siberia as they were.

After that many trains passed over the bridge. And much water passed underneath, until it froze and stood still. The trains kept on passing, but there was never one to start them on their way home.

While they were up there, four thousand Canadian soldiers arrived in Siberia.

Lieutenant Ross was glad. He was rather tired of having English officers stop by to tell him how to guard the bridge and what he ought to do to the peasants. Now that the British had troops of their own, they might stop trying to command other people's troops.

195

But that platoon never saw any Canadians. The American boys who did see them said the Canadians were fine fellows, and independent. They sized things up quickly and wanted to know what about all the allied promises of neutrality. And why so many harmless people were being murdered.

They said what they thought. And were sent home in the first transport that could be brought to Vladivostok.

The platoon stayed in the derailed box cars all winter, and got on each other's nerves. They stayed until the spring of 1919, when the Allies and Americans started guarding the whole Trans-Siberian Railway. In the reshuffle, the platoon was sent back to Vladivostok, where they did a spell in the railroad yards, wearing out good shoes tramping up and down beside box cars. Some of the beats could be walked blind-folded, but a nose-clip would have been more useful. There were trains loaded with some kind of fish that smelled higher and higher as the weather got warm. In the Trans-Baikal people went on dying of famine.

When the boys were lucky, they got a trip west, guarding military and American Red Cross trains. That was at first. Afterward they only guarded military trains. That was partly because of Alfred, and a Harvard man who tried to do his duty, and a child named Genya whom none of them ever saw.

# XII

SVETLANSKAYA, with flags limp in the September heat. Coolies darting through the crowds, sing-songing the latest extra. Pigtails lifting off their backs. If they ran fast enough, Alfred thought, the pigtails would stand straight out behind their heads. Things streamline when they get the chance; things wiser than people milling up and down hot Svetlanskaya. Maybe life was just a fever that matter sometimes caught. When people were cold, everything was all right again and there wasn't any more trouble. "God, don't let the flesh in these furrows ever be people again."

Funny he should have prayed; he hadn't meant to. Funny to have said that. He expected to be mad, but what he expected didn't have anything to do with it. What he saw didn't bother him then or afterward. Only he was troubled by the part he hadn't seen. The trainload of men and women, with no baggage, getting out into the empty plain which was their destination. That thick, black column marching quietly to nowhere. Smoke rising from the waiting locomotive. It started like a dream. Not the night kind; the kind that comes in a drowse on a hot day. The train crippling up to a little sunbaked station. Dust devils waltzing slowly on the plains. One turning to gold mist against the late, hot sun. Then dark again. Getting out on the platform to stretch the legs, without quite waking up.

"Sure," the Railway Service man said. "It's wherever they happen to stop, but this is part of it." He had started with the Northern Pacific in Tacoma, before Alfred was born; a big, solid railroad man with a thick gray moustache. "Looks like a lonely place, eh? You wouldn't guess how many colonists Semeonoff has settled out this way. It's queer, teaching these Russians modern train dispatching for that sort of traffic. A trainload passed through yesterday and stopped just up the line. In an hour and a half the empty cars came back. I wish you'd take a look for yourself. There's time while they fix the bearing. A mile back, I should say, and a quarter of a mile off to the left of the road. You can't miss it. There's some empty ammunition boxes where you turn.

"So far as I'm concerned, it doesn't matter. I've been in Siberia since the spring of 'Eighteen. You get used to things. Trouble is, you get too used to them.

"I'm scared to think about being home again, if I ever am. Suppose I'm inspecting the line between Tacoma and Lakeview. Beside the roadbed, I find them the way I do here. Proper thing would be to yell Police and Rape and Murder, and go to court in my best clothes to testify. What if I do what I'm used to, or forget where I am? Say to myself: 'One of Semeonoff's armored cars has been through here,' and let it go at that? I'd be disgraced. It'll be just as if I had a wooden foot no one must know about. I'll always have to be watching, ready to say 'Ouch!' when someone steps on the wooden foot that doesn't feel anything. That's why I want you to go, Sergeant. I want you to make a report. I'll have an affidavit ready. My name is Smith. I want you to make a report, and say that I protested!"

The Railway Service man was crazy, or a bad judge of distance. Alfred hiked back through the heat until the train and station were one dark block against the yellow sunset. He didn't find anything beside the tracks except a shred of clothing and a few scattered bones. He gave up in his mind and was ready to turn back when he saw the white ammunition boxes. It was dusk then, and suddenly chilly. On the plateau the temperature dropped with the sun like something shot.

Out on the plain he didn't feel anything except cold. There wasn't much to see but trampled ground. The last gleam of light from the sky caught by bright heaps of brass at his feet. Two long furrows of earth, black in the dusk. One dark ridge of earth telling nothing. The other, where they had lost their enthusiasm for shoveling, quiet enough.

That was the time he should have been mad, but couldn't make the grade. Still, he felt called on to do something official to justify his being there. He picked up a machine gun cartridge and struck a match, looking learnedly at Japanese characters which he could not read. . . .

In Vladivostok you heard whispers. When influential men criticized the Supreme Dictator, nothing happened at first. You were almost ready to believe there was free speech in Siberia. Then you heard the men had been arrested and sent west. Later you heard that they had disappeared on the way. "Sent to Semeonoff's killing station," people would whisper. They made it sound like a half-legendary, ghastly place. Really, it was peaceful enough when one was in a position not to mind the cold. Better than Vladivostok and the Maritime Province. Better than Svetlanskaya, with its crowds of hate and fear and hot activity. Russian officers without troops, glittering like Christmas trees, contemptuously returning the salute of an American. Jap soldiers inclining to the left to brush Russian civilians into the gutter, always with the air of it being accidental. Czech soldiers saluting Russian officers with something like contempt. "A Czech corporal knows more than a Russian captain. We did all their fighting. Now that we've quit, they're ----ed." English officers, impatiently polite to friends and enemies. A party of French officers, excited about something that concerned French officers. Chinese coolies shooting through the crowds, stirring up dust and heat, selling extras which stir up heat and dust in the mind; Roumanian money changers waiting for their soldier victims. . . . A dozen nations, and a hundred cross-purposes and double-crosses.

Not even the Americans could agree among themselves. That serious young Red Cross officer; Alfred had caught his eye and saluted. The officer returned the salute with a look defiant and appealing, the look of a conscientious man with something under his skin. He and Alfred shared what would never let them be strangers or friends.

The officer, Randall, was in charge of the Red Cross train on that trip west, Alfred in charge of the train guard. They had their meals together and got along all right at first. Twenty-two days from Vladivostok to Omsk in hot weather. The train always breaking down or being side-tracked. Plenty of time to get on each other's nerves. Randall was fair and slender, with a sensitive mouth and a little moustache. Alfred didn't like the deliberate, picking way he ate. He noticed it more after they stopped speaking. While they were on speaking terms he sometimes felt impatient with the way Randall fumbled around for just the right word. As if he kept such a big stock he couldn't immediately lay his hands on what he wanted. But they got along all right at first. Red Cross was a Harvard man, the first Alfred ever met. Not that he was riding on that reputation. Alfred only found it out by accident, asking if Cambridge wasn't in England. They were two serious young men, trying to make a good job of what they were doing.

They made out well enough, until they got on Russian politics. Then it was all off. The battle of the Red Cross and the Army, cock-eyed as everything else in Siberia. The Red Cross was all for military action, exterminating the Partisans. The Army was all for peace and mercy, healing the wounds of war. When the argument developed a hot-box, Alfred pulled out and wouldn't talk politics. Randall was pained at first. Then he must have seen it was the best thing under the circumstances. They cut out politics, though each was a little hurt that the other didn't see things his way.

That station was larger than some of the others. More Japanese soldiers and more Japanese flags. Young Cossacks on the platform with their girls. A line of tough little ponies tied beyond the end of the yellow station. A town, the prairies, and the clear light sky. Something like seeing the wild west as it had been years before you were born. The train had no business at that station. It stopped as it was always stopping, without your knowing whether it would be five minutes or half the morning. There was always something on the track ahead.

He didn't see where the Russian came from, except it was from the side away from the station. A flash of a Jap sentry, trying to bar the way with his rifle, then the Russian was on the platform of the car. George was barring the Jap's way with his rifle.

"*No, you don't!*"

The crossed rifles clashed and separated.

"It's all right!" Alfred called. Probably the Jap didn't understand English, but one didn't have to be bilingual to understand George with a rifle. The Jap shouldered his rifle and went on.

Alfred decided the Russian didn't look lousy, and led him into the guard car. He was a peasant, and it wasn't always healthy for peasants to be seen near the railway. A tall, stooping man, almost young, with a peaked cap at one end of his face and a little curling yellow beard at the other end. It made his face look a foot long. His big Adam's apple moved up and down while he talked earnestly.

"I don't understand Russian, old man."

The peasant had two carrots in the sagging pocket

of his muddy coat. They fascinated Alfred. To keep from staring at them, he offered a cigarette and matches. The peasant didn't light his cigarette at once. He opened a yellow horn-handled knife and slicked a match in two. Sharp as a razor. Then in four, with a piece of head on every splinter. You wouldn't think it of those hands. After that he lit up with one quarter of a match. A tiny spark of fire. Put the others in the box before offering it back. Whoa! That didn't seem right, getting back two more matches than he gave. Alfred motioned for him to keep the box.

"The corporal said there was a man you wanted to question." The interpreter was there, with Randall behind him.

"Sergeant, aren't you taking a chance on typhus, bringing peasants in here?"

"He looks cleaner than most, and he would be taking a chance on his life if they saw him."

"I don't believe a loyal Russian has anything to fear."

Loyal to who and what, you damn fool? Rumblings of the Red Cross-Army battle.

"Find out what he wants."

The interpreter chattered in Russian, then English, while the peasant turned his cap uneasily in his great hands.

"He says may your health be good. He is Mikhail Petrovich, from the village nine versts south. There is sickness in the village and people are dying. Fever and sore throat—"

"Malignant sore throat," Randall suggested professionally. "Plenty of it about."

"He has been hiding near the tracks since daybreak, praying for an American train to stop. He will pray God eternally for you if you send a doctor to the village—"

"Ask him why he was hiding."

The interpreter rattled questions as if he wanted to get through with the job. The peasant answering slow and patient, ending with a gesture of both hands. Like holding out a baby for them to look at. You see how it is.

"He says he was hiding because of the Japanese and Cossacks about the station. They have beaten some of the peasants who tried to ride on the railroad and killed others. He is more afraid of the Cossacks because they raid his village. Most of the time he is away hiding. Peasant men are afraid if they are caught they will be killed or sent to the army—"

"Oh, slackers!" The girlish Red Cross eyes met Alfred's. "We don't coddle slackers at home, either."

The peasant was talking to the interpreter, with his light gray eyes steady and pleading, his Adam's apple bobbing up and down.

"He says things are very bad in the village. Two weeks ago his wife went to gather mushrooms and didn't come back. When someone disappears, Mikhail says, you might as well look for the wind in the fields. Two of his children have died of the fever-sore throat, and two of the others are sick with it. His oldest girl was taking care of the others, but now she is sick. He says if you send a doctor he will pray God eternally—"

Randall cleared his throat. "It would be nice to

care for all the sick in Siberia, but we have to put in our efforts where they do the most good. Ask him why he and the other men in his village aren't in the army, fighting for Russia."

The interpreter translated, but in Russian it didn't seem to make sense.

"He says God bless you, he doesn't know what you mean."

"Do you suppose he's stupid, or doesn't want to understand? *Ask him why he isn't in the White Army, fighting the Bolsheviki.*"

The peasant looked surprised. His voice was protesting, almost shocked.

"He says may you live a hundred years. The only White Army he knows of is Admiral Kolchak's at Omsk. The peasants will never fight for the Czar."

"Doesn't he know the Czar is dead?"

The interpreter asked him that.

"He says the peasants know. And they want the Czar to stay dead."

"All right." Randall was frowning. "Ask him if he realizes what would happen if Admiral Kolchak were defeated and the Bolsheviki came in here."

The interpreter asked. Listened to the answer. Explained something that didn't seem to make any difference.

"He says God bless you, the Bolsheviki were here! They called an election at which the people voted. They elected three of their elders to the Soviet of Deputies. The village had law and peace until the foreign soldiers drove the Bolsheviki out. Since then no life has been safe."

Alfred listened, wooden-faced. Anything he said or did would make it worse for the peasant.

The peasant was talking again, more rapidly, with a deep note coming into his voice.

"He says the fever-sore throat is a bad business. His oldest daughter, Genya, nursed the children until she caught the disease herself. The neighbors have their own sickness and trouble. Fourteen in the village have been injured by hand grenades. Mikhail can only go home at night, like a thief. It is a bad business. If you would only send a doctor and some medicine he would pray God—"

'Tell him this," the Red Cross man interrupted. "Tell him if he were in the army, where he should be, fighting the Bolsheviki, he would not have to go about like a thief at night. And there would be doctors and a hospital for the people of his village."

The interpreter told the peasant. He stopped turning his cap in his big hands and looked down at his rag-wrapped feet, saying nothing.

"Tell him the Red Cross is not spending its own money. The American people have given us money to help the Russian people. What would they think of us if we spent that money helping Bolsheviki and criminals?"

Mikhail's answer was patient, edged with dignity.

"He says the people of his village are the people of Russia, and there are no criminals among them. There was a horse-thief, but he joined the Cossacks."

Wipe off the smile, you damn fool. Randall had seen it already and thought Alfred was laughing at him.

"Tell him that when he and others like him are

decent citizens, fighting the Bolsheviki, they won't have any more troubles." He did an about-face, not quite properly, and marched out of the car, like a Napoleon wasting his gifts carrying bed-pans.

The peasant went on talking earnestly. Now and then the interpreter put in a word or nod. He, too, seemed to think something was a bad business.

"What is he saying?"

"His daughter, Genya. He thinks there is something strange about her. I can't interpret it. Something in his mind. He says he never really noticed her until the last two weeks. Since something happened to his wife. He hardly noticed her, with four other children. At night he always came home tired as a horse, sometimes drunk. The children were a plague he had to put up with because God sent them. Genya was just a name for one of the children. It is true he never beat her, but he did yell at her when she let the geese into the cabbages. He only noticed her when she did something wrong. The way he only noticed the baby when it cried. He was always too stupid with fatigue to notice anything that didn't bother him.

"The Cossacks began making trouble for the village. When he wasn't working in the fields, he was hiding. The Cossacks would come to the village and beat the women with the ramrods from their rifles, or kill a few old men when they couldn't find young ones. They took whatever they wanted. There is no law, he says, and nothing to stop them. Once some Partisans came out of the marshes and fought the Cossacks. They killed seven. Mikhail would have gone with the Partisans if it hadn't been for the children.

Children are a great burden in bad times. Afterward he was glad he didn't go. A battalion of Japanese went after the Partisans and killed them all. Since then the Cossacks have it in for the village and the men have been hiding most of the time.

"Then the sore throat sickness came. His oldest son, Pieter, caught it first. The day after he was buried, Mikhail's wife disappeared. She went out early in the morning to gather mushrooms. There was mist on the common. Mikhail says he was sorry to lose her. She was a good, hard-working wife who made excellent cabbage soup and complained very little, for a woman. She disappeared with the mist."

The interpreter got more information in Russian, and shifted gears to English. "The night after she disappeared, Mikhail came home and found two of the younger children sick with the fever. It was late, but there was a fire in the stove and Genya was up, trying to nurse them. He didn't think his wife would come back, and he had to find someone to care for the children.

"Genya said: 'Don't worry, Papa. I can do all that Mama did, if I have a box to stand on and reach the shelves.'

"He didn't notice what she was saying then. He only remembered it afterward, when he couldn't find a woman to nurse the children. All the families in the village had more than their share of troubles. One woman did help when she could at first. Then she took sick, and there wasn't anyone for it but Genya—"

The peasant's face brightened hopefully at the name. "Genya." He told the interpreter more.

"Mikhail didn't think much about it at first. He had so many troubles and never knew but what it was his last hour. Then he saw that she managed to do everything. She lit the stove and made cabbage soup; brought water from the well. Sometimes she even chopped wood, though it took her a long time to cut a little. Genya had sensible ideas, too. That surprised Mikhail. He hadn't supposed children had any sense. She moved the baby into the other room. Mikhail thought that only made more steps for her.

" 'But, Papa, if I keep the baby away from Alexis and Vierochek, he may not be sick. I told Mama that about Pieter. She said *yes, yes*. But I don't think she heard what I said.'

"Mikhail decided there might be something in the idea, and he was proud of Genya. He had hardly noticed her until then, but he began to think about her, even when he was away hiding in the marshes. There's something about him—he's very religious or superstitious. After a while he decided it was a miracle. The way Genya did all the work and nursed the other children and was never impatient with them. If one of them woke at night and wanted something, she heard him as soon as he stirred and got up in her sleep. The children never called for anyone but Genya. When Vierochek died, Genya washed her and laid her out as she had seen them do for Pieter. She didn't call the neighbors until afterward. When Mikhail wanted to know why, she said it was because Vierochek liked her to do things for her.

"Yes, Mikhail thinks it was a miracle. The way Genya had strength for everything, and so much sense.

209

She was like a little woman in a world where everything was too big for her size. Only nothing was too
big for her spirit. And with a box to stand on to reach
the shelves and oven, she did everything. . . . ''

"How old is Genya?''

The interpreter asked Mikhail, then asked again.

"He says her name day is in August. Genya will be
eight, if she lives.''

"Genya . . . '' The peasant told him more.

"He says it was a miracle the way she never seemed
afraid of anything. She picked mushrooms on the common, where her mother had disappeared, and nothing
happened to her. Once the Cossacks searched the
house and barn for Mikhail. They said if Genya didn't
tell them where her father was they would shoot her.
Genya said they mustn't until she had fed the baby.
After she had done that, she kissed the other children.
The sick ones last. She could do that since she was
going to die. But when she went out the Cossacks
were gone.

"Another time they rode through the village and
threw a hand grenade into every house. Genya heard
the explosions coming toward her, down the street,
and carried the baby out. She was going back for
Alexis when a grenade came through the window.

" 'Papa, I was afraid to throw it back. If it hit one
of the Cossacks they would kill us all. If I threw it
out of the other window it might hit the baby. He
was out there on the ground. So I lay on the grenade
and shut my eyes tight and prayed that none of me
would hit Alexis.' ''

"It was a miracle, Mikhail thinks, that the grenade didn't explode. He thinks Genya is a saint—"

"Genya—" The peasant nodded earnestly.

"Yesterday Mikhail was fired at by a patrol of Japanese. He had a hard time getting away and didn't dare come home until very late. There was a fire in the stove and mushroom soup, and a large pot of gruel. Alexis and the baby were asleep, but Genya wasn't there. The pitcher was missing, so he knew that she had gone to the well for water. But she was a long time. He was going to help her when he heard a crash outside. There was starlight, and he saw Genya lying where she had fallen and broken the pitcher against the threshold stone. She didn't try to get up, and at first he thought she was hurt. When he picked her up, she said she wasn't hurt. But she was burning with fever through her wet dress.

" 'Papa, my throat is a little sore, but I won't be very sick. When I felt it coming today, I made a big pot of gruel for the baby. If someone else should have to feed him, he takes six wooden spoonfuls. Don't let Alexis or me use his spoon or red dish.'

"Mikhail says she was so thin and small that he couldn't feel her weight in his arms, and she was burning hot. It was the first time he had held her since she was a baby, and something happened in him. His heart was like that pitcher, broken on the threshold stone.

"He wasn't sorry the other children had died. They were better off. And he would have wished for the baby to die, only Genya liked to take care of him and was proud that he stayed well. He didn't mind about the others, but he thought Genya should live. She wasn't like a child, and nothing was too much for her spirit. If anyone lived through these terrible times he thought it should be Genya. She had earned the right. Her life meant more than his. That's why he came here, toward morning, and hid near the tracks until he saw a Red Cross train."

The interpreter coughed and wiped his forehead with a khaki handkerchief. The peasant went on talking with gentle stubbornness, his Adam's apple moving up and down; holding his cap in big calloused hands.

"What is he saying?"

The interpreter coughed again, shaking his head angrily while he coughed. "I'm human, Sergeant. I've interpreted too damn much already." He walked forward, out of the car.

Alfred stood there, thinking; gave Mikhail a pack of cigarettes while he thought quickly, planning what he was going to do. The peasant went on talking. Without an interpreter it was like the light gone from a stream he had been watching. He couldn't see it now, only he heard it, flowing in darkness, and knew what it meant. Now and then there was the gleam of something shining on the slow, dark current of words. "Genya—"

"Wait here." He motioned for Mikhail to wait, out of sight, and went out of the car; forward along the hot station platform; under the eyes of dingy neat little Japanese sentries, and insolent young Cossacks with their perfumed girls.

"Where you going, Baby?" one of them asked in

English. He passed without answering. She called after him, "Look out!" He didn't know whether it was a taunt or a warning.

The Russian engineer was leaning out of the cab, talking to a Cossack officer. A Japanese major looked on. Where even a Cossack's girl spoke English, it wasn't a place to shout anything important.

"Going to be held up much longer, Engineer?"

"About ten minutes, Sergeant."

"A train is coming through from the west," the Japanese major explained politely.

A black and white plume of smoke and steam was rising in the west, beyond where the rails dwindled to nothing.

Salute. "Thank you, Major."

He found George on the far side of the train.

"What's the dope, Alfie?"

"When we pull out, you ride in the cab. Have the engineer slow down when we're clear of the station."

"First good place for a man to make a getaway?"

"Right. If the engineer objects—"

"You know me, Alfie!"

"Now I have some business with the Red Cross, which I can handle alone—"

"Say, Sergeant!" Montana was lumbering down the steps of the nearest car. "Is it all right for the Cossacks to take that man—"

"Jesus Christ!"

"Can that!" Alfred said. George was shackling the bolt of his rifle. "Did they take him out of the car?"

"He just walked out as if he didn't care. And they nabbed him."

There wasn't anything that could be done. Bluff

213

didn't work. "This is Japanese sector," the major reminded him politely. "Japanese are here for law and order. We have sufficient guard. Japanese do not interfere with items Russians can liquidate."

"But, Major, he was our prisoner."

"We did not interfere. He is not your prisoner after he escapes, and you do not interfere. Now he is better guarded. You might let him escape once more." The Japanese major used his English in a small, deadly way, like a sting.

When they led Mikhail around the end of the station he walked steadily on his rag-bound feet, smoking one of Alfred's cigarettes. His face was calm and patient. Alfred thought of Genya, going out to the Cossacks after she had fed the baby.

He stood on the platform of the car and watched the locomotive from the west loom slowly bigger. Smoke and steam and steel. They'd made a mess of it. God damn the interpreter for leaving him in the lurch. Only it would grow just so large, then smaller again. Even if Mikhail didn't understand the gesture, he knew what would happen. Bigger and bigger. Montana said he walked out as if he didn't care. "Tell him when he and others like him are in the White Army, fighting the Bolsheviki, they won't have any more troubles." If everything was that simple we'd all be in the happy White Army. Bigger and bigger, as if it would fill the world. Probably took that as final. Burning up the rails. Like that pitcher broken against the threshold stone. Louder and louder. Racing wheels on steel. Come on! Drown everything out. . . .

He drew back from the blast of wind as the locomotive tore by like a great shout. A shout and the crack of a whip. Flying light with one armored car. Machine-gun muzzle sticking out from under the flaps. Smaller already, among dying sounds. It tried to fill the world with steel brutality. Almost did, but just missed. Something called perspective fooled it at the last moment. Slung it off into tapering oblivion. . . .

"Sergeant!"

Randall was there with the interpreter, hanging onto his nice Stetson hat. "Sergeant, where's your peasant?"

Mine? Peasants belong to the soil. "He walked off the train. Maybe taking your advice about joining the White Army!" Why not rub it in? "The Cossacks got him."

"Hell!" The young man looked dashed, fumbling a package. "I wanted to send some stuff for Genya's throat. On my own responsibility—"

So that was what the interpreter had been up to. Handled words so hot at last that he passed the blisters around.

"I'll explain that his children are sick. You shouldn't have let them— Where did the Cossacks take the man?"

"To the log storeroom behind the station." Might do him good to have a look. "I think he's still there."

Randall was shaking when he came back and crawled up the steps, like one of the flies on Mikhail's face. "I can't help it." He hung over the railing. Vomiting, he gasped, "My God, they shot him!"

"What did you think they'd do?"

"You needn't look at me as if I did it!"

215

Alfred didn't say anything.

Randall wiped his white, sweating forehead. "By God, this job's no joke!"

Isn't it? The locomotive whistled. Come on, come on! Let's get out of here!

"If you don't need me," the interpreter said, "I'm going to have a nap." He went forward with the air of being sure they wouldn't need him.

"It's hard to be just!" Randall's teeth were chattering, for all the heat. "I'm going to telegraph a report. Something must be done for those poor children! Genya— Did you hear?"

O, shut up, White Face, shut up!

"You mustn't look at me like that! When I said what I did, I meant I have my orders. I have to follow my orders, don't I? You follow yours. At headquarters they have to look at things in the bye and large. Put in their efforts where they will do most good. Kolchak is starting his big offensive tomorrow. And we're God knows how many weeks from Omsk! I'm supposed to be rushing summer underwear to his troops. On this crippled train! And we have to stop at Chita. General Semeonoff wants supplies—"

"*Semeonoff!* What are you taking him—butchers' supplies?"

"My God, I won't have you yell at me like that!"

The train started with a jerk, throwing Randall against the soldier. White face and pleading eyes and sour smell of vomit. Alfred shook himself out of the grotesque embrace as the Red Cross train gathered headway and panted west on its errand of mercy.

Mad? He was mad then. All the rest of the way to

216

Omsk and back he never yelled at Randall, or spoke to him. Being mad didn't last, though. The feeling went away. But he kept up the appearance out of stubbornness. He didn't intend to speak to Randall again unless it was a matter of duty.

And that didn't seem likely. Back in Vladivostok he made a detailed report of the trip. It may have been coincidence, but thereafter the guarding of American Red Cross trains was left to Cossacks.

That was the end of the summer of 'Nineteen, and they were feeling defeated. It isn't hard to defeat American soldiers. You only have to send them into exile, where there are no enemies to fight and no friends they can trust. Nothing they can get their teeth into. And keep them there until they break their hearts. Until their girls at home write impatient letters—as if they were staying in Siberia because they liked it. He had given up hope of finding out why they were there, in that world of shadows and collapsing rumors. Where you did something as useful as knitting without yarn. While others stumbled around in the dark, killing and fighting with shadows.

Everything that wasn't a shadow rotted and fell to pieces. The Ussuri Cossacks sickened of killing; sickened of bringing in men for Kalmykoff to kill, one at a time, in his peculiar way, in spasms of excitement. One of his battalions mutinied and came to the Americans for protection. White Russian officers grafted the supplies away from the Czechs who were fighting for them. Czech regiments mutinied and some of their officers killed themselves. Then their general, Gaida, vomited up the White Russian cause and came East. Vladivostok was ringing with his public and bitter comments.

And still there wasn't any talk of calling it a bad job and going home. The French and English had divided Siberia between them and started training camps. Cossacks rounded up the peasants and brought them in with the encouragement of knouts and bayonets. They were trained hurriedly and sent west in American Red Cross underwear and new British uniforms, with French and British rifles. Packed into trains and sent west. After that, one couldn't say. There were reports of great victories for Kolchak, and whispers that his army fell to pieces quicker than it could be patched up.

And the Americans just stayed, without even a bad reason. Going through the motions of guarding their sectors of the railway, like steadying a plank leading to nowhere on which the trusting and ignorant walked to their death. Giving Russians of every color equal rights of travel; sending them on to other sectors where radical and liberal suspects were weeded out and shot. Not doing themselves or anyone else any good, only earning hatred.

Not even a bad reason for being there, and a thousand good ones for going home. Some of them desperately personal. At home there would be Clarice, who had waited for him so long; patiently at first. There would be Clarice—instead of Olga Veronovna.

# XIII

ALFRED hadn't anticipated Olga. Not when he was in the forest with Clarice, nor for a long time afterward. This war was going to be short and sharp and full of danger. But it would be victorious. If a man survived the dangers he would go home to well-earned love in a better country. In a world that was a better place to live in.

He hadn't suspected then that war has no victory for the soldier. He couldn't have foreseen that his part of the war would have no fighting and no end. That he would only be a spectator forced to sit all night in the bleachers, under a cold, autumn rain, while teams he couldn't see played a scoreless tie in the mud. He hadn't foreseen that in the misery of that unforeseen night he would snuggle up to the strange woman next to him. Because he must have warmth, or die.

He found her very willing, because she, too, must have warmth, or die. Misery makes strange bedfellows, Olga.

Clarice still wrote to him, but no longer every day or every week. Sometimes her letters were disturbingly affectionate. Sometimes they were quarrelsome, blaming him for one thing and another; mostly for not marrying her. If he hadn't been so stubborn, she pointed out, they would have had a year together while he was at Camp Fremont. She could have attended Stanford instead of the University of Washington.

Sometimes the letters were neither disturbingly affectionate nor quarrelsome. She assured him that the intervention couldn't last much longer. Many Americans, including her father, were agitating to have the troops brought home from Siberia. Senators Borah and Johnson were doing all they could. And he mustn't give up hope. Clarice was fine and helpful, but he hadn't seen her for over two years. Remembering her was like listening for a voice very far away. When he heard, it was as clear as ever. But most days he could no longer remember what being with her had been like. When she wrote encouraging letters it seemed to him they were mostly for herself. That it was she who was giving up hope.

There wouldn't have been Olga if the war that wasn't a war hadn't gone on after it was over. The war that was to end war, but didn't know how to end itself. The war for democracy that couldn't end until Siberia and Russia were made safe for Admiral Kolchak, who had abolished democracy. There wouldn't have been Olga, except for the twistings of that war, and something that directed a sapling on one of those hills. The cherry sapling that had been knocked over and weighted down by high-explosive shells, flat on its face. In time, the top had turned toward the sun and become a tree. Not where it had taken root, but where it could. Life twisting and turning, accepting any compromise that allowed life to go on.

Olga was life going on where it happened to be.

She spoke English, which was a help at times. She was a technical assistant in the dental department of the big hospital. But she was in contact with more than the toothaches of war. What first attracted him to her was the way she walked, something like Clarice. She was about the same size, too, but her face was flatter and heart-shaped. They had an arrangement for the duration of the war, but she was always forgetting that part. As time went on he wondered if duration and forever didn't mean the same thing.

He didn't pretend to understand Olga. He didn't understand Clarice very well. And trying to understand a foreign woman beyond a certain point would be attempting the impossible in an unknown language. He got along very well with her by not being too sure. He never was sure how long he would be in Vladivostok. And there was a limit to the time he could spend with her. Soldiers had to have passes when they were out at night. And passes were infrequent.

So Alfred saw Olga when he could. They got along well and kept each other from dying of the cold. Sometimes an hour passed like a minute. That was an achievement in Siberia, where time was usually the other way round. They got along very well, perhaps because he didn't really love her. He was never quite sure whether she loved him or not. When she was most passionate there was something greedy about her love. Then she wasn't really aware of him. There was only herself, trying to take everything, and more.

Some days, when the atmosphere was just right, he had a warm, clear recollection of Clarice, who had been sweeter and more generous in love. And then he would feel sad because he had gone away from someone fine to someone not so fine, through no fault of his or hers.

But he and Olga got along. And she was generous in other ways. From her he heard many things about the White Russians. They seemed to lack something necessary to grown-up people. They did or didn't do things because they were afraid, or because it was to their advantage. But they didn't seem to have any loyalty, or to expect any. Semeonoff and Kalmykoff sometimes cut the telegraph wires to Omsk, confiscated trains or thumbed their noses at the Supreme Dictator. Kolchak put up with it and called them his generals because even though they were disloyal they might yet be useful. Behind backs, White Russians in Vladivostok spoke of Admiral Kolchak as England's puppet. Semeonoff, Kalmykoff and Rozanoff were the puppets of Japan. White Russians were contemptuous of the savage Cossacks who were the only Russians willing to fight for them. And they expected to keep the peasants in line through fear. If that didn't work, punishment. And if that didn't work, death. They didn't know any other way and weren't interested in learning.

It seemed to Alfred that by the time the White Russians had ruled out their leaders and the common people and the men who did their fighting, there wasn't much left but a myth. And what the remainder wanted, Olga couldn't tell him. Except that they wanted to rule Russia and have comfortable positions. Most of them agreed that that could only be accomplished with a foreign power to do their fighting. But they quarrelled among themselves as to which power, if any, they could trust.

The Japanese seemed willing to shed any amount of blood, but they were opposing Kolchak while pretending to help him. It hardly looked as if they wanted Siberia to have any government. The only White Russians who favored the Japanese were those in their pay. The others would willingly have let America fight their war. But America had done least of all for them, and they were bitterly disappointed.

Alfred had already gathered that from the newspapers. They had been bitter. Now they were becoming abusive. Along with accounts of Kolchak's victories, they published curious stories of life in the United States. The United States were mostly colonized by Russian Jews. All American men were degenerates. Most American children were illegitimate. All American women and girls who went out unguarded were slugged and raped. American men spent their holidays lying in wait for little girls, the way men of other nations hunted and fished. . . .

Olga, who was a White Russian, told Alfred that these stories were only a piece of strategy, not intended for belief. She assured him they had the approval of non-military Americans in Vladivostok. General Graves was expected to take action against the newspapers. He would then be relieved of his command for interfering with the freedom of the Russian press.

Alfred laughed and told Olga she didn't know Americans. Americans weren't like White Russians, who showed no real loyalty to their leaders. Americans didn't go knifing behind each others backs.

Olga was vexed with him for laughing. She couldn't stand being laughed at. "You think I made mistake," she challenged. "No. It is you do not know something. Listen." And to justify herself, she went on to spill other beans.

Semeonoff and Kalmykoff had been at Japanese Headquarters in Vladivostok early in September. Why? Because the Americans' neutrality was embarrassing to Japanese plans for Siberia. They were preparing a force to liquidate the American contingent in Siberia. The Cossack Atamans had already received many thousand *yen* on account. News dispatches were written, only the date needed to be filled in. The dispatches stated that when the Americans at Iman had been liquidated, after a treacherous attack on the Russians, conclusive proof had been found that they were cooperating with the Bolsheviki.

All the Cossacks lacked, she told him, was enough modern rifles with long range—

"Alfred, you fool! What do you laugh at? Because I love you, I tell you things they kill me for. And you laugh, you laugh!" Her flat and rather pretty heart-shaped face was passionate with resentment. And she was talking louder than she should. They didn't know who lived in the next room.

He wasn't laughing at her, and he couldn't tell her why he had laughed. He said: "I'm sorry, Olga. I was thinking of something funny that happened at barracks this morning."

She said, "Ha, ha! Something funny will happen at

American barracks at Iman, Spasskoe, Nikolosk, Suchan. . . . " Reeling off the names, she snapped her fingers close in front of his face, like a string of firecrackers. "Vladivostok . . . and you don't laugh any more. Ha, ha! By time something funny happens in barracks at Verkhneudinsk there are no more American fool soldiers to laugh, 'Ha, ha!' "

It took some time to quiet her, but everything was all right after he kissed her many times and said that she was a hero. And that she had saved the lives of all his comrades. That he would try to see that President Wilson sent her a medal. And he would love her forever. After that she was greedy and not really aware of him. There was only herself, trying to take everything forever.

And after that she was very generous and said she loved him even when he laughed. He was a brave American who laughed at death.

It wasn't that. Really, it was something more bitter.

Olga said not all the White Russians approved of the plan to dispense with the American force. Only a few of their leaders were supposed to know the plan. But one general thought it was a bad business. And in some way the word had leaked and leaked. Some of the White Russians thought it was a fine plan. Others thought they might still get something out of the United States. But what they thought didn't make much difference, because it was really a Japanese-Cossack affair. And everything was ready except good rifles. The Japanese were ready to pay for the rifles, but they wouldn't supply them. It might look bad if something went wrong. One of the allies had refused to supply them for the same reason.

Alfred knew he was going to be late, but it would be in a good cause. He said goodbye, handsomely, and hurried through the crowds on Svetlanskaya. He hadn't laughed at anything that happened at barracks. But it was a hell of a joke, and it was on all of them. As a side line to neutrality, America had begun supplying the White Russians with arms. The transport which came in that morning brought a hundred and fifty thousand Lee-Enfield rifles and six million rounds of ammunition. If Olga's story was correct, the Cossacks wouldn't have to wait much longer. And if American troops were liquidated with American rifles it could be proved suicide. Good old Uncle Sam! The international Santa Claus, answering the prayers of his enemies.

"That's interesting," his Captain said. "You're right, Tucker, to report things like this. Do you know the woman's name?"

"No, sir, she wouldn't tell me. Being a White Russian, I suppose she was afraid to take the chance."

"M'm. And you had never seen her before?"

"Yes. I think I once helped her in some way."

"Well, sometimes you get rewarded for doing good turns."

"Yes, sir."

"She just stopped you on the street and told you this?"

"Not quite. She drew me into a doorway—"

"A doorway, Tucker? What a place! Still, I'm glad you reported it."

That is about as much satisfaction as one gets in the Army. But it seemed to Alfred that his captain believed there might be something in the story. Nothing was said about his reporting late.

Afterward, he knew that Olga's story had been the real thing. Only he wondered at himself for believing that he might be the first one to bring it in. The delivery of the rifles had been refused that morning. And the Americans were standing double guard over them.

The rifles stayed in Vladivostok. The British general wrote blistering letters to the newspapers. He made it sound as if the Americans were delaying an important White Russian offensive and endangering civilization. And that was strange, because the British could not find enough White Russians to use the rifles they had on hand.

After a month, the rifles were suddenly shipped west in two trains with extra guards. They were to be delivered to Admiral Kolchak's forces at Irkutsk. That way, there was at least a chance of their being kept out of Cossack hands.

# XIV

THERE won't be any trouble," the lieutenant said.

"I shouldn't think so."

"The other train must have got through all right."

"We would have heard if it hadn't." In his mind Alfred was going over the location of the hand grenades, cached at convenient stations among the sandbags which were the improvised armor of their armored car.

"Sure the men would be able to put their hands on those grenades without having to look for them?"

"Yes, sir." Alfred touched a deep notch in the cross-beam beside him. "There's a notch above every station. They could find them in the dark."

Lieutenant Ross wasn't really interested. He was leaning over a sand-bag, looking out at the brown plain, where it was getting dusk. "Camels!"

A long procession of loaded camels and men who looked as if they were stuffed, Mongols or Manchurians, crawling toward the west, parallel with the railroad.

"I didn't expect to see anything but polar bears in Siberia."

The soldiers farther back in the car had seen them, too. They were arguing hotly, telling Seeley, who was new to the run, that he was crazy to think he saw camels in Siberia.

"This is where the railroad follows the caravan route," Alfred said.

"Lieutenant Ross!" Seeley had come forward and was standing at salute, swaying with the swaying car.

"What is it, Seeley?"

"There's a whole lot of camels out there, sir."

"No! The things on cigarettes?"

"Yes, sir. You can still see them. Back there!"

The officer stared. "My God, they do look like camels! Well, live and learn."

"Thank you, sir." Seeley saluted and went back to the others.

Alfred heard him, triumphant. "Lieutenant Ross says those are too camels!"

"Yeah?"

"Don't let him kid you!"

"Camels can only live in hot places."

"Where do you-all see any camels?"

Seeley was robbed of his triumph. The crawling caravan had been left behind. There was nothing to see but the gleam of a river, brown plains stretching away in the gathering dusk, the cold gleam of snow-covered mountains rising into the sky toward Lake Baikal.

It was dark when they rolled into Chita, going at a good clip. They weren't stopping if they could help it. Lamplight in the windows of log cabins. Electric lights. Stone and brick buildings that might have been in Seattle. Sliding by the glittering sign of what looked like a movie house. Nearing the heart of the city. They would be clear in a few minutes, going through without stopping. What would Semeonoff think, hearing they had passed through with a trainload of rifles? It was too unlikely that he didn't know.

They were jostled against the forward end of the car, which came back to meet them. Steam hissing and brakes grinding; the crash and growl of couplings as the train jolted to a stop.

"Find out what's stopping us, Sergeant, then get back here quick!"

Alfred was already dropping over the side; running forward near a railroad station dark with people. The engineer was out of his cab, swearing terribly in Russian. There was a man with a red lantern. Railroad iron across the tracks. A group of Cossack officers descending on the engineer. An officer, gaudy with decorations that glittered in the half-light; one swagger from his black, kaiser moustache to his brutal spurs; an overdone picture of a butcher on a holiday. That perfume alone would have identified him.

Semeonoff had come on board the time Randall brought him Red Cross supplies. He had been perfumed then, and boastful about his personal daintiness. He could not sleep nights, he said, if he missed his daily bath of blood. He had been talkative and very genial, but Alfred had not liked him. The man's swarthy complexion made him think of dusk at the killing station. And the perfume sickened him. In his mind the sweet smell of scent was mixed up with the sweet smell of blood.

"You have rifles for me on this train."

The hell we have! Alfred had heard enough.

231

"Semeonoff looking for rifles! There's railroad iron across the tracks."

Lieutenant Ross was on the ground before Alfred had finished.

"Get back up there and see that nobody touches any of the cars. I sent word to the rear." He was gone.

There wasn't much to do but hang on. The men about him in the open sand-bag car were on the job, all right. Every rifle as ready as a bee sting. Half a dozen others, rifles in hand, were patroling the tops of the box cars, from where they had a good view of each side of the track.

Montana came back after delivering the lieutenant's message to the rear sand-bagger. "They ain't likely to fool with that end of the train," he reported. "There was some Cossacks, but the corporal—your brother—told them to get out. They got!"

Still the lieutenant didn't come back. A platoon of Cossacks stopped beside the car, reckless-looking youngsters with smooth, girlish faces under fur hats like great muffs. They were accompanied by a ragged civilian interpreter who explained what they were after.

"This gentleman, the officer, says your officer says he is to take rifles from the first car."

The Cossacks started on with easy insolence.

"*Wait!*" Alfred leaned out over the sand-bags, with his pistol in his hand.

They waited, the interpreter clasping his hands nervously.

"Tell the gentleman officer I'll open the car when

my officer orders me to. If he touches it before then he'll get his hand shot off at the ribs!"

It was translated, more or less, and the Cossacks drew back a safe distance.

Worthington, from Georgia, grinned admiringly and inclined his head toward the rebuffed Cossack. "I mean he's told, ain't he?"

Lieutenant Ross came back and climbed into the sand-bag car. He looked worried.

"Are they going to let us go on, sir?"

He shook his head. "Semeonoff gave me thirty hours to turn the rifles over. After that, he says he'll take them. I told him there'd be plenty of fireworks. I hope it doesn't happen. If it does, we might as well get in as many shots as we can. It'll be good night, anyway."

"Yes, sir. We'll get in as many as we can." Alfred was listening to the panting of a locomotive. Hoping rather foolishly it would be a train that could help them.

"Here they come," the lieutenant observed.

A thick, dark column, pouring around the end of the station.

"Take charge of the rear car, Sergeant. Remember, no shooting unless they rush the train. If they do, give them all you have. Better go along the ground."

Alfred dropped over the side of the car and ran between the tracks. The headlight of an approaching locomotive gleamed on the rails.

"Sergeant Tucker coming up!" Just to make sure some enthusiastic member of the rear guard didn't toss a hand grenade.

233

"I'll be damned, Sergeant!"

"We thought you'd gone to the movies."

They were glad to see him.

"What are the orders?" George wanted to know. There were two other corporals in the car, but he had been in charge since the train stopped.

"Don't start anything," Alfred warned. "But if they rush us, work fast with your rifles and grenades."

The battalion of Cossacks, four deep, reached from one end of the train to the other, the front rank about twenty feet away. A wall of shaggy fur hats cocked over reckless young faces. Coarse overcoats with leather belts. Riding boots. Long clumsy rifles with ramrods. No wonder they wanted something better.

Pink Byers said modestly, "I think I could hit one of them if they came closer." He was like a cat-shy mouse finding courage in the presence of the whole cat family. The worst thing he could have imagined had already happened and there wasn't anything more to fear.

The locomotive headlight flooded the dark air. No train, only a locomotive drawing a box car. Box car, hell! The muzzles of machine guns bristled from ports in its steel sides. One of Semeonoff's raiding cars. It rolled by and stopped somewhere near the head of the American train. While they were still looking after it the headlight of a second locomotive shone on the rails and flooded the night. The engine crept by and came to a stop, flanking them with the steel side and bristling gun ports of a second armored car.

They were in a nice mess. Fifty American recruits behind a few sand-bags, sandwiched between a battalion of killers and two armored cars. There was nothing to do but watch both sides, and wait.

George was scowling back at the steel wall beside their car. "I don't suppose we could even dent that stuff."

"I wouldn't waste any bullets on armor plate."

Later Alfred was called back to the first car. The American Consul was protesting the seizure. If they held on long enough, there might be a chance of getting through. The lieutenant was going into town to join the row. While he was away they were to sit tight and bluff it out.

When he was on the point of leaving, Lieutenant Ross was very grave. "Hang on with everything you have," he told Alfred. "If we give up those rifles today, some of our men may be killed with them tomorrow. I'd hate to be the one who supplied them." He dropped over the side and brushed through the ranks of Cossacks as if he didn't see them.

Looking after that brisk, straight figure, something flickered in Alfred's mind. This business wasn't real. Ross wasn't a soldier. He was a young lawyer, with a wife and child in Boise, Idaho, which he said was a swell town. He had a Ford car, and in summer he and his wife sometimes drove over to the Snake River to go swimming.

If something happened, it would be embarrassing trying to explain why it was necessary for Ross to be at Chita, Siberia, ten thousand miles from home, trying to prove that Americans shouldn't have to furnish the rifles with which they were going to be killed. If Ross got his throat cut under those circumstances, it could hardly be said that his death was due to natural causes—or unavoidable ones.

At ten o'clock the lieutenant wasn't back. They were still sitting tight, between the Cossacks and the armored cars. Dark coal smoke and snow white steam from a locomotive, rolling up and flying away in the night. Derisive yells from the Cossacks stirring impatiently. Impatient young faces under wild, shaggy fur. A string of electric lights along the station. On the platform, neat little Japanese sentries walked up and down, guarding the railway.

At eleven o'clock it was the same, except that the railway guard had changed. And other, identical, neat little Japanese sentries walked up and down the platform. Keen-eyed for little scraps of paper, which they picked up and put in a basket. Too short-sighted and hard of hearing to observe what was happening on the track beside them. A train of their allies, blocked and surrounded by howling bandits.

It was the same at midnight, only someone brought coffee. And while they were drinking it, a woman screamed in the armored car beside them. A high-voltage scream that sounded as if it would go on forever—and ended as suddenly as if it had been chopped off with an axe.

One of the boys thought it was their duty to investigate. He didn't get any support. The Cossacks traveled with their women and their horses. Their own or any they picked up. And they weren't responsible to any-one for whether they coaxed them or used spurs.

Past midnight the lieutenant returned. He looked tired but relieved to find them hanging on. He had

236

called Semeonoff's bluff about being authorized to take the rifles. Got a wire through to General Graves in Vladivostok. The General had wired back, "Don't give up a rifle."

Semeonoff said he would take them anyway.

"If we have to, we'll hold on until the rifles aren't fit for anything but a museum."

Earlier, there seemed a certain advantage in having thirty hours of grace. Now it had a touch of cruelty. The Cossacks were relieved by another battalion. The Japanese sentries were relieved. The city went to sleep. And the same fifty Americans stood to and looked at the same things all night. Smoke and steam of the locomotives blowing in the icy wind. The muzzles of guns from the armored cars on one side, and the restless Cossacks on the other, waiting for them to weaken or fall asleep.

Daylight came with the first early droshky drivers, looking for fares at the station. The second battalion of Cossacks was relieved by the first. They looked spiteful and yelled their annoyance at a handful of Americans who made them do so much standing in one spot. The irritatingly neat Japanese sentries were replaced by others like them, intent on carrying out the less important duties of a railway guard to perfection.

The train guard took turns at breakfasting, going by squads to the diner under the noses of the champing Cossacks, carrying their rifles with them.

The city stirred and woke up. More rattling droshkies and four wheeled carriages. Waves of people in old clothes, with old, anxious faces. Dashing motor cars, carrying Japanese and Russian officers. A flock of school children, carrying books, muffled in old clothes and older furs, crossing the railroad on their way to school. A regiment of Japanese soldiers on the march. Expressionless and dingy-neat, like factory-made toys of wood or lead. A caravan coming in: long-haired camels shambling under mysterious bales, Mongol drivers in quilted clothes. Maybe the same camels Seeley couldn't quite believe without an officer to verify them.

They stood guard all day, with a few minutes off for meals. An hour or two of sleep snatched in the lee of sand-bags. Just enough sleep to leave a poisonous taste. Tempers were growing shorter, eyes heavy, and faces black with stubble. The feeling and taste of a derelict ship being fouled with sea growth. The battalion of Cossacks was relieved. The Japanese railway guard changed and changed again. The flock of children crossed the tracks on their way home from school.

It was night again. They swayed on their feet, dozed and woke with a start to look at the same scene forever. The muzzles of guns from the steel wall beside them. Dark smoke and snow white steam. Wild fur hats and reckless young faces. The lights of the station. Hatefully neat little Japanese sentries marching up and down the platform. Raw nerves and hollow eyes, feet swollen from twenty-odd hours of standing.

The deadline had been set for three in the morning. A few minutes before, Alfred and George routed out the men who had slumped to the bottom of the car; got them on their feet, with their rifles in their hands. Pink, more than half asleep, wanted to fight George for waking him, went to sleep altogether, with his fist drawn back, and had to be wakened a second time.

At three o'clock the guns from the armored cars were swung experimentally, trained to better advantage. The long line of Cossacks swayed and yelled, their gray fur headpieces like the crest of a sea about to break and engulf the train. Neat little Jap sentries marched up and down the platform, pausing to pick up imaginary bits of paper and put them into a real basket.

Three o'clock passed. Four, with the Cossacks threatening but not attacking. Waiting, maybe, for the Americans to be tortured into striking first. Or until they all dropped from exhaustion, when the cars could be plundered without protest from the sleeping guard. It never occurred to them that Semeonoff might be waiting for them to decide they had enough, and give up the rifles. Probably no one in the train thought of ever giving up.

Daylight came back again, with the first droshky drivers. The Cossacks were relieved once more. The Japanese sentries changed. The city stirred and woke up. More droshkies. Dashing motor cars with Japanese and Cossack officers. Waves of people with old, anxious faces. The flock of children crossed the tracks on their way to school again. Japanese soldiers marching, wooden-faced. A caravan of silly little ponies seen through bleared eyes, awake since the beginning of time. Life so old and stale and poisonous. Like looking at something rotten, out of a grave.

The men in the rear car were cracking under the

strain: falling asleep on their feet, or slumping to the floor. When they were aroused, they wanted to fight. It didn't matter much whom. Toward noon George wanted to end his misery by jumping into the wave of Cossack faces with a pistol and grenades with the pins pulled. Alfred had to argue him out of it.

One o'clock in the afternoon. Thirty hours had drawn into forty.

Montana came reeling back over the tops of the box cars, red-eyed, his face black with two days growth of beard, looking like the corpse of a hobo tottering back into life. He fell into the sand-bag car.

"Lieutenant says be ready to move!"

Move, where? It seemed impossible that they would ever go anywhere, or see anything but the hateful life of Chita, rotating through endless days.

The train jerked and sent them reeling; jerked again and started rolling. The armored cars and the station slipped behind them. They yelled defiance at the howling Cossacks until they fell behind and were gone. Then they dropped in the car as if they had been shot, their rifles clattering on the floor. They slept like the dead as their train rolled out of Chita.

Alfred couldn't understand how they had escaped; why the Cossacks had let them go. It didn't seem possible that fifty Americans behind a few sand-bags had bluffed themselves out from between a sandwich of armored cars and Cossack battalions.

The lieutenant couldn't understand it at first, either. Then, as recent events fell into place in his mind, he thought he saw a very clever piece of strategy. The

Consul at Chita had told him that Japanese Commander Oi was in town, conferring with Semeonoff. The lieutenant gave his own general credit for knowing that, and timing the rifle trains accordingly. If Semeonoff had liquidated the guard and taken the rifles, in a Japanese sector with the Japanese general in town, the responsibility would have been nailed squarely on the Japanese High Command. There could have been no alibis.

They had a smart general. And after catching up on their sleep they thought rather well of themselves. If anyone wanted rifles kept out of Cossack hands, they were the boys to do it.

They felt an almost alcoholic glow for two weeks after they got back to Vladivostok. Then they talked with the guard of an American train which had just come through from Omsk, and the glow vanished. The guard told them that at every station in the Trans-Baikal, Cossacks had jeered their train and held up new Lee-Enfield rifles.

They might almost as well have let Semeonoff take the rifles when he asked for them. Well, not quite. And the Cossacks' jeering must have been a little sour.

The towns along the Trans-Siberian were gray with soldiers of the Czech Army, said the guard. The Czechs had given up the White Russian cause and were gypsying East in their echelons, taking their own sweet time about it. Having a look at the kind of democracy they had brought to Siberia. The ones who spoke English could give you an earful. And they did, by God! Siberia, they said, was a peaceful place when they captured it. Now it was turned into a living hell.

The Czechs were bitter against the Allies, who had talked to them about democracy—and betrayed them into fighting for a dictator. They were more bitter against the White Russians who had grafted away the shoes for their feet and the food for their horses, while they were suffering and dying in the Ural Mountains, holding back the Bolsheviki. But they were bitterest of all against the Cossacks who had stayed thousands of miles away from the front. The Cossacks who had done no fighting, but a sickening amount of killing.

The guard on that train didn't know about the Japanese-Cossack plan for liquidating the American force. But what they said about the Czechs made it sound as if it was no longer a good time for that plan.

Nothing much happened for a while after the delivery of the rifles. Except that the Allies and White Russians hated the Americans more than ever and went out of their way to show it. Not the Japanese, who are a polite people. And not Olga. Women do not understand politics very well. And they consider love more important. In that way they are more intelligent than men.

Around the middle of November the American railway guard between Spasskoe and Iman was strengthened. That was not on the Trans-Siberian line, but up north. Alfred and George's platoon had the misfortune to be sent. They were supposed to leave on the morning of the 18th, but there was a delay about trains. And they could not use the Vladivostok railway station because General Gaida was using it for a revolution. Gaida was the Czech general, but the Czech

242

soldiers did not help him because it was a Russian revolution. These Czechs were the ones who brought democracy to Siberia. And they did not want to bring anything else noble to anyone else's country, but only go to their own and mind their own business.

The Russians did not seem interested, either, and it was not a very good revolution. George and Alfred saw a little of it from the railroad yards, where they were pretending to look for their train. Cossacks were lighting cigarettes and shooting at the station from behind the trucks of cars. The Americans could not tell if they hit anything. But gunboats began firing from the bay, and shells dropped into the station. George thought that when they did get away for Iman, it would not be in very good style.

General Gaida surrendered that morning. The only ones who seemed to take the revolution seriously were some Russian boys who had helped Gaida. They wore blue arm-bands and belonged to some patriotic boys' club. After the surrender, the Cossack General lined these boys up in front of the railway station. It was sleeting, and the sleet was falling into the station where shells had gone through the roof. The boys' clothes were torn and they were bareheaded. One of them had blood on his face. But they did not seem to notice the sleet or feel cold. There was a big crowd watching. General Rozanoff questioned the boys, one at a time. Alfred and George did not understand Russian, but they knew the boys were giving the general the razzberry. The boy with blood on his face looked as if he might cry. They could see him moistening his lips when it got near his turn. But when his turn came he shouted back and gave the Cossack the razzberry. Then the boys were marched back into the station.

There were dead and wounded lying outside the station, and it looked as if the Cossacks weren't going to do anything for them. They were left lying in the sleet for several hours. When the Americans finally left for Iman, the Cossacks had got around to the wounded and were killing them.

On the Iman sector their platoon lived in two derailed box cars and guarded a railway bridge. It was not the bridge they had guarded the year before, when a train stopped with news of the Armistice, and they celebrated because they thought it had something to do with them. But it was the same kind of bridge. Trains passed over the bridge and much water passed underneath, until the water froze and stood still. And time stood still. But Alfred knew it was not the year before, because now he had two girls to write to.

He did not write much to either, but he saw Olga in December. He and George got passes to Vladivostok to have their teeth overhauled. After that they were separated.

# XV

IT WAS almost time for the train to Iman when he found George shooting crap with some quarter-master boys in the back room of the Man Hung. His big sheepskin-lined coat and fur cap were on a chair beside him, as if he had just stopped for a minute. Probably hours ago, when Alfred went to Headquarters. He was down on one knee, imploring the bones, with his face flushed and a lock of yellow hair hanging over one eye.

"Come on, Seven! Come on, you seven-spotted bastard!"

Alfred touched him on the shoulder. "We'll have to snap into it if we're going to make the train."

George threw a pair of deuces and looked up, aggrieved. "I lost twenty-two roubles," he explained, "and I was just going to win them back." He had been drinking, and it annoyed Alfred.

Not that he would have minded a skinful himself. It would be a nice change to get roaring drunk and stay that way for a week. Forget the whole Siberian mess. Wash out the ugly taste of what he had read in that San Francisco paper at barracks: a story hinting that the whole American command in Siberia was infected with Bolshevism. That General Graves had held up the rifles to spite the White Russians for publishing the fact and the United States Government had

245

repudiated his action. That hurt more than bullets. America repudiating an American general for not being snappy about supplying rifles to massacre American troops! Alfred was as angry and bewildered as the boys at barracks. If your own government goes back on you. If your own square-shooting general gets hell for not turning you over to those Cossack butchers. . . .

It was an occasion for getting drunk and staying that way. But not a safe time. Before leaving Spasskoe Alfred had been cautioned to watch his step. He had been cautioned again in Vladivostok. The White Russian papers were full of attacks on America and Americans. It was getting unsafe for small groups in towns and small detachments outside. There were growing threats of attack everywhere, and actual attacks in some places. Near Iman the Cossacks had arrested an American captain and a corporal whom they beat almost to death with the knout. The Americans' offense was traveling without passports. Not that anyone ever heard of soldiers with passports. Near Lake Baikal one of Semeonoff's armored cars had stopped at night and fired a machine gun point-blank into a box car where American soldiers were quartered, killing some of them. If that was how Semeonoff treated sleeping Americans, their action at Chita didn't seem so foolish: staying awake and bluffing it out for forty hours.

This was no time to take chances. George walked straight and talked clearly, but his face was flushed and he had a vodka breath. No doubt he had drunk plenty. And the cold night air might get him into trouble.

"You said you wouldn't go to the Chinaman's," Alfred reminded him.

"That was early in the week," George said. "Before we went to the barracks." He had seen the San Francisco paper, too. But Alfred knew that wasn't the whole trouble. His brother had been jolted by something in one of his letters, and from then on his temper had been spoiled. He didn't say what it was. Siberian exile hadn't gone so well with George. The action and battles he had dreamed about had let him down. Changed to inaction, while he watched the senseless butchery of peasants who didn't know what it was about. He could only watch and do nothing, without knowing what it was about, either. And he was beginning to suffer from the homesickness that had got nearly everyone else long ago. He had spells of being reckless, or sullen and moody. Then he didn't even tell his brother what he was thinking.

George's skinful seemed to have been good for him. At least it made him feel better. As they walked down Svetlanskaya he took in the scene with good-natured contempt. "Vladivostok!" he said. "Siberia! What a joint!" After another block, he asked, "Do you know what Siberia is like, Alfie?"

Alfred could imagine, but he hoped George would be careful about what he said. Probably that Russian officer didn't understand English. Even if he did, he wasn't likely to know what a "joint" was. But he had turned his head sharply at the mention of Siberia. He must have caught the disparaging tone. And an M.P. was watching them from across the street.

"Remember those Cossacks we saw, raping a girl near the railroad tracks?" His choice of subjects hadn't improved, but at least he'd taken the warning and dropped his voice.

Alfred remembered.

"I figure when we saw that we saw the whole show. Siberia's a husky peasant girl—dumb and husky—getting raped by a bunch of crazy Cossacks and cigarette-butt nobility. She could throw them all off if the Allies weren't holding her down. That's why we're in bad. We won't help hold her down."

The comparison was terribly appropriate. Too appropriate for Vladivostok, where the fact of their being Americans was enough to attract ugly looks. Alfred tried to get his brother's mind engaged with something safer. Resolutely, he began talking about Alaska.

"Yes," said George after a while, "there's a good country, Alaska. A good thing we took it away from Russia, or it would have been another mess!"

Alfred was annoyed, and beginning to be alarmed. "We didn't take it," he corrected sharply. "We bought it." There was no use looking for trouble, saying things that weren't so.

His brother scowled thoughtfully, maybe thinking up something else to quarrel about. Then his eyes twinkled, and he grinned. "Don't mind me, Alfie. Good old Alfie! You save my neck every now and then."

Alfred grinned back at him. "You started the habit, George, when we were kids. Remember the cougar?" In the snow and stinging cold, he could feel back to that day. Cold and deep snow. The two of them going up the hill, under gigantic trees. George so big and strong and grown-up. He must have been about ten. Pa hammering in the barn, building a sled for Hyak, the buckskin pony. Before they started for the school they never reached, they had seen Mrs. Harper being rowed across the bay. The day Clarice Jackson was born. The American flag, and gold-white firs at sunset. . . .

"Hell," George said, "do you think I could have stood around and done nothing? Or held you down while a cougar ate you?" He scowled fiercely at the thought. "If I held my brother down while a cougar ate him, it would have been like—"

Alfred knew what he was going to say. Like the Allies holding the Siberians helpless for the Cossacks. But George didn't say it. He staggered slightly, beginning to feel the effect of the clear, cold air. But he was being as good as gold. Talking pleasantly, and trying not to offend anyone.

"Remember our cave, Alfie? On Baranov, back of the glaciers?"

Alfred remembered. "We found it just as it started to rain cats and dogs. We moved our whole camp inside."

"We made a fire," George reminded him. "We cooked pancakes with blueberries in them, and bacon, and coffee. . . . "

"We'll go back there when we're in Alaska again."

" . . . and we built up a big fire and lay in front of it."

"Yes. And the rain was nearly washing the valley away outside, but it couldn't touch us."

"It sounded like the ocean," George thought. "But we were dry and comfortable. Remember, when the fire burned up big, we saw those old-timers sitting against the side of the cave? Just outside the fire-light."

Alfred smiled, remembering back. "It gave me a start, all right."

"Me, too," George confessed.

"But after a little while it didn't seem to matter."

"*Memaloose!* No, it didn't seem to matter."

*Memaloose ancuttie man*, sleeping forever in the cave. The old-timers who had made their way from Asia to Alaska for some forgotten purpose.

"We went to sleep listening to the rain." George yawned. Lurched and regained himself quickly. "Went to sleep without having to worry about any reveille." He yawned again. "Speaking of sleep, I could do with some right now."

"You can sleep on the train going back," Alfred said. If they hadn't missed it.

The train was late. The train was always late, if it ran at all. Even then it might turn out to be some other train.

George thought they should try the waiting room. The platform roof hadn't been fixed since Gaida's revolution. The platform was dismal with patches of night sky above patches of trampled snow. But Alfred persuaded his brother to stay outside. If George

250

did find a place in one of the stuffy waiting rooms, crowded with officers and refugees, he would go to sleep immediately. And once asleep, he couldn't be wakened without a scene.

Come on, train! The same old crowd, standing about on the bare platform and in the patches of dirty, trampled snow. Parties of officers, mostly Japanese, with a few White Russians and British. Japanese merchants. Refugees with their bundles and waiting faces. American, Czech, Chinese and Japanese sentries. The Canadians had stood guard there once. The Canadians who called a spade a spade, and thought a promise should mean something. They had been hustled home before Alfred had a chance to see them, long ago. Lucky fellows, rewarded for their honesty!

It looked as if the Czechs would be next to go. The Czechs who had started things by capturing the railway and fighting the Bolsheviki in the Urals, under the impression that they were fighting Germany. They guarded part of the railway now, but they did no more fighting. Now their Council was speaking from the shoulder. Telling the Allies they had been betrayed. Used as tools for autocracy. Made an accomplice in crime. And they were demanding that they be sent home—or allowed to stop the butchery of the Siberian people.

The Americans hadn't called a spade or murder by its proper name unless privately, to each other. They hadn't mutinied. They tried to be good soldiers and did all they were ordered to the best of their ability. And an American newspaper branded them as Bolsheviki because they hadn't taken part in the slaughter into which they had never been ordered!

By God, it would be good to get drunk and forget that lie! But this was no time for it, and one member of the family had drunk too much already. Steady, George. The train should be here any minute. Come on, train!

George had behaved very well since they reached the station. But he was getting tired waiting. His face was sullen and moody again, probably thinking of whatever it was in the letter that upset him. Alfred had a letter from Clarice, which he hadn't opened. Not when he was seeing Olga. He would read it on the train.

A train pulled into the station, but it was Chinese Eastern. Porganichnaya, Harbin, Manchuria Station. Japanese officers and merchants bustled into the first-class coaches. The third-class doors were unbarred. Refugees poured down the steps of the station, into the coaches. A solid black stream, with bundles floating on it.

When the Harbin train had gone, the platform seemed half deserted. There was room to move about. George and Alfred walked up and down at the far end. It wasn't as bad as Alfred feared. George was gloomy and silent again, but he showed no sign of making trouble. And when he lurched now and then, no one seemed to notice.

They passed it twice, walking up and down. First on George's side, then Alfred's. An empty, weather-beaten box left by the refugees for Harbin, probably brought for one of the children to sit on. A pathetic, childish relic abandoned on the snow-trampled platform.

They passed it twice, a kind of registration mark.

Alfred was betting with himself about how many times they would pass it before the train came. He had bet twenty and hoped he would lose by the train coming sooner.

The third time, George lurched and stopped with the box at his feet. "Damned carelessness," he grumbled, "leaving rubbish on the platform!" He drew back one foot.

"*Don't!*" Alfred tried to draw him away. He had a premonition of the box hitting one of those Japanese officers on the shins and starting trouble. In the distance he heard the whistle of their train, coming out of the yards. George mustn't spoil it.

*Thump!* The box skated across the platform and disappeared over the edge.

George dusted his gloved hands, although it was his foot that had contacted with the box. "Things were neater when we were on guard here."

"Come on," Alfred urged him. The locomotive headlight was streaming past the platform and the bell clanging.

Then they were aware of the Russian colonel, standing close beside them, glaring at George.

"You drunken swine!" he said in English.

George saluted, good-naturedly.

The Russian looked as if he might have had a few drinks himself. His face was flushed and his eyes blazing with hatred. "You damned American Bolsheviki!"

George saluted again, cheerfully. His thumb came half an inch nearer his nose than the regulation salute called for, but the colonel seemed to miss it. He went on pelting the two of them with abuse. The Japanese officers had come up close, listening with expression-less faces.

It was a nasty ordeal, but Alfred sensed it was almost over. Their train was coming into the station. The White Russian colonel was no doubt taking the same train. And he seemed to have run out of ugly words without making a dent in George's cheerfulness.

The colonel glanced toward the oncoming engine, ready to give up his attempt. He took a parting shot, with his face near George's. Lips and moustache drawn back from his teeth.

"You Bolshevik swine. *Your own government wants you to be killed!*"

Alfred winced. He had been prepared for anything, he thought, but that was almost too much, coming on top of that story in the 'Frisco paper.

The effect on George was terrifying. His face went white, under the sting of the words. Then he flushed darkly. "You—"

Alfred saw what was happening and pushed his brother's arm aside. The blow missed the officer, but it was already too late. He should have let George strike his blow. He should have reached for his own pistol first. Now it was too late. His arms were being twisted up behind his back. Blinding pain, making everything unreal. The locomotive rumbling past the platform forever. The hiss of steam and a great clanging bell, filling the world. Japanese officers, no longer expres-sionless, showing their faces at last. Eager and triumphant, crowding forward to shake hands with the Russian colonel over something on the platform, where there was blood on the trampled snow.

# XVI

REMEMBER the Bolsheviki Bird? It took refuge on the *Thomas* in the Sea of Japan. That was a year and some months ago, by time. So much longer by other measurements. There was a numbing distance between that nothing could cross.

The bird was tame or exhausted enough to be caught by hand. Someone nicknamed it the Bolsheviki Bird because of its red wing-feathers. And it was searched for propaganda. George almost got into a fight with the sailor who camouflaged it. "To hell with the color! You ought to know that paint's no good for a bird."

That time, so long ago that you could never get back to it. Farther away from now than it had been from the first thing you remembered. There was still innocence and faith when the *Thomas* steamed up Golden Horn Bay. You thought you knew why you were there. Hanging in the crowded rigging and cheering as you came into the dock at Vladivostok. Only a little puzzled as you marched down the gangway with your company. Soldiers with sea legs. Between dark Russian crowds. Searching your faces wonderingly. Silent, or calling one question. An interpreter explained that the Russians wanted to know what great thing had happened to make the American soldiers cheer as they came in. They had never heard that when Americans land everything is going to be all right. They should have known that. Or the Americans should have known the very special and well-rigged hell they were landing in. Then there would have been no cheers.

You can't unlearn things and go back to the time you were as innocent as a lost bird, taking refuge on a transport of war. The most you can do is to fumble your way back, with pain, to something like what it felt then.

The mast and halliards were the starting point, glimpsed from the narrow-gauge railway to the storehouse. It was something like the lost bird. An innocent sailboat lying at Vladivostok. Alfred had noted its location and come back to investigate.

There was a little snow in the hollows, in the chinks of a landscape of rusting shrapnel and explosive shells. Red outlined in white. But there was no ice on the bay, and the weather was mild with a touch of sun.

He found her at an old dock, astern of a little, rusting passenger steamer—a sloop of about thirty feet, on the beamy side. Her flush deck was broken only by the companionway and a small skylight. The sheets led aft, close to the hatch. There was plenty of deck, and nothing much to trip over on a dark night.

A young British officer was there before him, standing on the dock, smoking a pipe and looking her over. Another Britisher who would give him a line about the unimportance of the Russian common people. Alfred looked glumly at the sloop, thinking she was something like the *Tyee*, and hoping the Britisher would go away.

"Her lines are a bit coarse," the officer observed. Then his eyes lit up, meeting Alfred's. "But she's a boat!"

"Yes." After a while he said, "We have one something like her at home. She behaves very well."

"Did you manage any long cruises?"

"We got as far as Alaska."

"From where?"

"Puget Sound."

"You've something to look forward to, when this is over."

"I don't know. It won't be the same. I sailed with my brother. He's dead, now."

"I'm awfully sorry. Was it the war?"

"Whatever you call this. He was murdered. Ten days ago, at the railway station."

"I'm frightfully sorry. A Russian officer, wasn't it?"

"Yes. They called it 'self defense!'"

"I don't think White Russians are mature enough to be trusted with firearms." Then he observed, "You could say that about the human race."

Alfred wondered if he had heard right.

The officer sighed, looking at the sloop. "I never managed a boat of my own."

"But you've sailed."

"Rather! On college vacations I sometimes chartered a cutter on the Severn. A seven-tonner. Once we got a good slant in the Channel and held on until we raised the Isle of Wight. Coming into Cowes, I felt like the King himself. Another time we got only as far as Milford Haven, where we were stormbound for a week. But wherever we went we always had to turn back too soon, because chartering costs money."

Alfred found himself hoping that some day the officer would have a boat. It was a long time since he had gone out of his way to wish an Englishman good luck.

"Shall we look her over?" He caught one of the shrouds and dropped lightly on deck. Alfred followed him. All at once they were like two boys on a holiday. The lieutenant tried the long, limber tiller. "I like that!" he declared. "One could feel everything she's up to." One hand on the tiller and his arm at the angle that comes only with experience. "You chaps steer with a wheel, don't you?"

"We have a tiller on our boat," Alfred told him. "But we were hardly yachtsmen. We built her ourselves and never wore brass buttons."

"Good for you!" He let go the tiller. "There's nothing as safe as bare feet on deck."

"That was our style."

"And nothing else as safe as being naked when you're working on deck in a hard squall." He leaned over and knocked the ashes out of his pipe, against the sheer strake. "It stands to reason that when the wind's too strong for sails a man's safer under bare poles."

"We never thought it out," Alfred said, "but we found it easier to dry ourselves than our clothes. Of course, we didn't do it in freezing weather."

"That makes me think of unpleasant things."

"Did you ever try it?"

"No, but I saw it tried on others. I was in Omsk last December when there was an uprising against Kolchak."

"I heard about that. Did they really run the rebels through the streets at forty below?"

"It was only thirty-eight, but they looked like men running in fire!"

"Was it true they promised to let them off if they named their leaders—and shot them, anyway?"

"I don't know what they promised. At any rate, it must have been a relief to be shot." He got up, swinging his arms. "I didn't mean to talk shop."

Alfred succeeded in raising one side of the skylight an inch, and squinted below. "Everything looks ship-shape."

"I'd trust a yachtsman of any race to be tidy."

"Any idea who owns her?"

"I asked the watchman. He's on board that steamer. It seems she belonged to some city official who's been liquidated. He was rather vague, but so's my Russian. Shall we have a look below?"

"The hatch is locked," Alfred said regretfully.

The lieutenant dug into his overcoat pocket and brought up a key, buoyed with a cork. "It's wonderful what a few kopecks will do!"

The boat smelled all right below, only shut up and stagnant. Aired out, she smelled as clean as a wild bird.

Alfred admired her construction, while the Englishman tinkered with a brass stove. The flush deck

259

barely allowed sitting headroom. But she would be the stronger for it, and a better sailer.

A match cracked and flared. Then blue flame, and the queer, arid smell of burning alcohol. "There's nothing as good as a Primus. Hang one in gimbals, and you can cook everything in weather when you're too seasick to eat anything."

"You're having fun, aren't you?" Alfred was enjoying himself, too.

"Yes. This is a bit of a holiday. I'd expected to go it alone, but company tops it off." After a minute he worked the pump and the stove roared like a blowtorch.

"Think you'll have a boat when you get back?"

The Englishman looked grave. "I hope so, but it's hard to say. I'll be looking for a job, long after the others had their pick. The war came the year I went down at Oxford. It's taken five years out of my life. Not that they're all lost, if you live through."

"The war hasn't done me any good," Alfred thought.

"War's not supposed to, but it happens." The lieutenant's thin young face was ruddy in the loud flame that was beginning to drive out the chill. "War gives you something, if you're lucky. The trouble is, it keeps on until you lose it again. Once in Arabia, when we were having it out with the Turks, I saw a shell uncover a flight of stone steps that seemed to lead underground. The next shell covered them again. We advanced after that and I was never able to go back and find what was there, under the desert. It was a grief to me, because my field is archaeology."

260

"You were with General Allenby?"

"Yes," investigating a locker. "I saw the Holy Sepulchre."

"I've only seen the Crucifixion."

The Englishman admired a jar which held part of a black brick of tea. "Before long you'll see the Resurrection," he predicted cheerfully.

"We could have tea!" He got up suddenly and bumped his head on a beam, without denting his cheerfulness. He put the jar and a tin of evaporated milk on the berth. "All we need is water."

"I'll find some." Alfred came to with a start, and bumped his head. They both laughed.

"That makes it even! But you stay. I've some credit left from my ten kopecks. And I invited you to tea." After a moment he called down. "You might give me a boost up on the dock. The tide's been falling while we talked."

"Interventions end after a while, don't they?" Alfred asked over his third glass of tea. It was hard to believe that the thing hadn't ended that afternoon.

"Right-o. I believe this one is almost over." After a while he remarked, "Your men seemed to behave well in a nasty situation."

"They've been fine. Only they're plenty homesick."

The Britisher drew himself another glass of tea. "I dare say being heroes is a dull business."

"Heroes?" What the hell? The officer didn't seem to be laughing at him. "I didn't know there were any heroes in this mess."

"You chaps carry out your general's orders."

"Sure, doing railway guard, and barracks duty."

"I rather think we have the handsomest general," the Englishman decided, stirring his tea. "But yours is the hero of this show."

It had never occurred to Alfred that General Graves was a hero any more than he was. They were both in a dull and unprofitable mess. "How—"

"By keeping neutral, of course."

"But America promised to be neutral."

The Englishman laughed. "The Japanese promised to send twelve thousand soldiers, and keep neutral! They have seventy or eighty thousand here, censoring Russian thought with bullets and protecting their hired bandits. Everyone promised to be neutral. Your general kept his country's word."

"I suppose that's something."

"Here, let me warm up your tea! Damn it, man, I've got to warm you up somehow! I'm making a hero out of your general, and there may be a little left over for you."

Alfred smiled and felt warm. "I'm glad we've been neutral. But I can't see that we've done any good."

The Englishman was laughing at him now. "And you one of the Trojan heroes! Of course, things have been a bit mucked up. But intervention was doomed from the minute your general took his stand. Maybe I have a perverse sense of humor, but your general is my hero of the war. Don't you see? This was to be another Siege of Troy. All the promises of neutrality were the wooden horse. And damn it if your general didn't really keep neutral! He stayed in the belly of the wooden horse, when he had been counted on to open the gates and let in an army. The Italians and

Chinese stayed with him. After a while the Czechs joined him. That changed history. I don't doubt it's been dull—"

"Dull as hell!" Alfred assured him. "With just an occasional peek out from under the horse's tail."

They laughed together. Then the Englishman turned grave, hugging his knees and smoking his fine-smelling pipe. "This is all nonsense," he said. "Your general may have saved a few million lives. But if he had come out of the horse, the final result would have been the same. Only there would have been more death and dishonor than you could pass around."

Alfred found himself trusting the Englishman as he would have trusted George. Why couldn't he have met one like him earlier, before he had wasted so much hate?

The lieutenant gave the stove another pump. "We have a tidy little ship." His eyes were shy and friendly. "If Englishmen and Americans didn't always do their duty, I would suggest that we buy or steal her. Say '. . . the war,' and cruise south."

"By God, I wish we could!"

"But we won't." Regretfully. "There's a fatal integrity about all people. That's why history is a solemn thing. That's why this intervention is so stupid—and so damn fascinating!"

"If you know what it's all about," Alfred said, "I'd like to hear it! I've given up trying to figure it out."

"As I see it, this intervention assumed that the Russian Revolution was the coming off of a wheel that could be put on again. That's silly! The government was ripe with incompetence and graft. It was knocked over with one kick. The Bolsheviki finished the job with another kick. The people were ready to try anything that promised them peace and bread. And they would die rather than go back to something that had been dead and rotten on its feet.

"The Allies weren't interested in what the people wanted. And they didn't like Socialism. They must have thought they were Joshuas who could make the sun stand still. They made it, too. Only it's the earth that moves." The lieutenant grinned at Alfred. "You don't have to listen unless you want to."

"I do."

"Thanks.

"This mess was going to be a clear-cut demonstration that history doesn't mean anything. The Allies lopped off a piece of Russia and wiped out the Revolution. Put the nobility in power again. Took away the peasants' bread and let them watch aristocratic ghosts eat cake. Rather an unholy experiment: tampering with history that was already written.

"They might have foreseen that when they went back to before the Revolution they would have it over again. The White Russians gave a perfect performance, like old times. Used the Cossacks and the knout on the people. Clapped a 300% tax on sugar which we supplied at cost. Bickered over their graft while food rotted all along the line and people died of famine. Grafted until the foreign army which had given them their holiday, mutinied and quit. They hadn't forgotten a line of their old part, or learned a new one."

"That's something I can't figure out," Alfred said. "You'd think the Revolution would have taught them something."

"There's never been a revolution explicit enough to teach anything to the side that was overthrown. When you dust off the fallen and put them back in power, they feel at home in the familiar saddle—and use the spurs until they're thrown again. That's what I mean by the fatal integrity of people. It's easy to look on, and say they should do this or that. But people can only act what they've learned. Did you see the Gaida Revolution?"

"I saw part of it," Alfred said.

"The young Social Revolutionists with arm-bands? The ones they caught in the railway station?"

"Yes. I was sorry about them."

"I wanted to spank them. Like a troop of Boy Scouts, weren't they? I think even Rozanoff was touched. Otherwise he wouldn't have given them the chance to join his forces. That wasn't a bad offer, for Siberia. If they'd had any sense, as you and I see it, they would have joined up and waited for something else to happen. But, no. They had to stick out their hairless young chests and wave their arms and shout that they would die by torture before they served with cut-throats. The poor, brave fools! Their exhibition wouldn't have been worth tuppence at a cinema. That's when someone should have taken down their pants and spanked their B.T.M.'s. I wanted to shout to them: 'You're not in comic opera. Those rifles are loaded!' They knew it, of course." He drew the back of his hand across his eyes. "One can't always keep his perspective. To my taste, it was the rummest kind of comic opera. But those poor, dead boys couldn't have done any different. That was integrity."

The swell of something that had passed stirred the sloop and creaked her mooring lines. They might have been at the Sitka dock, with a Seattle steamer coming in. Not at the edge of a city where smooth-faced youngsters made dramatic speeches—and were butchered in a cellar.

"These White Russians have their own fatal integrity," the Englishman observed. "In their way, they're just as stupid and heroic as those boys. Making all the old, ghastly mistakes. Demonstrating how they were incompetent the first time, and going down to final defeat."

"You think Kolchak will be defeated?" Alfred asked.

"I rather think Kolchak knew that himself, from the beginning. That's why one used to see two Russian officers to every enlisted man. They were able to handle mutinies that way."

"But he ordered the mobilization—"

"Ah, yes. When his hand was forced by the Allies. It shows he had some guts, signing his own death warrant. And it proves our leaders had plenty of faith in their own judgment. Misplaced, of course. But faith is always touching." He gave the roaring stove a few more pumps.

"If Kolchak is going to be defeated," Alfred said, "I hope he gets it over with soon. Then they might let us go home."

"I rather think we are making merry waiting about

for the Admiral to die." The Englishman smiled around his pipe, with small, even teeth. Smiled more, then chuckled.

"I'm cursed with a disrespectful imagination," he explained. "It used to make me laugh in church when I was a boy, and get me into no end of trouble. Here, I'm attached to the training camp. Business is slack, now. But I helped drill the All-Siberian Army. I did my best, too. England has had better soldiers, but none more conscientious. Still, I couldn't help a disrespectful imagination, drilling those poor devils who were rounded up like cattle and driven in on the hoof. They were good material, too, when they had lost some of their fear. I did what I could to take the fear out of them and put confidence in them. I taught them how to meet the enemy in the most effective manner. That was my job of work, training them for the day when they would face their enemies—What are you laughing at?"

"Did you tell them which enemy?"

Their eyes met with an amused gleam.

"I think you have a disrespectful imagination."

"That makes it even," Alfred pointed out.

The Englishman rinsed the tea glasses and began putting things away neatly for the liquidated Russian official who wouldn't use them again. Alfred wondered if he had been sent to Semeonoff's killing station. It wasn't as bad as it sounded, once you were in a position not to mind the cold. Still, it didn't seem right for a yachtsman, so far from any sea.

"We'd best be getting along," the Englishman was looking at his wrist watch. "It's after six."

"You don't know how much this has meant to me, Lieutenant. I never expected to feel this good again."

"It's good to settle the problems of the world while you're young. When you grow older you only see things mucked up." He opened a valve on the stove and the roaring flame collapsed and wheezed out like a pricked balloon of light and sound. The gray twilight of the cabin seemed to bring them closer together. Two living and trusting shadows.

"What about the Japanese?" Alfred asked. "They seem to be the only ones here who know just what they're after. And they don't give a damn how they get it."

The lieutenant sighed. "It's no secret that they've been promised Eastern Siberia in return for destroying Communism. Maybe it would be worth part of another people's country to liquidate something you don't like—if it stopped there. But that precedent's a handy gadget. Now, the Japanese are claiming to have driven Communism out of Manchuria—"

"Where do you suppose it's likely to stop?"

"It needn't you know, for a few thousand years."

"But, Jesus Christ!" It was almost dark in the dead man's boat.

Outside it was still and cold, with snow patches in the twilight. They stopped a minute before a mountain of rusting shells, having drunk a good deal of tea.

"It's all they're good for now," Alfred said.

"Or ever were," his companion said. "This is an act of deliberate disrespect, out of loyalty to the human race." Afterward, as they hiked into

268

Vladivostok, he said. "You must forget everything I've said. Prophecy is nonsense. And I admire the white race. It's developed the sailboat to perfection. That is the noblest work of man."

They parted on Svetlanskaya, with a look and a salute. Alfred walked slowly to barracks, thinking. When men love each other they haven't any way of showing it. You'd think a man and woman had the best of it, with so much at their command. But it didn't seem to work out that way. It was a high-geared, fragile business that wouldn't stay put. About the time you thought you had the hang of it, it went to pieces with a monkey wrench in some part you'd never heard of. Love must have been built by a woman, with a woman's frightening ignorance of mechanics. A woman who will hang a heavy mirror on a tack, or drive nails with a loaded shotgun shell. Yes, you damned cobble stones of Svetlanskaya, cemented with horse manure and snow, I know every one of you by name. And I'll tell you this much: love is an impossible, haywire thing, built by a woman. Ten-ton sprockets driven by a garland of roses. There's nothing you can say in defense of love, except that it can be very sweet. Sweet, trying the impossible.

Clarice and he had loved each other, had tried the impossible of being so close that they would always belong. There in the forest where there was no time, for a little while. In a second-class Tacoma hotel where time devoured everything. She had written him that she was sure he would understand. He understood nothing except that she had married an officer hero of a war that had a beginning and fighting, and an end. Their disagreement which had seemed nothing had been everything. Her enthusiasm for some scheme for returned veterans. Trying to get him interested, while he was still wondering when in hell, if ever, he would be a returned veteran. They were organizing to make America a better place. He answered with a line that he would be very well satisfied with America the way it was. That was a quarrel. And she was married to someone she had known at the University.

He and Clarice had loved passionately and never quarreled when they were together. Five thousand miles apart, they quarreled fatally with each other. Or with the five thousand miles. She was married to a young ex-officer who knew just how to improve on America. And he was expected to understand.

He didn't know what was in that stained letter in the American Cemetery on the hill. Clarice might have commissioned George to see that his brother took the news sensibly and didn't try to get himself killed. No doubt she was sure that George, too, would understand. More likely, he understood nothing, getting drunk and caught off base forever.

# XVII

THE others were asleep. Montana, who had been made corporal in George's place, slept face down, as if he were trying to hide his big hulk from life and death. Willoughby, with one arm thrown out, and his face turned toward the ceiling. Pink Byers, folded up, smaller than ever; a dim little shape under blankets, with his knees drawn up and his close-cropped pink head bowed down, like a baby waiting birth. Worthington, with his thin, fine face as sagging as his empty clothes. Potter, snoring in the far shadows. . . .

Alfred had been disturbed by some early noise downstairs, and couldn't get to sleep again. He was lying on his cot near a barracks window, looking at the dawn, a wide, dim crack of light in the gray sky above the hills toward Suchan. As romantic as being in a meat safe and having someone open the door and let in a gleam of light. While his sleep-solemn eyes looked, his mind talked to his brother.

George, I don't suppose you're anything now. If you could remember, you would remember that time the *Tyee* lay at Bering. So near the top of the world that distant continents almost touched; where the sun only made a gesture toward the horizon to indicate night. So far away that a few shacks became a city. Walking toward Point Spencer, we were alone at the top of the world. Only flowers, the crying of a million birds, and the pale sea tumbling on the arctic littoral.

The world had never seemed so clean and honest, so safe. But it was a trap. We were seen there on the beach, throwing smooth stones into the arctic sea. Across Bering Strait, a mirage lifted the continent of Asia. The coast of Siberia raised a headland out of the sea, like a great animal, and looked; then sank slowly down behind the horizon.

We argued about it afterward, without being able to decide whether or not we had seen Siberia. But it saw us, and in the end it got you. It's got a good deal of me. To this day, I can't make out why we were ever sent here, why we have been kept here. But it looks as if we would go home at last—those of us who can. George, I'll tell them all the dirty trick. that was played on us. . . .

That band of sick light in the sky above the Suchan hills was the coming of the last day of January, 1920. And things were cracking at last. New shapes were moving on the snowy plains of Siberia, where it was still night.

Kolchak had fallen. The Supreme Ruler had become an ordinary man, running for his life. His fall seemed to be the signal for going home. Half the American force was in Vladivostok. More detachments were coming in. Officers denied rumors that they were going home, but denied them cheerfully. And the Allies had the air of giving up. Their war on Communism hadn't been a great success. Except for Communism, which seemed to grow on punishment; particularly on the punishment of innocent people. That disillusioned observer from the broken Ural front said that about the only difference between the White Army and the Red was the officers. When opposing forces met there wasn't always a battle. Sometimes they patched up their differences by dispensing with the White officers.

That picture the observer gave. On the road west of Kurgan he had tea with the colonel of a White Russian regiment that was going up to the vague front. The colonel was a stout, gray man with a limp; a veteran of the Russo-Japanese War and a decent, homely man with no pretense about him and no illusions. His regiment was less of a rabble than some the observer had seen. He praised it because he liked the old colonel and was sorry for him, being sent to a front where things went so badly and looked as if they might go worse.

The colonel thanked him, but he seemed to be thinking of something else. Or didn't want to talk about his regiment. But he did. When the orderly had taken the tea things away, he went back to the subject. "They will make good soldiers," he said, "but I shall never really command them. They are Bolsheviki to a man!"

"Good God! You know it, and can't do anything?"

The colonel said, "What can I do? I was given this regiment to command. I was ordered to the front. The discipline has been good. The men are willing to go to the front; too willing. I know that at the first opportunity they will go over to the enemy. They are the enemy. But what can I do? If I told my commanding general that they are Bolsheviki, he would say, 'So is the rest of the White Army.' He might have me shoot some of my men as an example to the others. But I have always tried to treat my soldiers nicely. I do not wish to shoot any of them. It is not their doing that they are here. I am only here because I have commanded troops for so many years that it has become a habit. So we shall go along together and see what happens."

It was time for the regiment to move on. They shook hands and the colonel said, "Think well of me. Live a hundred years!" He could not have expected to live as many days.

The last the observer saw of him, he was riding west at the head of his regiment. A decent, honest human being who would have made someone a nice grandfather, leading a Bolsheviki regiment against the Bolsheviki with no illusions in his tired old heart.

Tragic jokes like that, because someone didn't want to believe that the White Russians had no soldiers to fight for them.

Pulling on his clothes because he couldn't sleep any more, Alfred thought how thoroughly he had misjudged everything at the beginning. Then he had thought of the Siberian people as helpless and doomed because they were unarmed. He hadn't guessed the power of a people's just being. Hadn't foreseen that Kolchak, with the sympathy and wealth and munitions of the world behind him, would turn out to be the helpless one. Doomed because he had no people to fight for him. Forced to camouflage his bankrupt cause by arming his enemies. They were numberless and made a fine showing—until everything blew up in his face.

Now there was yellow in the crack of light above the Suchan hills. Light caught by the face of Golden Horn Bay, seamed with the paths of ice-breakers. One breaker still at it, backing and charging. A black, high-bowed silhouette, with navigation lights burning: a piece of night staying longer than the rest. There would be hot coffee in the galley, and a bunk to sleep in on a watch below. It was good seeing work done. Good, with a touch of homesickness and shame. Alfred had been in this country part of three years, without having done anything useful.

He looked about at the exiled men, sleeping in the dim, stone room at dawn. Good Christ, he was homesick! Thinking of these wasted lives and wasted years in an alien country. American men, with their own great country waiting, forced to spend these years watching the Allies try to help someone who must help himself, or die. Watching them try to help Admiral Kolchak lift himself by his boot straps. And when all of them lifted, they had only succeeded in setting the Admiral on his ass, for good and all.

The business would have been a joke if it hadn't eaten up part of men's lives. If it hadn't swallowed some lives whole. For what? *For what?* He looked about in a kind of helpless rage, wanting to tear something. Then he thrust himself into his Alaska coat, caught up his fur cap and went out quietly. There was no useful work he could do. But he could walk. And maybe he could help other spectators watch the Japanese. They were digging in around the station and setting up machine guns along the railway toward Nikolosk, where they had crowded into the American sector, ready to observe their pledge of neutrality when the Bolsheviki echelons rolled in to capture Vladivostok.

Downstairs he almost ran into his captain and a first lieutenant from Company C. They looked very warm and hearty, buttoning their big coats and pulling on gloves. And they looked slightly surprised.

Returning his salute, the captain said, "You must like the Army, Sergeant! Up an hour before reveille."

"It isn't the Army, Captain. I want some fresh air."

"Well, there's plenty of that."

"And cold as hell," Lieutenant Lanning put in.

Outside there was the noise of a car. Lieutenant Ross came in on the run, looking very fresh and brisk and pleased with himself. "I got it, Captain!"

"All right, let's go." He said to Alfred, "Come along, Sergeant, if you'd like to take your air having a look at the British."

Alfred didn't know what the joke was, but he went along. They piled into an Army Dodge, with Lieutenant Ross driving.

"Did you have to use force, Ross?"

Shifting gears, Ross said, "I had to threaten to use it."

The captain's voice observed from the back seat, "We're just like a staff car, Lanning!"

Alfred didn't know where they were going, and he didn't want to look his gift ride in the mouth. He knew Ross would have told him if they were alone.

At first he thought it had something to do with the expected Partisans, and the Japanese along the railway. But Ross passed the station, a block away, and turned west at the head of the bay, driving with alert fury over light snow, through sleeping streets, away from the railway.

There was no traffic. Even the signs of traffic were disappearing. The snow in the wide street was marked by only a few droshky tracks. Ross drove faster. The speedometer flirted with sixty and the motor roared as they flew up and down hills.

"They've kept her in good shape," Ross said.

Two dark, shaggy ponies galloped out of a side street ahead of them. The roar of the motor sank and the brakes squealed faintly. Ross's face was concentrated. The *izsvostchek* driver, standing up in the act of lashing the ponies, sat back, surging on the reins. His mass of whiskers and spectacles took on a look of academic, dignified panic.

"Son-of-a-bitch!" Ross spun the wheel with gloved hands. The little Dodge swerved in the snow, brushed by the rear of the four-wheeler, plunged on, slipping and swaying, with the young lieutenant coaxing the wheel.

From the back seat the captain called cheerfully. "Remember, Ross, you're not on the Snake River!"

They were in the outskirts of the city, and Ross drove more slowly. "They must be near here, Captain."

"We're far enough out, I believe. Try cruising around."

They made a right turn and drove several blocks,

without seeing anything but the daybreak on snow and scattering houses. Then two left turns. Coming up to the street they had left, Ross stopped the car suddenly.

"All right, hold it!"

The early light picked up gleams of metal in the endless column of fours, pouring down the street.

"We might as well get out and stretch our legs," the captain said. "It'll give us a good appetite for breakfast."

They piled out, Alfred wondering. The captain had said they were going to have a look at the British Army. The British had only officers and a few orderlies in Siberia. They couldn't be sending an army at last, when everyone was getting ready to go home! But there wasn't any mistaking those smart British overcoats, puttees and shoes. That jaunty British cap among the fur ones. The Sam Brown belt on a file-closer who wore no overcoat, but looked as if he were padded with two uniforms. And those were Enfield rifles.

The unbroken snow squeaked at first, then hardened under the tramp of British shoes. The squeak of compressing snow changed to a low, muffled drumming. Company after company, battalion after battalion, rolled through the sleeping street and swept on into Vladivostok.

"Down there, too!" Ross said.

The next street was dark with marching men, bright with the gleam of sunrise on British rifles. The captain and tall Lieutenant Lanning were watching the incoming army, and talking comfortably between themselves. Alfred didn't listen to what they were saying, but he saw the puffs of steam coming out of their mouths, like speeches from the mouths of people in a funny paper.

He and Lieutenant Ross watched without saying much. The scene spoke for itself: the cold light of a new day shining on British uniforms and arms, and bearded peasant faces.

Alfred would have liked to say something, but it was so big that he couldn't find words to go round it. Saying it would have been like trying to pick up a windrow of hay in his arms. It had something to do with lies and fears coming true, if you pretended hard enough. Long ago they had been sent here to keep an imaginary German-Bolsheviki army from capturing Vladivostok. Now a real Bolsheviki army was marching in, and there was no one to oppose it. The Allies and White Russians had worn themselves out fighting with shadows. Fighting an imaginary Red Menace so hard that it turned into a real one. And then they were licked.

He wanted to explain to Lieutenant Ross and to himself that while this was a real army, it was also an imaginary one. In 1918 these peasants wanted only bread and peace. They weren't interested in politics. They had sworn they would never march again. They would still be on their farms if they hadn't been tortured and shot for Communists when they didn't know what the word meant. They had become a Red Army because frightened people imagined a Red Army. They had imagined every part of what was happening and tried so hard to prevent it that it happened. To make the imaginary army complete, the British had supplied uniforms and rifles. That was because fear and hate kept them from seeing what they were doing. When the imaginary army was real and prepared, it was marching in to capture Vladivostok, because the Allies had once pretended that would happen.

That was what Alfred wanted to explain to Lieutenant Ross and himself. But it was all so loose that he would have needed to put the word-ideas in a hay press. So he just looked at the passing battalions and commented on their discipline, which seemed to be good.

After they were all cold, standing in the snow and watching, they piled into the car again. Ross drove slowly back into Vladivostok. By the time they got there, the first Bolsheviki regiment had ridden in on the street cars and captured the city without firing a shot. All that happened before breakfast.

That afternoon he stood on Svetlanskaya, watching another regiment march in. The uniforms made him think there must be some truth in the story that was going round. That the Bolsheviki leaders had wired their thanks to General Knox for drilling and outfitting a hundred thousand of their men.

A voice beside him said, "This comes of a disrespectful imagination!"

His English friend was there beside him. His face looked finer and paler than ever in the cold, but he had a lovely smile, although that bitter January day was no triumph for England. He said, "This makes me look at my own uniform and wonder, 'Am *I* sound?'"

He stayed only a few minutes. And because of the

people about them they exchanged ordinary news. How there hadn't been any violence in the sections guarded by their nationals. And they hadn't heard of any anywhere else. The lieutenant said the Cossacks had fired one piece of artillery at the Partisans, who hadn't replied. That was the only shot fired in the capture of the city. It might have been messier, he thought, if the Japanese hadn't been concentrated along the railway, while the Bolsheviki hiked in from the other side of town.

He stayed only a few minutes, but it was good to have him there. It seemed to Alfred that the lieutenant was a genius who had managed to get something very lovely out of the ruin of war. He must have been charming to start with, but there was something about him like a comment on his military history. He had fought under General Allenby and helped capture Palestine for the Jews. From there he had been sent to Baku, on the Caspian, where the Bolsheviki were fighting to save the great oil port from the Turks. There the British fought side by side with the Bolsheviki. Good soldiers, he said, and conscientious men. When that show was over, he was sent to Siberia, where the British were blaming the world's woes on the Jews and planning the extermination of the Bolsheviki.

Some of those contradictions were in his lovely smile and in his amused eyes that had seen the last crusade, and the Holy Sepulchre. A flight of marble steps leading down under the desert, uncovered and covered again by bursting shells. The honoring of the Jews in one place, and their damnation in another.

The Bolsheviki presented as comrades in arms and as beasts to be exterminated, according to the complicated and shifting needs of Empire. He had seen and remembered everything and turned it all into a wise and haunting sweetness that mightn't always be comfortable for everyone. Sometimes one glimpsed the razor edge.

That was really the last day in Siberia. Alfred's company didn't go home until six weeks later, but nothing happened after that. The fever had gone out of the crowds on Svetlanskaya, and everything was very tame. Contrary to Allied prediction, no women or children were killed; not even any men. The Partisans renounced the right to military executions, and even arrests. Everything was left to the city government. It seemed there had been a government all the time, only it hadn't been working because Admiral Kolchak had forbidden it to discuss matters of government.

After that day, Vladivostok was a good deal like any other city, only tired and quiet. Even the White Russians seemed glad that it was all over.

The tameness was the worst part, the hardest to bear. It made everything that happened seem so unnecessary. Two years of misery and slaughter, to save Siberia from going over a terrible precipice. And when it happened anyway, the precipice was only two inches high! The footfalls of soldiers getting ready to go home seemed to cry, "Cheated, cheated!"

After the first orderly, tame week, the British had an explanation. They had discovered that the men who captured Vladivostok weren't Bolsheviki at all. They were only peasants. And they had rebelled against treatment that really had been too rough.

Alfred thought there was a lot of truth in that. But if it was true, it seemed a pity that so many thousands of peasants like them had been butchered through mistaken identity. And if it was true, Alfred was going home without being sure that he had ever seen a Bolshevik. The real thing stayed as shadowy as the phantom Germans they had come to fight. To the very end, Siberia was like that. On closer inspection, everything turned into something else. There was never anything into which you could get your teeth.

# BOOK FOUR

# XVIII

E was home for the spring of 1920. Before the end of the summer he had learned to keep his mouth shut. In a war you put up with a good deal, knowing it won't last, believing that when it is over you can go home. You don't find out until afterward that when a war is over neither the dead nor the living can ever go home. You come back to something else. It doesn't sink in at first. For a while you blunder around, hurting yourself against things that weren't there before. How could you know that while you were gone the rules had been quietly changed, when people who had been there all the time didn't realize it?

Things change at home as well as in the country where the war is going on. You see things happen, horrible and senseless, and you keep telling yourself: "When I get back to a clean and decent country, I'm going to tell about this. I'll help see that such things can't happen again." And later, when you get used to horror, you tell your tough conscience: "I'm not doing anything to stop this. But when I get back to a clean country, I'll remember." What you don't know is that all the time you are saying that, people at home are being prepared to doubt you, and worse. Their ears are being sound-proofed against what you have to say.

287

He woke that night and found his mother in his room. It must have been very late, but she was still dressed, sitting in the chair beside his bed. It had been dark when he fell asleep. Now the moon was high. The inlet was silver, with salmon jumping and falling back in the moonlight. There was silver on the top of the sweet apple tree outside the window. His mother was sitting in the rawhide chair. The moonlight was all outside the window, but her hair was silver in the half-dark of the room that was too big.

When Alfred came home, George's bed was still there. He wondered if his parents had debated about that. Whether it would be better to leave it, empty, or have it put away, admitting there was no place for George, even if he came home from the hill overlooking Vladivostok. In the end his mother had suggested that he take the bed apart and put it in the attic. Then she had gone quickly downstairs, not wanting to hear the groan of the bed as it came to pieces.

Now she was the shadow of a mother in the rawhide chair beside the one bed. With the gleam of her hair which had started going white when she was still young, in the rooms of this house. A hundred times, looking up when she thought she was alone—and finding strange Indians who had come in like ghosts.

He reached out his hand. "Mother, you should be asleep."

Her hand felt fragile and cold. "I find I don't need so much sleep as I used to," she said. "I have more time to think."

Was she going to ask him again if he was quite sure that George had died without pain? Go to sleep, Mother. What I told you was true. Go to sleep, Mother. George is asleep. I was, too, until you woke me. Let's not go over it all again.

"I wasn't going to wake you." The fragile warmth of her hand, with more lasting love than hotter ones. "Alfie, do you mind if I ask you something?"

"Anything you like, Mother."

"Alfie, are you a Communist?"

It was such a shock that he felt nothing, no surprise or pain. "No, Mother." Then, as it sank down in his mind, he felt hurt, and let go her hand. His own mother.

She took his hand again, with both of hers. "Don't misunderstand me, Alfie! I wouldn't blame you if you were. It would serve America right! Keeping you in that terrible place nearly two years after the war was over. Keeping you there for nothing, until George lost his life and you lost the girl you loved. I wouldn't blame you if you were a Communist!"

"Well, I'm not. I'm an American, if that means anything."

She hardly seemed to hear him.

"You think I'm an old woman, Alfie?"

"No," he protested, "you're just the same, Mother."

"I could see it in your face when you came home. You thought I had aged in three years. I am nearly sixty. But sixty doesn't seem old when you get there. Maybe no age does. George was just a baby when I came out here from Iowa to join your dad. In some ways, that seems a long time ago. In some ways, it might have been yesterday. I don't feel much older, Alfie. I don't feel too old for life. Not too old to learn, or to start over."

"You have the pioneer spirit, Mother."

She said. "I want you to understand how I feel. When you're older you can remember what it was like to be young. But when you're young you haven't any way of knowing what it is like to be much older. You can't know how little different one feels inside."

It was hard to believe that, even though he could see she meant it. "I believe you, Mother. You will always be young." The salmon were jumping, ceaselessly, and falling back in the moonlight.

His mother was saying. "I didn't ask you that because I didn't trust you. I only wanted to be sure that you trust me and understand how I feel. Alfie, if you are a Communist, I'll be one, too, if I can. Even if I can't, I can help you better if I know. If it would help for us to move somewhere else—I'm not too old to start over. And Dad will go wherever I go."

He sighed. It was only painful to see such loyalty wasted on a false scent. "But I'm not a Communist, Mother. If Siberia taught me anything, it was to love America. I don't mean the way things are now. I mean the way things were before the war, when Americans had confidence and self-respect. That can't all be gone. I'd live through a good deal to see it come back."

She said, "I don't know what it is, Alfie, but something is terribly wrong."

"Being a Communist wouldn't help," he pointed out. "We're too full of European hate and propaganda already. By God, I'd be the last person to bring in any more!"

"I'm glad of that, Alfie." She held his hand tighter. "But if it had been the other way, I would have been with you."

He said: "The thing that kept us going in Siberia was our faith in America. As far as the Army was concerned, America was on the level. She didn't promise one thing and do the opposite. It's a queer feeling, coming home and finding we're in bad because we weren't used in a piece of dirty work that would only have disgraced our country."

It helped, talking about more general things. But whenever he thought of it, his mother's question hurt. Not so much the question; the fact that it had been possible for her to suspect him. "Mother, why should you have thought that?"

"I didn't think so," she insisted. "I only thought you might be—"

"Why . . .?"

"The newspapers said the American boys were infected with Bolshevism—"

He choked. The lie that had killed George, poisoning the mind of his own mother! "I didn't see any sign of it," he said at last. "So you got your opinion of me from the newspaper?"

"No, Alfie," she insisted. "I didn't believe it at all at the time, not about you and George, anyway. But tonight, when I couldn't sleep, I got to wondering. You've told all the dreadful things the White Russians and the Japanese did—"

"Not all, Mother. There are some things I can't tell. Some I wouldn't want you to hear."

"And you never talk about the Red atrocities—"

"But, Mother, I can only tell you what I saw, and what was reported by reliable people."

"Didn't the Bolsheviki do terrible things, too?"

He pointed out. "You know as much about that as I do, Mother. They may have murdered people in Russia. But in Siberia, in a year and a half, I didn't see anything of the kind. No one I knew saw anything of it."

His mother's look was strange in that dim light. He knew that she wanted to believe him, but couldn't, quite.

"I don't understand, Alfie—"

He said, "I don't pretend to. But then, I'm not even sure I ever saw a Bolshevik."

She looked more bewildered, not even trying to believe him.

He explained. "You haven't any idea how mixed up things were. I saw plenty of peaceful people who were killed for Bolsheviki, though they insisted they weren't. At the end I saw the peasants who captured Vladivostok. They claimed to be Bolsheviki. But when they turned out to be very humble and peaceful, and didn't hurt anyone, the Allies insisted that they weren't. You can make anything you like out of it."

His mother sighed. "It's the strangest thing I ever heard of, Alfie. I'm glad it's over and you are home."

"So am I, Mother." Only it seemed to him that it

wasn't over, and he wondered if he would ever really be home.

She said, "I don't see why it had to happen the way it did! It was so much worse than if George had been killed in the war. O, I thanked God for the Armistice, with both of you alive and well! The boys came back from the training camps and France—most of them—but there wasn't any word of your coming home. There seemed to be something secret about it. No one could tell us anything. After a while it was a year since the Armistice. I was really frightened then. George's letters sounded so homesick. Then Clarice married Lloyd—I don't like him, Alfie! —and two weeks after that we got the telegram over the telephone—" Her voice broke and she stopped, but did not cry. After a while she said, "It wasn't fair! If only you could have come home after the Armistice—"

"I know Mother." But it didn't happen that way. Some shadowy "They" wouldn't give up. We had to wait for the death of a corpse. While Admiral Kolchak rotted and fell off the foreign bayonets that held him up the way sticks hold up a scarecrow.

"Clarice wasn't happy about it," his mother was saying. "When I saw her just before, she looked desperate, reckless, anyway—"

"There, Mother!" He gave her hand a little shake. "I'd rather not hear."

But she wasn't to be put off. Her look was as unfathomable as the dusk in the big room. "Alfie, I'm an old-fashioned woman. I believe in the sacredness of marriage. But if you love Clarice, I think—"

"Mother!" He patted her hand. "We don't have to go into that, do we?" Perhaps she was glad to be interrupted when she had said the meaning, before she had said the words.

"No." She kissed him on the forehead. "I never meant to wake you." She got up to go. "You'll be able to sleep again, won't you?"

"Yes, Mother. I can sleep anywhere, any time. Now you go to sleep."

"Yes, Alfie." She hesitated, very tall beside his bed in the dusk, with her hair dim silver. "And you're not mad at me for asking—what I did?"

He took her hand and kissed it. "Of course not, Mother! I couldn't be. Now you go to bed."

For a long time after she was gone, he lay awake, watching the salmon jump in the dying moonlight. Thinking, no, brave Mother, I could never be mad at you! Even if what you asked hurt. But what have they done to you, that you should come here in the night, on a gentle Red hunt in your children's room?

# XIX

I T's lucky we talked things over beforehand!"
Burke said. The big locomotive engineer had
been a captain in France, and he was Commander of the Veterans' Post. "It's damn lucky.
This wouldn't do, brother."

"But you asked me for a talk on the A.E.F. in
Siberia." Alfred stared at one of the brass cuspidors
in the hotel lobby, where Burke had kept him waiting. "I've stuck to facts."

"I can't dispute you there," Burke said, "but people have certain ideas about Russia. It's a bad policy
to upset their ideas in shaky times, just after a war.
It wouldn't do you or anyone else any good."

Alfred wanted to know what he objected to in the
notes.

"Just about everything, buddie. Right off, everything belittling about the White Russians." He spat
toward the shining cuspidor, then gave Alfred his
friendly and undivided attention. "I don't doubt
they were bastards. All foreigners are. In France, if
we'd followed our personal feelings, we'd have probably fought the Frogs instead of the Germans. That's
confidential. We knew the Frogs better. But in a war
you have to stand up for your allies."

"We were in a different situation," Alfred pointed
out. "We were neutral. The White Russians could

not have been our allies any more than the Bolsheviki."

Burke looked at him glumly. "I know there was some funny business there. America was backing the White Russians, and the A.E.F. wasn't. Isn't that about the size of it?"

"The Government and the A.E.F. promised not to take sides in Russian affairs. I can't speak for the Government, but so far as I saw, the A.E.F. kept America's word and went through hell to do it."

The big engineer fixed the cuspidor with a scowl, then spat in it. "If you weren't supposed to fight, what in hell were you there for?"

Alfred laughed. "That's a fair question. Only we never learned the answer. We were sent to help the Czecho-Slovaks get out of Siberia, and to fight the Germans and Austrians. But the Czechs had captured most of the country and didn't want to leave. And there weren't any Germans or Austrians, except in prison camps, and never had been."

Burke said, "There was a lot of criticism of you fellows for not fighting the Reds."

"We were never ordered to."

"I dare say it wasn't your fault. Didn't you have a crazy general who wouldn't fight them?"

"Not half as crazy as the Allied generals. They drilled and armed a hundred thousand Bolsheviki whom they mistook for White Russians. Our general only followed orders from the President."

Burke yawned and shook his mouth against his fist. "Wilson—" he said. "That's over with. Wilson and his idealism! We don't have to be afraid of any idealism from Harding when we elect him."

"Getting back to this talk," Alfred said patiently. "There were about seven thousand Americans who served their country in Siberia, which was no clambake. They stayed a year and a half after the war was over, while other men got the pick of jobs at home. When they finally did get back they found they were under suspicion because they had gone where their country sent them, and followed their orders." The jarring rumble of a logging train echoed in the hotel lobby.

"You boys had tough luck!"

Through trembling plate glass windows, Alfred saw the first car sail heavily into view across the street. A brakeman standing easily on pyramided logs, dark with rain from the foothills though there was smoky sun in town. . . . Maybe tough luck began at home, like charity. He raised his voice above the crashing roll of cars. "Isn't it about time people heard the truth about the Siberian A.E.F.?"

"I wish to hell there was some way!" Burke shouted. "But I don't see how you can do it without being un-American!"

Endlessly passing rain-dark logs. Brakemen in stag shirts and "tin" pants, trundled past against a sky of sun and smoke. The noise of the storming train blurred speech and hearing. He raised his voice again:

"Can't a man tell the truth and still be an American?"

"Not if it's anything good about Russia!" Burke

shouted. Soundlessly rustling Alfred's notes. "Not if this is the truth! Don't you see, it would help Communism?" His earnest eyes intensified his noise-faded words.

"I don't see what that has to do with us!" Jolting wheels and heaped logs passing forever. Speech pale before the might of their insistent thunder-crashing. "Isn't it more important to clear the names of Americans than to hurt foreigners who have nothing to do with us?" The black locomotive, panting behind the last log pyramid. Silence following, cautiously.

"They have a lot to do with us!" Burke's voice grew bigger among the dying sounds of the train. "Take the situation here. The logging camps are full of radicals stirring up trouble. They're agitating for a strike right now. They'll never pull it, because our boys have learned a few things overseas. We're organizing the ex-service men to drive all the radicals out of the county. And, what's more, we don't care who knows it."

Again Alfred had the feeling of being in a strange country. One he didn't know anything about. At home it used to be that the County Sheriff and the drunken Constable could handle all the trouble that ever came along. "Haven't you any laws?"

"Laws are too slow, buddie. We aren't going to wait for laws when Americanism is in danger!" Burke's eyes had the quiet, steady glow of a remembered light. "We didn't fight in a war for nothing. The Wabblies are going to find that out pretty quick. They won't get a chance to hide behind fancy lawyers when we can run them out in one day with a few Winchesters."

"I don't get you," Alfred confessed. "You start out fighting for Democracy, and end by backing up a wage cut in the logging camps with Winchesters."

"Jesus Christ," Burke rumbled, "do you think we'd fight to cut our own wages? Wages have nothing to do with it. The Wabblies are only using that as an excuse. What they're after is to stir up trouble and destroy the country. Don't you get the idea? America's in danger and we've all got to be unselfish and pull together." He smoothed Alfred's notes on his big knee. "That's why this talk of yours wouldn't do, buddie." Burke put his big, solid hand on Alfred's arm. "You don't know how bad I feel about George. If we could get the bastard who killed him, I'd be the first to help string him up. Our Post sent your mother flowers on Decoration Day. Hell, that's nothing! I mean that in a way George died for his country—"

"Sure. So it's our duty to make people think he was a Communist and a traitor—"

Burke struggled like a wounded bear. "Jesus, Alfred," he rumbled, "that hurts! You *try* to get me all wrong. I mean we have to defend the America that George—"

"*You leave George out of this!*"

Burke sighed, with a thwarted look. "Alfred," he said kindly, "I know you're on the square. But I wish you could see that our first thought has to be about America. If you told things like this, just when the boys were pepped up to drive out the radicals—don't you see, it would confuse things and hurt America?"

"It might hurt someone," Alfred said, "but it wouldn't hurt America."

"If I hadn't believed in you," Burke told him sorrowfully, "I wouldn't have invited you to give this talk. I still believe in you, but I wish you could see things my way." He frowned heavily at the linoleum and the cuspidor. "Why couldn't you talk about just one part of the intervention?"

"You mean like the help the Y.W.C.A. was to the boys?"

Burke flushed, but appeared to go on thinking. He'd been decorated for bravery under fire. "You've a note here about the Bolsheviki taking Vladivostok. I suppose you were there?"

"I was."

"Why not tell about that?"

"If you like." There was surprise in his voice.

Burke looked at him. "You'll tell everything about the capture of the city?"

"Everything I saw, and I had a pretty good view."

"Fine!" Burke said. But he still looked uneasy, as if he expected a catch somewhere. "You'll tell how they executed everyone with money or education."

"They didn't execute anyone."

Burke's jaw dropped. "But I saw it in a Seattle paper!"

"They may have butchered thousands—in a newspaper."

"It said the gutters flowed with blood!"

"There was mention of blood," Alfred explained. "The Partisan leaders said that too much had been spilled already. It looked as if they were willing to give up their revenge in order to stop it. Anyway, they didn't execute anyone."

"What in hell did they do?"

"They left justice to the civil courts," he explained. "The courts had been suspended while the Kolchak government executed about three hundred people a month in Vladivostok. People of wealth and education who criticised the dictatorship were kidnapped and killed outside the city; or sent to one of Semeonoff's killing stations."

"I'll be damned!" Burke said.

Alfred met his baffled eyes. "So you want me to tell about the taking of Vladivostok?"

Burke was looking at the cuspidor again. "You know damn well I don't."

He walked with Alfred to the door and put his big, solid hand on his shoulder. "I believe in you, buddy," he said. "I wish to hell there was some way of telling the truth—"

"Some way that wouldn't be un-American," Alfred suggested.

"I guess we understand each other, after all," Burke said, shaking hands. "Some way that wouldn't be un-American!"

# XX

BURDENED with the heavy new logging chain, Alfred thought, make something in the form of a snake, and it's like a snake. Cold-slithering, with the instinct to fall in coils. Logs made with the instinct to roll. Across water and mud flats, a train on a black tressel. Logs rolling into the bay with the sound of thunder, born to roll. Men in this country born to roll logs. Come on, keep her rolling. Tear your heart out! He and his father were tackling a new acre of clearing. Clearing land is quieting to the bewildered heart.

The *Tyee* was waiting for him at the public dock, with a man standing there, looking her over. Alfred had taken the mast and bowsprit out of the sloop, cutting her down to a stumpy power boat. The stranger would probably say knowingly: "A sailboat once, wasn't she?" Alfred would answer: "I guess she was," as if he hadn't owned her until afterward. He didn't like to be reminded. The change had taken the life out of the sloop.

He had seen the man in town once or twice. Short, dark, with a serious face; neatly dressed. He waited while Alfred dumped the slithering chain into the cockpit.

"You're Alfred Tucker, aren't you?"

"Right."

"My name is Smith." They shook hands. "From the Department of Justice." He showed his badge. "I've been investigating you."

The hell you have! Alfred stared at the old stern-wheel steamer, *Forest Queen*, lying at the Company pier. "You've been investigating me?"

"That's what I said. And it's lucky for you that you don't seem to have had any dealings with the I.W.W.'s."

He felt impatient and flippant. As if some fool had set a mouse trap for him in a corner where he didn't go. "When you look at things that way, it's lucky for you that you haven't got into card games with strangers."

Smith's face was hard and serious as his straw hat. He didn't look like a man who ever had time to think anything was funny. "This isn't a joke," he pointed out. "The fact that you seem to have kept clear of the Wabblies is the only thing that's saved you."

"Saved me from what?"

"You aren't a child," Smith said, "and this isn't funny. You might as well know you're getting out by the skin of your teeth. You were in Siberia, and you've been shooting off your mouth pretty freely. One more link, and you'd have been in the net with the other Reds."

"Someone gave you the wrong dope," Alfred explained. "I went to Siberia because, in the Army, it's healthiest to go where you're sent. I wanted to go to France."

"Maybe you did. But the fact is you've been in

Siberia, exposed to Communist propaganda. That makes you a marked man. And don't you forget it."

"That isn't fair. I volunteered for the duration of the war, not to be a marked man for the rest of my life!"

"I'm not placing any charges against you," Smith reminded him. "And if you keep your mouth shut, nobody is going to bother you."

Alfred stared at the disused *Forest Queen*, rotting on the still water beside the Company pier. You were good enough in '17, when you took me to enlist. I was good enough. He looked down at Mr. Smith's dark, solid face. "If I've said anything wrong, it's because I'm almost a stranger here. I didn't get back until this spring. We used to have free speech."

Smith said, "You'll find out how free you are to shoot off your mouth about Russia!"

"You've got me wrong there, too," Alfred told him. "I'm not trying to sell Russia. I think countries can look out for themselves. Siberia doesn't interest me except in relation to some Americans who were sent there, and slandered because they went."

"Forget it," Smith advised, "and you won't have any trouble."

Alfred's mind was going over recent events. "Do you read Russian, Mr. Smith?"

"No. Have you something Russian?"

"No," Alfred admitted, "but I had until last Saturday night. It was a famous document. One of the posters they put up in the Siberian railway stations after the Omsk coup. As it was translated to me,

Admiral Kolchak abolished democratic government in Siberia. He proclaimed himself Supreme Dictator, with death to anyone who opposed his government, and twenty years hard labor to anyone who criticized him. My brother took a chance getting a copy of the poster for a souvenir. I hope to get it back. And I apologize for not having any Red propaganda for you."

"What are you trying to insinuate?" Smith looked toward him sharply, with only his eyes moving, like a pair of turret guns.

"I'm talking about Saturday night, when we were all away at a Grange meeting. You said you've been investigating me."

Smith said, "Don't be a fool, Tucker." Afterward he said, "You'll find out you can't be so fresh and independent in a crisis like this. You know the woods are full of I.W.W's."

"I've heard that," Alfred admitted. "Personally, I don't know anything about them except what I've read. You've been investigating them. Tell me, what makes them so dangerous? Or is that a secret?"

"Don't be funny," Smith advised him. "You know what makes them dangerous. They're trying to overthrow the Government. They're a Bolsheviki outfit, getting their orders from Moscow. We can prove that."

"Wasn't there a big round-up of Wabblies—during the war?" Alfred asked.

"You're damn right! And most of them are still in jail."

"But they were convicted because you had proof

that they were part of the Kaiser's spy system, taking orders from Berlin," Alfred pointed out.

"That was war hysteria," Smith explained. "We know now that it was Moscow."

Alfred thought of the letter he had received from Pink Byers the week before. "Your Department is rounding up dangerous foreigners," he observed. "Have you caught Nazorovsky?"

"The name doesn't mean anything to me. Who is he? What did he do?" Smith sounded impatient, but alert.

"He was one of Semeonoff's generals, and he killed some American soldiers."

Smith looked sceptical. "What were the Americans doing?"

"Sleeping," Alfred told him. "I don't think he would have had the courage otherwise. He was in an armored train and our boys were asleep in a wooden box car. They were part of the railway guard near Lake Baikal. He stopped his armored train beside their car at one o'clock in the morning and cut loose on them with a machine gun. Some of them never woke up. The thirty-five who were left woke up quick. They piled out where it was fifty below zero and had a running fight for about two miles. The train had started rolling again, but not quick enough. In the end they captured the armored train and General Nazorovsky and sixty Cossacks, alive and dead."

Smith whistled with surprise. "How in hell did they do it?"

"Someone got a hand grenade into the cab of the locomotive. The ones who were lucky got on top of the armored cars, where the machine guns couldn't reach, and dropped hand grenades through the ventilator ports.''

''They had plenty of guts, I'd say.''

"When the American lieutenant questioned the prisoners, they all told the same story. They'd been out raiding ten days. During that time they'd picked up around fifty men, whom they robbed and killed without asking their politics. They also got three women. They raped them and cut their throats afterward.''

Smith looked uncomfortable. "A pretty outfit. But what do you expect me to do about it? We can't go to Siberia after them.''

"How about California?'' Alfred wanted to know. "One of the men in my company wrote me that General Nazorovsky is living there. He was welcomed to America when Siberia got too hot for him.''

"I'll make a note of it,'' Smith said, "though it isn't in my territory. Then he pointed out. "It's no good for you men to go whispering among yourselves, stirring up trouble. If what you told me is true, your friend could have reported to the proper authorities.''

"He did. And he was given the advice that you have given me: to keep his mouth shut about things that happened in Siberia.''

"It's good advice, too. Don't forget it. Listen, Tucker, you may have reason for personal feelings. But in a national emergency we can't have everyone putting in his two cents' worth.''

That would come to a little better than half a cent a year for the time he had served his country, Alfred figured. And it meant that George's life had gone rather cheap. George, and half dressed men who had piled out to die in a bitter Siberian night, grappling an armored train with bare hands that froze to the steel and left the skin behind when they dropped off. They rotted in disgrace, while their killer enjoyed the blessings of America.

He started the engine with a vicious jerk of the bar, and cast off from the dock while Mr. Smith watched him glumly. With his hand on the clutch lever, he was struck with a doubt. Above the thudding of the engine, he shouted: "Mr. Smith, *what department did you say you are from?*"

"*The Department of Justice!*"

Alfred slammed in the clutch and thumped away from the dock, with Mr. Smith staring after him, angry and puzzled.

On the way home, he thought, what the hell? Once he helped save American soldiers from being killed with rifles furnished by America. That should have taught him that a man has to look out for himself, even in his own country. He should have known a democracy isn't perfect. A rough and tumble affair. Always with the chance of getting knocked on the head on one of the off days. It depended on who had the upper hand at the moment. Maybe it was a democracy one day, and not the next. At least you couldn't always see it. Like Mount Rainier, up there above the jagged treetops of Skookum Point. Seventy-five miles away, and still so big that it filled the sky to the southeast. Its base lost in the distance. A steep, dim-shining snow cap floating at an incredible height. Only a few times a year the sky was clear enough to see "The Mountain That Was God.". . . Who remembers the names of the Seattle man and the Tacoma man who had a fight over it? One calling it Mount Rainier and the other Mount Tacoma. They beat each other up and both went to the hoosegow. For the honor of a mountain that wasn't honored or dishonored. . . . Mr. Smith, with his hard face and hard hat, snooping a week in town. Finding out everything, doing everything in a week. Going away, without having learned anything or done anything. A country wasn't made or broken by detectives.

He liked to think that America was always there, like that mountain, even when the sky was too smoky to see it. Serene and unshakable, while men called names and went to the hoosegow with bloody noses. Names were cheap and snow was soft. But anyone who tried to tamper with the mountain itself would be broken on solid rock. . . . "One more link, and you'd be in the net with the other Reds." They might kill him and a few others with cheap snow-balls, but if they went too far they would be broken on rock.

A light, westerly breeze, rippling the inlet. Blue when you were out on it. Green with reflected trees near shore. Light west wind, with fir incense and salt on its breath. If only the *Tyee* had sail, now. Low in the water, plodding home to the thudding of the old Atlas, she had no wings to feel the wind. He had cut her down because he and his father needed a work boat. But you have two reasons for everything. The other reason was Alaska, which was almost America, and where everyone was almost successful. He'd been tempted all spring to fit out the *Tyee* and shove off for Alaska, where men had so much hope in their hearts and where years slipped away, inconclusively. Partly, he had cut her down to make sure he would stay where he belonged. When you can't get away from things, it's better to make your stand where you belong than where you half belong. . . . In the parlor at home, in the little metal chest the Indians had brought with Jimmy, a yellow letter from General Pickett, written after the Civil War. "They offered me the command of the armies of Egypt. . . . We could all be together there, and wouldn't have to worry about money. When you grow up and love your country you will understand why I could not go." Understand why his father turned his back on the life of a prince to sell insurance, and die in poverty in the ruined South. . . .

Blue inlet, between little farms and forests. More forest than farms. Three points of land, with great firs coming to the water's edge. Siwash and Thunder Bird and Skookum points, going away into the distance where Mount Rainier floated hugely in the sky. One wooded point repeated three times. Green, blue-green, and blue. Substance and shadow, and shadow of a shadow. The inlet winding past them like a river. One boat ahead, going his way. Mrs. Harper's large figure in the stern; Oliver standing up and facing forward to row, fisherman fashion. Just as he and George had seen them from the beach twenty-some years ago, on the morning of the winter day that Clarice Jackson was born. The day he got his scars.

Mrs. Harper, who had withdrawn from the neighborhood for so long, was getting about again, visiting her old neighbors, having people over, disproving the legend that she was a bitter old hermit. It seemed nearer the truth that she had been thinking things over, mellowing in her ivy-covered house on the southern slope of the hill. She was keen as ever, but sweet and gentle, with the old-timer's feeling that all the young ones belonged a little to her.

West wind, with salt and incense on its breath. Blue inlet, rolling away from the low sides of the *Tyee*, like a song.

> *Oh, Shenandoah, I love your daughter,*
> *Hoo-ray, you rolling river!*

His father was the quiet one these days. There were things he never talked about. But he found his voice in that chantey, while they rolled logs in the new, fire-blackened clearing.

> *It's full ten years since first I sought her. . . .*

For three times ten years his father had been wooing the stubborn earth of these shores. Earth twenty fathoms deep under fir forest. Not knowing how to behave, naked to the sun for the first time in a million years.

He throttled down the engine and threw out the clutch, coming up with the Harpers.

"Ahoy, there!"

Oliver turned, resting on his oars; tall, in dark,

formal clothes, with grave friendliness; looking about the same age as ever. Mrs. Harper turned more slowly, but with eagerness in her sweet, wise old face.

The *Tyee* was heavy and carried weigh on her for a long distance. Alfred backed the clutch and stopped her beside the path of the other boat. Oliver shipped one oar, then the other as they drifted together.

Mrs. Harper said, "Our New Bedford whaling ships used to stop like this for a gam at the ends of the earth!" She held onto the *Tyee*'s rail with one long hand. Alfred remembered her hands from childhood. Steady and precise, threading curved needles with white thread, to sew him up.

Oliver said, "You and your father aren't going to leave any woods on your place, the way you're going at things up on the hill!"

"There's still plenty. It looks as if an acre a year is our speed now, with working the farm."

Mrs. Harper said, "An acre a year is a great deal! If we had done as much, we would have nearly fifty cleared by now."

Lighting his pipe, Oliver observed, "If you'd wanted that much, Mother, you'd have had to get out and help me roll logs. The way Mrs. Schmidt does."

She shook her white head and her old black hat with its modest flowers. "Rolling logs is much too heavy work for women."

"Or for men," Oliver said.

"Or for horses!"

They laughed, with blue water wrinkling past their boats, drifting together in the sun.

After a while Mrs. Harper said, "You're probably in a hurry, Alfred."

"No, but I'm keeping you. Won't you come on board? We can go on with our gam under weigh."

Her large bulk stirred with a sigh, while she smiled. "Thank you, Alfred, but I'm a heavy old woman. I don't know if I should risk changing boats in midstream."

Oliver said, "Nonsense, Mother! You're as active as ever. I'll hold the boats together and Alfred will help you. Up you go!"

She was slow, and heavy. But she had been out in boats in all kinds of weather, and knew how things should be done. When she was on board and settled on a cockpit seat, Alfred told her:

"If you'd weighed only ninety pounds, you would probably have stepped on the gunwale of your boat and gone into the drink." He opened the throttle and kicked in the clutch. They went on, towing the heavy skiff.

"This is going home in style," Mrs. Harper said. "I suppose people have to keep up to date, Alfred. But I did regret seeing the mast and sails go from your boat."

"There isn't much chance to use sail here."

"I suppose you're not old enough to remember the *Plunger*."

Alfred could just recall the ruins of the craft, covered with green slime, showing near the cove at low tide.

"Mr. Walter and Jimmy used to do all their marketing with the cutter," Mrs. Harper said. "They would

314

sail as far as Port Madison. That was when there weren't enough people in Olympia and Tacoma and Seattle to buy all the fruit from your orchard."

Alfred said, "There aren't enough people there now."

The old woman sighed. "Mr. Walter used to make a good thing of it. Though he gave up the long trips in the cutter after Jimmy went away to school."

"Jimmy wasn't much help," Oliver recollected. "Mr. Walter used to complain that half their load would be horse-clam shells. Jimmy drew on them with charcoal. Everything he saw. He wasn't much of a success as a mate!"

"No," his mother agreed, "but he was company. After he went away to art school, the *Plunger* wasn't used much. Mostly to bring Jimmy from Olympia— or take him away again.

"The Walters' place never seemed complete without a sailboat," she went on. "Boys and sailboats!" She was an old woman, but her eyes had a young, flying look. Then she sighed and looked old again. "Though mostly the sailboat was waiting in the cove, with the boys away somewhere. The *Plunger*, with Jimmy away. Then the *Tyee*, with you and George at war. Every day an old woman looked at your boat from across the bay and said to herself: 'The boys will come home soon, and sail again!' Alfred, you don't know what it did to me when you came home, alone, and took out the *Tyee*'s mast!"

He didn't look at her, but felt her compassionate hand on his arm.

"It was like waiting for some beautiful young tree to bloom, and seeing it cut down instead."

He turned and looked at her gravely. "That sometimes happens."

"It shouldn't!" Then she smiled, but her eyes remained sad. "I'm only seventy-one. Maybe I'm not old enough to be philosophical."

"You are very wise." He swung the *Tyee* toward the Harper's house. Windows looking out of deep ivy, against a background of forest. Green on green. Except for the windows, you hardly knew a house was there.

Mrs. Harper was saying, "I'm not wise, Alfred. I am only a sentimental, match-making old woman."

Oliver cautioned him. "She can't make matches worth a cent. Look at me, single as ever!"

"I only make matches in my mind," she explained. "It's up to the young men and girls to do the rest."

Alfred threw out the clutch and let the *Tyee* glide in toward the clean, steep gravel beach. "Have you a girl picked out for me?"

Her large bosom stirred with a regretful sigh. "No, Alfred."

Oliver smiled triumphantly, pulling the big skiff alongside. "You see? We'll both be bachelors. Mother can't make matches worth a cent!"

Almost as if she didn't want her son to hear, Mrs. Harper said, looking shrewdly at Alfred, "But I had a girl picked out for you once."

He didn't ask who she was or what became of her.

Mrs. Harper was very wise. And there wasn't any use in joking past the joking point.

He promised to bring his mother over soon for some of the peaches that were ripening against the southern slope of the hill. Saw Mrs. Harper and Oliver safely ashore. Then thudded across the bay toward the boat shed in the cove, where he had once dashed in with thunder and lightning.

# XXI

OMING up the hill in the rain, with the grapes, he raised the schoolhouse—blackened shingle roof and white walls against a background of young firs very green in the gray rain. Smoke was coming up from the chimney, but the rain beat it down again. Because of the rain, the smoke looked gray, but it was good smoke. It made the schoolhouse look not desolate. The other times he had seen it since coming home, there had been no smoke from the chimney. No children playing in the yard or clattering the ship's capstan which had done for a merry-go-round. Then he passed without stopping because the empty schoolhouse was haunted the way every place where people have been is haunted. And childish ghosts are trusting and still hopeful and very nosey. They turn the soul inside out and drag out things dying quietly and painlessly in the dark. Things that grow green for a minute, and hurt when they are put away to go on dying.

There wasn't anything wrong with the building, except that it wasn't a school any more. The district had been consolidated and the children were taken to town in a bus. The spring he and George had come home to enlist was the end of the last term. That night he struck matches while Clarice put their Indian pipes among the children's maidenhair fern and bleeding hearts. Everything was over then, only they hadn't known it. The schoolhouse was used only two or three times a year, for an election or a sociable. This time it was the harvest festival.

From the stile the schoolhouse wasn't against a background of firs. They were beyond the fence, and the building was in the middle of its barren acre of ground in the rain. But the smoke made it come alive and there was a car in the open shed. It looked very comfortable in where it was dry, with rain falling on the roof and the ground very wet outside. The car looked like the Packard in which Clarice Jackson and her husband sometimes drove down from Seattle. He knew Clarice had come home for a week, alone. But he had not seen her. Knowing that she was at the schoolhouse did not make any difference to his mind. But his body thought it was a fine thing. His body was romantic and thought of her as its own true love. His mind didn't often think of her one way or another.

In the schoolhouse everything was warm and alive. The dry smell of books and maps was away behind the smell of fruit and corn. Eve Miller met him at the inside door. She had red in her cheeks, and good, bright eyes, like the nice part of autumn. Blocking his way while she selected a bunch of grapes, Eve said: "You're just in time, Alfred! Clarice and I have been praying for a man."

From a stepladder against the blackboard, Clarice smiled down at Alfred, very brightly, and with dismay. "Speak for yourself, Eve!" She scrambled down.

"We wanted a tall man," Eve explained, eating grapes.

"With a polygamous heart," Clarice suggested, shaking hands.

"Clarice!" Eve reddened. "We wanted a man to help with the decorations." She reddened more, and Clarice held a red apple beside her face for comparison.

Alfred said, "You shouldn't have raised my hopes."

It was nice, helping the two young women make the bare room rich with massed stalks of corn, dark green Hubbard squash, golden pumpkins and baskets of apples redder than Eve's face had been. The fire was bright through the eyes of the stove, and the room cozy. Rain roared steadily on the roof and shut the three of them away from everything else with a curtain of sounding water. It was hard to think of there being anything else beyond the room, shut in with rain. While it lasted it was like keeping house with two wives. He thought the others felt it, too. Eve hadn't been thinking that when she said they had been praying for a man. She expected other people to know what she meant, and didn't worry herself about double meanings. Clarice had only made fun of her because the opportunity was too good to miss. But it became partly real as they worked in the rich warmth, shut in by rain. Each was nicer to him and more thoughtful than if the other hadn't been there. Trying to outdo each other, very quietly, because the combination wasn't equal. He tight-rope walked, without thinking much about it, because that was instinct under the circumstances. Anyway, it was only real until someone else came in and changed the combination.

Eve found a secret to tell him. It seemed to him she had been trying to think one up for some time. Marching him to admire the way she had arranged small shocks of corn and pumpkins at each side of the door, she sank her voice: "Alfred Tucker, I almost lost my reputation because of you, last week!"

He couldn't see how that had happened.

"I told the friends I was visiting in Olympia that one of the nicest men I know is a Communist. They just about mobbed me!" Her healthy face was confiding and excited.

"What has that to do with me?" Alfred asked her.

"Aren't you a Communist?"

"No."

Her eyes rolled up at him, wickedly. "You don't have to pretend with me, Alfred. I'm your friend."

"If you are," he said, "don't say things that aren't true." He wanted to spank her sturdy behind.

"Anyway," she decided, "I think you're nice."

Clarice called, "When you have time, will one of you tell me how this looks?"

She had heaped a big tray on Jimmy Pickett's table with apples and yellow pears and blue Concord grapes cleverly arranged, with different, bright colors next each other.

"That's swell, Clarice!"

Eve sighed loudly. "O, dear, it looks good enough to eat." She sat on top of a desk and looked at the autumn richness. "If we could only sell the things we raise!"

322

Clarice stood back to admire her work, smiling. She was something like Olga Veronovna, only much sweeter. "We'll add a footnote to our prayer of thanksgiving. An envoi, asking God to look into the distribution of the fruits of the earth that he so kindly sends!" She sat on another desk and became grave. Watching her, Alfred thought she wasn't as pretty as she used to be. She was thinner, and too tense. She could be gayer than ever at times, but then there was something reckless about her. And she changed very quickly to being sad and quiet. When she was like that, she stirred him more than at other times. It puzzled him that she was more appealing when she wasn't so pretty. Here the children used to sing lustily: "Believe me if all those endearing young charms—" It wasn't like that, but there was something in the funny old song. Maybe, for a while, women became more beautiful as they got less pretty. Sometimes, now, everything about Clarice was in tune together. Her look and voice and what she said. A caressing autumn richness, that left frost's sting of regret.

She was saying, "Do we really have to buy and try to sell? We come so near raising everything we need! Why can't we go the whole way? We would be so much happier." Clarice was married to the son of a wealthy lumberman, but she was talking as one of the inhabitants of the neighborhood, faced with the half-solved problem of making a living.

Eve said, "We've all been trying to get along without money. It's no fun."

"Not really," Clarice insisted. "We've always

counted on buying flour and meal, when we could grind our own wheat and corn. We've counted on buying our clothes, when we could just as well raise sheep and spin our own wool."

"Wool wouldn't do for summer," Eve said, "and we can't raise cotton."

"Do we need clothes in summer?"

"We need to be decent!"

Clarice appealed to the man. "Alfred, if you had this neighborhood to run, couldn't you take it through a year without anyone starving or freezing?' She seemed very anxious for him to agree with her.

He said, "The people could do it themselves, if they planned the crops and work. I don't know what they would do for a doctor and dentist, though."

"We'd get them," Clarice insisted. "They would come here just to study the fine, healthy people we raised."

Alfred knew that only dreamers and loafers would go in on such a scheme. But he saw that there would be possibilities—if Americans were different from what they were. "One seine boat with a good crew could keep the whole neighborhood in fish the year round. Fresh and salted and smoked."

Clarice brightened. "We'd salt the backs and smoke the bellies, the way they did in the old days."

"Why not smoke one half and salt the other?" Eve was only three years younger than Clarice, but those three years made all the difference. She had no memory of the delicacy.

"If you'd ever had smoked salmon bellies, you wouldn't ask."

Clarice said, "They couldn't have weighed more than a few ounces each, and they looked like strips of curled, black bark, but they tasted better than anything else."

"We'd smoke clams, too," Alfred said. "George and I picked it up from the Indians. I guess we were the only white people who ever did it."

"Were they good?"

"Tough. But if you liked them, they were very good."

"We'll have expeditions after huckleberries, with all the children to help," Clarice said, "and a community kitchen for canning."

Eve was becoming bored with the talk, and sleepy with the warm room and the steady roar of rain. She got up, stretching. "This doesn't decorate any schoolhouses."

"We'll have a community boat yard, too," Clarice said. "We'll build a boat bigger than the *Tyee*. One we can sail in anywhere to trade things we have for things we need. We'll arrange it so the people who want to can take their vacations that way."

"You're both alike!" Eve said. "You're a couple of crazy Communists."

"George and I used to dream of something like that," Alfred told her.

"Did you, Alfred?"

"We had plans for a schooner. It was to be a kind of training ship. We were going to take boys from around here on cruises. Alaska or the Hawaiian Islands. We would have done it, if the war hadn't upset our mining plans—and everything else."

325

From the bench of the folding camp-meeting organ, Eve said pointedly, "I'm decorating as much as you two."

Clarice asked: "Did you have a gold mine, Alfred?"

He said, "It came in as part of the Tanana Strike, but we weren't there to do anything about it."

She looked sad, without speaking.

Eve began playing the wheezing organ, singing:

> *Lavender's blue, diddle, diddle,*
> *Lavender's green.*
> *When I am king, diddle, diddle,*
> *You shall be queen. . . .*

"We'll have the boat, just the same," Clarice said. "It'll be a training ship and trading ship, too."

Alfred didn't know what to say. It was fine planning things with her. But she seemed to forget that they were not children, and that she had a real and practical husband.

> *Call up your men, diddle, diddle,*
> *Set them to work.*
> *Some with a hoe, diddle, diddle,*
> *Some with a rake . . . .*

Eve was enjoying herself, being as objectionable as she could.

Clarice didn't seem to hear her, but her enthusiasm for a Tyee Bay civilization died. She became grave and anxious, but still very sweet. "Alfred, did you ever get that clipping I sent you?"

"Yes." Something about the Soviet government wanting men to introduce modern logging methods

to Russia. "I'm afraid I didn't thank you for it."
He hadn't figured out why she sent it to him.

"Did you do anything about it, Alfred?"

"No."

She was looking down, without saying anything.
He thought she was disappointed. Then she slid from
the desk. "We must finish with these decorations."
She led him to a large, undistributed pile of corn and
vegetables. "The Rogers were coming to help. But
we can't expect them, walking, in this rain."

Eve was still at the organ, pumping hard with both
feet. Bearing down on the keys with both hands.
Letting her voice go:

> *Some to make hay, diddle, diddle,*
> *Some to cut corn.*
> *While you and I, diddle, diddle,*
> *Keep ourselves warm.*

"Where are we going to put all these?"

Alfred wasn't tight-rope walking any more. He
didn't mean anything to either woman, except for the
hour when they were shut away from the world by
walls of rain. But he saw that for that hour, Clarice
wanted his company. What she wanted, she got.

There was the noise of a car coming into the yard
and stopping in front of the schoolhouse. Eve was
helping again.

"There's Dan!" she said. "I'll have to run." She
kissed Clarice. "You don't really need me."

"Won't Dan come in?"

"I don't think so. He's a little bashful, and it's
raining hard. Goodbye, Alfred."

"Goodbye, Eve. It was nice to see you."

"Did you see me?" As if to make up for being slighted, she put her hands on his shoulders and kissed him warmly, with something like mockery.

They went with her as far as the porch and saw her leap through the waterfall from the eaves into the car. Dan waved to them, with his face solemn. Eve threw a kiss, and they drove out of the yard, the car going very fast on the wagon track between the huckleberry bushes and shiny black tree trunks in the rain.

"They're going to be married in the spring," Clarice said.

He looked at the rain, and the disturbed puddles in the yard settling back into place. "There's no end to marrying and giving in marriage."

They went back into the warm, autumn-rich schoolroom. "Once it was almost us," she recalled, kneeling and sorting stalks of corn.

Through the rustle of leaves and roar of rain he heard the dry creak of his hands clenching themselves.

"But you wouldn't have any strings on you while you served your country," she said to the corn.

"No. I wouldn't have you tied to what might come back."

"I told you that you would come back all right. Think how different everything would have been."

He started to touch her, then drew back his hand. "I'm sorry, Clarice."

She half turned, looking up at him with defensive surprise. "Don't think I'm complaining! I love Lloyd.

Our marriage is quite satisfactory. I wouldn't change anything. This is only a kind of game, trying to figure things out from the standpoint of ourselves at the time you went away."

A hell of a game!

"You must admit it was very foolish of you to insist on waiting."

"I'm sorry I insisted. But knowing the chances, I couldn't have done anything else. Unless I had been forced. Why couldn't you have found you were going to have a baby? I couldn't help wishing that would happen." He hadn't quite wished it then. He wished it now.

"You didn't tell me."

"That wouldn't have been fair. It would have been encouraging you to do something about it."

She carried an armful of corn and leaned it against the wall. One stalk fell over, but she didn't seem to notice. When she turned to come back, he saw that she was crying.

"Clarice!"

She dropped onto a desk, sobbing wildly. "You don't care! You had a good time with me! You only think about yourself! It doesn't mean anything to you!"

When he tried to comfort her, she dashed his hands away. "Don't touch me! I'll kill you if you do! You made me suffer enough. I hate you! Let me alone!"

Later, when she was quieter, she said, "I'm sorry, Alfred. I didn't mean to. Only I had told myself so often that if I could only cry in your arms—"

He put his arms around her.

"It's too late, now," she reminded him. "I'm through crying."

He held her a minute, belatedly.

"Now you must let me go, Alfred." She gave him a very gentle kiss, flavored with salt. "Anyone is likely to come in."

He let her go.

"We must be sensible, Alfred. I want to talk about you." She was bright and smiling again, almost as if she had never cried. "Why didn't you try for one of the Russian jobs?"

"I have plenty to do here," he pointed out.

"I think you should go to Russia."

"You, too?" he asked, smiling faintly.

"What?"

"Trying to make a Communist of me."

She said impatiently, "Don't be scared of a word! Russia is a new country, and you are a pioneer. Russia is going to be a very great country."

"I think it will be."

"Why not go, Alfred?"

"Because I am an American, and not a Russian."

"No one will believe that, Alfred!"

He winced. Then said grimly, "I don't have to ask other people what I am. I know what I am, and I belong here."

She said passionately, "No one belongs where he has to keep quiet or be destroyed!"

"Where you belong depends on how you feel inside," he told her. "What other people say can't change that."

Cradling a dark green and gold squash in her arms, she looked very small and dear and tender. She smiled at him from a distance.

"Alfred, if you will be sensible and go to Russia, I will go with you."

His body was alive with the sensation of flying, but his mind was heavy and kept him down. "What about Lloyd?" his voice asked. He took the heavy squash away from her and put it down, holding her gently.

"It wouldn't matter if I could go away far enough," she said breathlessly. "We get along like cat and dog. Lloyd cheated me, without meaning to. He came back full of enthusiasm. He was going to see that things like the war couldn't happen again. He was going to help make America a better country. I got excited about helping him. And I was disappointed in you. You wrote me so shortly that you were satisfied with America the way it was. I didn't know that Lloyd's plans would boil down to organizing the veterans to crush labor in his father's logging camps!" Clinging to him, she said, "I'm heartsick when I see their cynical destruction of men! Their cynical destruction of this beautiful country. Taking what is easy money, and burning up the rest. Leaving a barren land to be washed into the sea. Lloyd laughs at me when I talk about that, and I hate him for it. He says there is no money in reforesting. There'll be plenty of land for us to be buried in. Alfred, I don't want to die! I don't want to think about where I'm going to be buried. I want to think about the country where our

331

children are going to live!" She was clinging to him desperately, while the rain walled in the schoolhouse with its gray roar.

"Alfred, I meant it when we were planning a community where people worked together and used the earth wisely. I meant it when I said we would raise beautiful children. We couldn't do it here, with all the greed and destruction. We couldn't do it here, where you are spied on. Where you have to keep quiet or be destroyed. That's why I want you to take me to Russia. It's a great, new country. . . ."

But it isn't our country, he thought.

She was warm and heartbreakingly lovely in his arms. His body cried out that it would never let her go. But in his mind he knew that he could not tear up his roots that went down to the beginning of things here. He had been an exile once, and wasn't going away again.

Footsteps thundered on the porch. They kissed each other and went back to work. They were alone for a minute longer while the Rogers took off their wet coats in the outer room. Clarice and he worked together, arranging the harvest of squash and pumpkins and yellow corn. They smiled at each other, and her look had that caressing autumn richness, while his nostrils felt the sting of frost. It seemed a pity that crops could not be sold, that she could not belong to him, and that he was something of an exile. But everything that made up life was there in a rich harvest. And it was good to be with the woman he loved, among the fruits of the earth of his own great country.

J...
Cat 38

Date Due